MADISON'S AVENUE

Also by Mike Brogan

Business to Kill For

Dead Air

Hi neighbors...
Hope you enjoy!

MADISON'S AVENUE

Mike Brogan

Mike Brogan

Lighthouse Publishing

This book is a work of fiction. Names, characters, businesses, organizations, places, events and incidents either are the product of the author's imagination or are used fictitiously. Any resemblance to actual persons, living or dead, events, or locales is entirely coincidental

For Kate and Emmett,
my parents.

ACKNOWLEDGMENTS

So many have made this book possible. Especially all you advertising professionals in the United States and in Europe who over the years have provided me an abundance of unforgettable experiences and characters to draw upon in writing *Madison's Avenue*. Some of the events in this story actually happened. Names have been changed to protect the guilty.

Special thanks also to my writing colleagues: Shamus Award winner Loren D. Estleman, and distinguished writers like Frank Wydra, Pete Barlow, Phil Rosette, Len Charla, Jim O'Keefe, Annick Hivert-Carthew, and friends like John and Mary Ann Verdi-Huss. Your helpful comments, suggestions and guidance have helped make this story better.

And finally, thanks to my wife, children, friends who expand greatly the meaning of patience.

One

BOSTON

Madison McKean checked her list. Two more client matters and she was done for the day. First, she had to reassure a nervous client that the jogging bra advertisement would run in the marathon section of Sunday's *Boston Globe*. Then, she'd review some rough-cut television commercials for Norwegian Skin Care Products before tomorrow's presentation.

As the account director on Norwegian Products, a major client at Boston's CPR Advertising agency, Madison was responsible for all aspects of the Norwegian Products advertising. And her recent promotion to Group Account Director had made her responsible for some other agency clients as well. It was a lot of work, at times overwhelming, but she loved it.

Suddenly, she remembered Hanna and Emily, her new copywriter and art director team. It was their first day on the job and she'd been too busy to see how they were doing. She hurried down the hall and leaned into their joined cubicle.

"So, by now you two have probably whipped up some fantastic ads for Lunch Munchies, right?" Madison said, smiling.

They smiled back, but their smiles faded fast.

Madison sensed something was wrong. "Problems?"

"Sorta," Hanna said.

"Like?"

"Like our first assignment. It's not Lunch Munchies. It's *weird!*"

"Why weird?"

"Because Mr. Kasdan, the creative director, and his associate asked us to work on that ... *new* Norwegian product."

Madison hadn't heard anything about any new Norwegian product, and as account director she would know. Her antenna went on prank alert.

"What strange new product?"

Hanna and Emily seemed surprised that she didn't know.

"Well, you know about Norwegian's feminine hygiene spray...." Hanna said.

Madison nodded.

"Well, they told us that Norwegian is introducing a hygiene spray for *men*. A genital spray. They want *us* to name it and come up with a theme line for it."

Madison's laugh exploded from her mouth.

"Excuse me, but there is no new Norwegian male genital spray."

"*What?*"

"The boys were putting you on, initiating you new girls."

Hanna and Emily blushed, then began to laugh.

"That's too bad," Hanna said.

"Why?"

"We came up with a cool name and theme."

"For a male genital spray?"

"Yeah."

"What?"

"*Umpire ... for Foul Balls!*"

———

Madison buckled over with laughter and had to steady herself on a nearby chair. "I love it! Stick that line over the photo of a male crotch, then show those bozos!"

They smiled.

Suddenly, Madison sensed someone behind her. Turning, she saw Elaine, her assistant, looking concerned.

"Your father's on your private line," Elaine whispered. "He says it's very urgent."

Her father, Mark McKean, didn't make urgent calls. He hadn't made one to her since the day her mother died six years ago. Madison excused herself, hurried down to her office and grabbed the phone.

"Dad...?"

"Sorry to interrupt, Madison. But I...." He sounded short of breath. "I still can't believe it!"

"Believe what?"

"Someone at my agency sent me an anonymous e-mail accusing me of misappropriating 8.7 million dollars of company money. It's absolutely preposterous!"

She was stunned. "Of course it is." Her father, chairman and CEO of Turner Advertising in Manhattan, was the most ethical man she'd ever known.

"I haven't taken a dime! Ever!"

"I believe you."

"Our CFO just checked *all* agency financial records. There's not one red cent missing anywhere."

"You're fighting this?"

"With everything I've got! But the memo demands that I resign now. I wanted you to hear all this from me, and not through the agency grapevine, or worse, the newspapers."

"Any idea who's behind this?"

He paused. "No, but the $8.7 million figure seems familiar. I saw it somewhere in the company recently. In someone's office, I think. On a file, or computer maybe. But there's so much happening so fast, I can't remember where. I'm even concerned my office phone may be tapped.

That's why I'm calling you on my cell phone." Her dad, always cool-headed and unflappable, sounded very anxious.

"Dad, listen, I'm taking the next flight home tonight."

"That's not necessary, Madison."

"I'm coming. Don't try to talk me out of it."

He took a deep breath.

"What's wrong?" she asked.

No response.

"Dad, what the hell's going on there?"

"I'm not sure. Just be damn careful, Madison, please!"

"Dad...?"

The phone connection went dead.

Two

The Yellow Cab inched through evening traffic on Manhattan's Park Avenue. Her father still wasn't answering his cell phone, or his office and apartment phones. Madison was growing concerned.

In Central Park, she passed a horse-drawn carriage with an attractive bride and groom. Madison smiled at them and they smiled back, which reminded her that tonight her father would once again ask if she was dating anyone special. And once again she'd tell him no, say she was just too busy. She would not mention that she hadn't even been looking for Mr. Special for more than two years.

Ahead, she saw her father's corner apartment building and thought back to the day he moved into it five years ago, just months after her mother's death. He'd complained that their family home in Larchmont had become too quiet without Kate fussing around the kitchen. He'd really meant *too painful*.

So he purchased the Manhattan apartment at Seventy-Sixth and Central Park West, and as usual buried himself in work at his agency – an agency he'd transformed over the last thirty-two years from a tiny creative boutique into a powerhouse advertising network with blue-chip multinational clients and offices in twenty-six countries.

She was proud of his achievements, but she still felt their caustic effect at times. His sixteen-hour workdays, working weekends, and constant business travel had left little time for her and her younger brother, Thaddeus, as they were growing up. Even when her father was home, he was often working at his desk. Even when he was chatting with her, she could tell he was thinking of agency matters. And it had hurt.

The disturbing thing was that *she* was becoming him. She was working crazy hours, traveling on business, working late at home and on weekends in the office.

But the difference was, her long hours weren't hurting anyone.

Yet someone was trying to hurt her father. And destroy everything he'd achieved.

The taxi rolled to a stop in front of his charming old building. She liked its red marble walkway under the canopy, the white bricks arching like halos over the windows and the pink azaleas hanging from the penthouse roof garden. She paid the driver and hurried through the entrance as an elderly couple she recognized held the door open for her. She thanked them, took the elevator up to her father's floor and headed down toward his apartment.

At his door, she saw a man presumably chatting with her dad inside. The slender man in his mid-forties wore a dark suit, shirt and tie, and thick-soled black shoes buffed to a military shine. His narrow face was dominated by large dark eyes, thick brows and black hair combed straight back off a high forehead.

He turned toward her. "Do you live here?"

His tone made her heart beat faster.

"No. My father does. I've just arrived from Boston. Why?"

He blinked, looked away a moment, then slowly turned back. "I'm Detective Pete Loomis, ma'am," he said softly, showing her his gold and blue NYPD badge. "And this is Detective Archie Doolin." A fifty-ish, sandy-haired man stepped from her father's apartment, nodded at her, then quickly looked at Loomis.

"Why are you here?" she asked.

Detective Loomis hesitated. "I'm sorry, ma'am, but your father appears to have had an ... accident."

Madison stopped breathing.

"Thirty minutes ago," Loomis continued, "we found an empty rowboat on the East River just off Clinton Street. In the boat was a suit coat with your father's wallet in the inside pocket."

Madison felt her knees buckle.

"We haven't found him yet. But we found this on the kitchen table." Loomis handed her a folded sheet of gray paper.

Dad's stationery!

She caught her breath, unfolded the note and began to read.

Madison, Thad,

Please forgive me for what I'm about to do. But recent baseless accusations that I mentioned this afternoon, and other outrageous insinuations have simply overwhelmed me. Being forced to resign over these vicious and false assertions is more than I choose to bear, or more importantly, have you bear. I refuse to have our family name, and your names, destroyed by cruel lies in the media.

I wish there was another way, believe me, but there isn't. I love you both, far more than I've ever told you, so please, I beg you, find it in your hearts somehow, someday, to forgive me.

Your loving father

"Is this your father's handwriting?" Detective Loomis whispered.

Clinging to consciousness, she slumped against the wall, tears filling her eyes, and nodded.

* * *

Outside on Seventy-Sixth Street, Harry Burkett, a muscular man in a dark Lincoln, leaned close to the rearview mirror and checked for cops. He saw none.

Burkett reached into a bag of salted red pistachios, crammed some into his mouth and licked the salt from his fingers.

Suddenly, a shadow moved across Mark McKean's apartment window. Burkett cranked up the volume on the laser eavesdropping device. He'd heard every word of the conversation between McKean's daughter and the two cops.

Obviously, she'd flown in from Boston because her old man had told her what was happening at Turner Advertising. Did he also tell her who he suspected was behind everything? Probably.

The daughter was a problem.

But every problem has a solution, Burkett thought, looking down at his SIG-Sauer 9mm.

Three

Madison felt the two detectives easing her down into her father's favorite chair. Her mind was reeling, her eyes blurring. She struggled to remain conscious.

"Some water, Ms. McKean?" Detective Loomis asked.

She managed to nod, trying to focus through hot tears on her father's suicide note.

How could you do this?

How could you do this to Thaddeus and me?

"We're very sorry, Ms. McKean," Loomis said.

Detective Doolin handed her a glass of water and she tried to sip some, but her throat closed shut. Cold perspiration dampened her skin and she forced herself to take several deep breaths. Finally, she dabbed her eyes and looked up at the two somber-faced detectives.

"What happened...?"

Loomis flipped open a small notebook. "An NYU coed was jogging in East River Park around six thirty. As she ran along the dock, she heard something bump it. She looked and saw it was an empty rowboat, just kinda drifting in the water. The boat had a man's suit jacket folded on the seat. She saw no one in the boat, or in the water, or on the dock. So she became worried, afraid someone had fallen in. She called 911 on her cell phone. We got there six minutes later. As we pulled the boat to shore, a big wave hit and the jacket fell in the water, but we pulled it right out. In the inside pocket, we found ... your father's wallet."

No....

"We assumed he might have slipped and fallen overboard. But when we got back here, we found this note."

She looked back at the note, her eyes blurring. *Impossible! Dad would not write this. He would never take his own life. He was always positive and upbeat, even when times were bad.*

She turned to Detective Loomis. "This afternoon my father was extremely upset over something at work."

"Over what?"

"Someone there falsely accused him of stealing 8.7 million dollars from his own company and was forcing him to resign."

"Is that what he meant in this note by these 'recent accusations'?"

"Yes."

"The allegations obviously pushed him over the edge."

She shook her head. "No, Detective. My father would never take his life. Certainly not over a bogus allegation or a forced resignation. *Never!*"

"But his note says he did."

"But that note ... it's simply not *him!*"

"Even though it's *his* handwriting?

She studied the writing's slant, the deep-loop g's. "Yes, it's his writing."

Loomis stared at her as though she couldn't face reality.

"Maybe," she said, "he confronted his accuser...."

Loomis blinked. "And then the accuser *forced* him to write this suicide note, and killed him?"

She nodded.

Loomis flipped a page in his notepad. "But a resident here, a Mr. Lawrence Gardner, saw him go up to his apartment alone tonight. Later, the building surveillance video shows your father leaving alone."

Her throat felt like it might close off permanently. She looked out the large window at Central Park. Darkness had descended on *their* tree, the huge, sprawling oak that she and her father often gazed at from this same room. The tree soared heavenward, spreading its long, leafy branches wide as though drinking in large gulps of air. They'd called it their 'Wishing Tree.'

Tonight, she only wished she'd wake up from this horrific nightmare.

"We have his wallet and coat down at the station. A personal identification of his effects would help. Do you feel up to it?"

"No. But let's go...."

* * *

Some fifteen minutes later, Loomis and Doolin led Madison into a small interrogation room in the NYPD Seventh Precinct station on Pitt Street. She glanced at herself in the room's two-way window and was shocked by her appearance. Her light-brown, medium-length hair was tangled and hung down over her forehead. Brushing it back, she saw that her green eyes were rimmed with red. Mascara tears had streaked down her cheeks and stained the collar of her white blouse. Her charcoal suit was badly rumpled. She looked like she felt: numb, frightened, and very much alone.

She sat down at a wood table marred with scratches, cigarette burns and a coffee stain shaped like Florida. The air smelled like cigarettes and sweat. And although the room was warm, shivers crawled down her back.

"Would you like some coffee or water, Ms. McKean?" Loomis asked.

"No, thank you."

A uniformed patrolman walked in and placed a large transparent bag on the table. He reached in and pulled out a soggy men's blazer with a piece of seaweed on the lapel. River water trickled out of the sleeves.

Slowly, she opened the wet lapel and saw *M J M,* her father's initials, stitched in dark blue on the inside pocket. He'd worn the blazer to their dinner two weeks ago in Boston. *Our final minutes together....*

"It's his."

"And this?" Detective Loomis placed a soaked wallet on the table.

"His." She opened the wallet to his driver's license. Next to it was a photo of their family – her mom, dad, brother and herself on a North Carolina beach six years ago. A terrific family vacation. Seven months later her mother died from pancreatic cancer.

Detective Doolin walked in and handed Loomis a sheet of paper.

Loomis read it, then turned toward her. "Your father's fingerprints were on the rowboat oars."

"How'd you find out so fast?"

"AFIS matched them to his prints as a Naval officer in Viet Nam."

She felt her last ounce of hope drain away. "Do you expect to find him?"

Loomis shrugged. "Hard to say. Tidal currents in the East River are very strong. They may carry him out to sea."

The image of his body being battered against rocky ocean reefs brought fresh tears to her eyes. Suddenly, she felt incredibly hot. The walls of the cramped, stuffy room seemed to close in on her. She leaned back and drew in a deep breath.

"We're done here, Ms. McKean," Loomis said, gently ushering her from the room.

Back out on Pitt Street a light rain was falling. The cool rain washed away her tears. She wanted it to wash away any memory of this painful night. But of course it wouldn't. This night, like the night her mother died, would be branded in her memory forever.

She got in the police car, and minutes later, it stopped in front of her father's apartment building.

Detective Loomis turned to her. "The NYPD and the Coast Guard will keep looking for him."

Madison nodded.

"Do you have someone to stay with you tonight?"

No, she thought. "My brother's in Paris and most of my friends are in Boston, but I'll phone someone, Detective. Don't worry."

Loomis nodded, but concern lingered in his eyes.

She stared up at the dark, empty apartment. Never again would her father's smile brighten the rooms. Never again would his contagious laugh bounce off its walls and cheer everyone around him. *Never....*

She stepped from the police car and walked toward the entrance, fresh tears filling her eyes. She thought of all the good times she and her father recently spent in this apartment. Their talks had been therapeutic for her, like she was catching up on all the time she'd missed with him growing up.

Here, she told him how badly his absence had hurt her. He listened patiently and said he now recognized that he'd failed her and asked for her forgiveness, which she had gladly given him along with her tears and hugs.

He then revealed that his father also had been too busy for him due to long working hours, constant travel and weekend golf games. She was surprised by her father's revelations.

Then he told her how much her refusals to work with him at his agency had hurt. She apologized, explaining that she'd joined the Boston agency to prove to herself that she could make it on her own before she came to work for him. He said he understood.

* * *

Harry Burkett watched Madison McKean step inside the apartment building *alone.* Then he watched the taillights of the police car fade away down Seventy-Sixth Street. Smiling, he sipped some aquavit and looked up at Mark McKean's apartment window.

A light came on.

Her tall, shapely shadow moved behind a curtain.

First, papa deserts you ... and now the two cops desert you.
How convenient.

Four

"Throw it now!" Mark McKean shouted at the seaman in the Coast Guard rescue boat.

The tall seaman leaned over the railing and tossed him the orange life ring. It splashed into the water fifteen feet away. McKean swam for it with everything he had, but a huge wave pummeled him down into a vicious current. He gagged his way up to the surface, but the ring was now forty feet away.

The seaman tossed him another ring.

Much closer.

McKean swam hard for it. Five feet, two feet.... He touched the slippery ring – but a monster wave swept it away, then pushed him deep beneath the surface. He fought the raging, churning currents, but they only forced him *deeper....*

Now, he was upside down, thirty feet under, on the other side of the Coast Guard cutter, caught in a whirlpool swallowing him even deeper.

His lungs screamed for air. His arms and legs felt like frozen icicles.

He was being dragged deeper into the freezing black abyss....

"DAD!" Madison shouted, bolting upright in bed, trembling in her sweat-soaked nightgown.

A nightmare, she told herself. But real. Like her father was alive and calling out to her. She tried to wipe the terrifying images from her mind, but they lingered. Her clock read 5:17 a.m. Sleep was impossible. But continuing to search for her father's accuser was possible.

Easing herself out of bed, she noticed that she'd knocked the phone off the bedside table during the night after talking to her brother in Paris. She placed the phone back in its cradle and headed to the bathroom. After showering, she toweled off briskly, and got dressed.

In the living room, she walked over to the window and looked out at the rays of dawn now touching the top branches of their Wishing Tree. Suddenly, the reality of her father's death hit her again and she began to weep uncontrollably.

As she looked away from the Wishing Tree, she noticed the same parked, dark Lincoln she'd seen the previous night. The driver stared straight ahead. Probably a chauffeur. He sipped something from a silver flask.

She walked to the kitchen, made coffee and took a steamy mugful into her father's study. She sat in his soft leather chair where he'd always sat, reading the newspaper, puffing away on his briarwood pipe stuffed with Mixture 79. The sweet tobacco scent was still present, unlike him....

She looked back at the green folders on his desk. Last night, she'd gone through them twice, searching for any hint of who might have accused him. She found nothing.

Over three decades, her father had built Turner Advertising from 54 employees and $68 million in advertising billings to 1,920 employees and $2.4 billion dollars with 24 affiliate offices around the world. Today, it was one of the largest, most profitable independent advertising agencies in the country. No wonder ComGlobe and other conglomerates were drooling over the possibility of acquiring Turner Advertising.

Two weeks ago, her father told her that he was still opposed to the ComGlobe merger for sound business reasons.

Did his opposition frustrate someone so much that they accused him of misappropriating funds to force him to resign – a resignation that would have guaranteed the ComGlobe merger? Did his opposition cause someone to stage his fake suicide?

Certainly, in today's ruthless, agency-merger environment, with billions of dollars at stake, certain individuals might go to any extreme, including blackmail and even *murder,* to acquire the cash-rich agency of their corporate dreams.

As she placed her coffee on the table, she noticed a red emergency button on the wall. She wondered if any of the old red buttons, installed in each room over twenty years ago for an invalid woman, still worked today.

The phone rang. She saw *NYPD* on Caller ID.

They've found dad's body....

"Hello."

"Detective Loomis, here."

She squeezed the phone tighter.

"How you doing, Ms. McKean?"

"So-so, Detective."

"I understand. I just called to tell you the Coast Guard hasn't found any trace of your father yet. They said yesterday's rapid tidal currents probably carried his body out into the bay."

... and then into the Atlantic, she thought.

Detective Loomis went on to tell her the NYPD and the Coast Guard would continue searching for the next seventy-two hours. If the body was not found by then, they would be forced to discontinue their investigation.

Madison thanked him for his update and hung up. She understood Loomis's position, but it meant *she* would have to find out who'd accused him and forced him to write the suicide letter.

She began searching his desk, drawer by drawer, examining each scrap of paper, looking for a name, a hint, something.

After four hours, she had found nothing suspicious. Fortunately, her brother Thaddeus, an attorney with UNICEF, would arrive from Paris tonight. It would be much easier with Thaddeus here.

Madison walked over and stared out at sun-drenched Central Park.

As she turned, she noticed the same dark Lincoln parked in the same spot across the street. The driver seemed to be looking up at her window, but when he noticed her looking at him, he leaned back into the shadows. Could the man be watching this apartment?

The tiny hairs on the base of her neck stiffened.

She double-checked the locks and re-set the alarm, then went back to reviewing her father's files.

Twenty minutes later, the doorbell chimed.

She walked into the foyer, looked through the peephole and saw no one. She turned the tiny telescopic hole to the right and left and still saw no one. Her pulse kicked up a notch. Had someone left a package?

Keeping the chain on, she opened the door a bit and saw a man's back. He was bending down, reaching for something.

Her heart started pounding.

As he spun around, she froze.

She was staring at her brother's handsome, but tired face. His light-brown eyes seemed strained with worry and his six-foot-three-inch frame appeared to have shrunk a few inches.

"How'd you get here so fast?"

"Caught an early Air France flight."

He hugged her tightly.

"It's just us now, Maddy."

She nodded, slowly, burying her face in his shoulder.

They sat down in opposite leather chairs and stared at each other in silence for a few moments.

Thaddeus pushed his dark brown hair back off his forehead and loosened his tie. "I should have spent more time with Dad. Called him more often. I assumed there'd always be time...."

"Me, too."

He nodded. "I talked to Dad's attorney, Chester Beale, last night.

He just phoned me back in the taxi from JFK. Very interesting conversation."

"Why?"

"Chester is filing a petition with the Probate Court to request that Dad be officially declared dead."

"But I thought the Probate Court required seven years if the person's missing?"

"Generally they do, but Chester feels certain the judge will grant the petition now, in view of dad's handwritten suicide note, and because the Coast Guard has just officially stated that it's highly unlikely Dad's body will ever be recovered."

She nodded, but held onto the unrealistic hope that her father was still alive, perhaps clinging to driftwood somewhere.

"What happens after the Probate Court grants the petition?"

"Chester can execute Dad's will, which as you know splits everything fifty-fifty between us."

She recalled her father telling them that after their mother's death.

"Chester really surprised me though."

"About what?"

"How much stock Dad had acquired in Turner Advertising. His working agreement permitted him to increase his Turner stock holdings every two years, and Dad did that religiously."

She didn't know anything about the stock.

"I thought he owned about 40 percent of the stock," Thad said.

"How much does he own?"

"Chester said 79 percent."

She sat back, astonished at the amount. "I had no idea."

"Dad kept it quiet. Mr. Turner's widow retains 10 percent of the shares, and the remaining 11 percent are owned by the top ten Turner EVPs."

Her mind was spinning. "So ... you and I split 79 percent of Turner stock?"

He nodded.

She thought back to how her father had always wanted Thaddeus to work at the agency with him. But Thaddeus only had eyes for international law, much to his father's dismay. Thad had recently become serious about a beautiful woman from Brussels. Madison had met her two months ago and liked the blonde linguist instantly.

"Seventy-nine percent gives you and me some *serious* voting leverage," she said.

"*You.*"

"What?"

"You, not me! The voting leverage is all yours, Maddy."

She stared at her brother, wondering what he meant.

"I told Chester that I'm assigning the proxy to vote my shares over to you. *You're* the adwoman. You know the ad biz. I don't. Besides, my job has me traveling to remote places around the world, half of which are difficult to reach by phone. So congratulations, sis! You now control the voting rights to 79 percent of the stock in Turner Advertising. And you know what that means?"

"What?"

"That you could be named chairwoman."

She was too stunned to respond.

"But I'm not ready for – "

"You're a fast learner, sis."

"Not *that* fast!"

Suddenly, his eyes tightened with concern and he looked away from her.

"What's wrong?" she asked.

"I'm worried."

"About what?"

"You."

"Why me?"

He looked back at her for several moments. "The person who stopped Dad from using his 79 percent, will probably try to stop you."

Five

E van Carswell, the thin, gray-haired vice chairman, and a close friend of Madison's father, counted each raised hand slowly, then smiled at her.

"Congratulations, Madison. You've just been elected to our board of directors of Turner Advertising. We're delighted."

Except for my father's accuser, she thought. *Probably one of you.*

"Thank you all very much. It goes without saying that I'm honored to be on your board."

Two days earlier, the New York Probate Court had officially declared her father deceased, based primarily on his handwritten suicide note and the Coast Guard's final report that it was very unlikely his body would ever be found.

She looked out at the other directors, five men and five women, the governing body of Turner Advertising whom she'd chatted with briefly earlier in the morning. The directors developed the agency's corporate goals and the strategies to achieve them. They also controlled the various agency departments: namely, the account service people who dealt with the clients, the media personnel who bought the advertising space and time for the clients, creative people who dreamed up the ads, production specialists who made the ads, and others.

As she looked around the table, most directors smiled at her with friendly, welcoming faces. A few smiles, however, reminded her of hungry crocodiles. Everyone sat around the gleaming cherry wood conference table in the lavishly appointed, multi-screen, high-tech board room.

Carswell rested his hand on the empty chairman's leather chair and faced the group. "Now, to our most important task. The election of our next chairman. The floor is open for nominations."

"I nominate you, Carswell," Leland Merryweather said. Merryweather, she knew, was the agency's Executive Vice President of International Operations. He looked distinguished thanks to his tanned, patrician face, gray hair, trimmed moustache and a black velvet eyepatch over his left eye.

"I second it!" said Finley Weaver, the short, hard-charging, redheaded EVP of direct mail.

A number of directors nodded approval.

"Forget it," Carswell said. "You all know I'm retiring in ten months. My grandkids, my 30-foot Catalina, and several large-mouth bass have invited me to come play in the Florida keys. And I'm damn well going to. I'm *not* the person to build our agency's future on. And that's final!"

Inga Kruger, the EVP chief financial officer, a heavy-bosomed woman in her fifties with large black-rimmed glasses and brown hair that hung down over her ears like tiny springs, raised her hand. "I nominate Karla Rasmussen."

"Seconded," someone said.

Madison looked down the table at Rasmussen, a nice-looking but stern-faced woman around fifty. She wore a dark blue wool suit with braided trim and what looked like a Hermes burgundy scarf. Thick Joan Crawford eyebrows arched over steely, close-set dark eyes. Her hair, lustrous and black, was pulled back tight in a bun at the nape of her neck. The namecard in front of her read, 'Karla Rasmussen, EVP,

Director of Media Services.'

Madison recalled her father telling her that Rasmussen was a brilliant, hard-working executive whose abrasive remarks sometimes created problems, and on occasion, enemies.

"Any discussion?" Carswell asked.

Halfway down the table, an attractive woman in her early forties, with long brown hair and high, sculpted cheekbones raised her hand. She wore a gray striped business suit. Her nameplate said, 'Alison Whitaker, EVP, Director of Client Services.' Madison's father had said that Whitaker was a consummate professional who handled things no matter how difficult.

"Karla," Whitaker said, "You know I have great respect for your abilities and all you've done for this agency over the years. But you also know a number of our major clients have voiced concerns about working with you. So, my fear is that these clients would not be comfortable with you as our Chairperson. Their discomfort might risk our business with them."

Rasmussen stared daggers at Whitaker. "Which clients?"

Whitaker named six.

"Their concerns were minor," Rasmussen shot back, her eyes blazing.

"Not if they asked to have you moved off of their accounts."

Rasmussen scowled back, but said nothing.

"Any more discussion?" Carswell asked.

There was none.

"In that case, all those in favor of electing Karla Rasmussen as our new chairperson, please raise your hand."

Merryweather, Kruger, Weaver and Rasmussen raised their hands.

"Those opposed...."

Six other directors raised their hands. Madison did not need to vote since the majority had already voted down the motion.

"Motion fails," Carswell said. "Other nominations?"

Madison looked around the room, waiting.

"In that case," Carswell said, "I would like to nominate someone I believe can take this agency to even greater successes in time. I nominate Madison McKean to be our new chairwoman."

Muffled gasps broke the silence.

"I second it," said Alison Whitaker, smiling at her.

"It is moved and seconded that Madison McKean be elected chairwoman of Turner Advertising," Carswell said. "Any discussion?"

Madison felt tension hovering over the room like a high-voltage wire. She waited for an avalanche of objections decrying how young and inexperienced she was to take control of a 2.4 billion dollar global advertising network. Frankly, she *was* young and inexperienced, and she had serious concerns about whether she was up to the job. But when Evan told her earlier this morning that he might nominate her, she quickly developed a transition plan she thought might compensate for her relative inexperience.

Karla Rasmussen raised her hand, revealing a chunky gold bracelet the size of a man's Rolex.

"Madison," Rasmussen said, "How long have you worked in advertising?"

"Nine years." Madison knew how pathetically few that was compared to the seasoned professionals surrounding her. Beneath the table, her knees began to shake.

"In which departments?"

"Two years as a creative copywriter, one in media, and the rest as an account director working with a range of clients."

"That's good experience," Rasmussen said, adjusting her scarf, "but it does not seem, ah ... commensurate with the skill-sets and experience required to manage a multi-national advertising network of Turner Advertising's 2.4 billion dollar size, in my opinion."

"Nor mine," Leland Merryweather said. "And what about international experience, Madison? Have you had any?"

"Quite a bit, actually. I've coordinated multinational advertising for some Gillette products, and for Proctor & Gamble in European and Asian markets. In three years P & G sales increased 44 percent and 78 percent respectively."

Merryweather appeared taken aback by her experience and began to fiddle with his eyepatch. Carswell had told her that Merryweather, who managed the international agencies, was respected internationally, but rumored to have once received huge kickbacks from the Lebanese newspapers where he'd placed ads.

"What about Internet and social media, consumer-generated communications?" asked Alison Whitaker.

"Six years for various clients: airline, pharmaceutical, hotel, banking and automotive."

Most directors seemed impressed.

Karla Rasmussen did not. "All good experience, Madison, but again, do you really believe your nine years in a small agency has adequately prepared you to run a massive, global advertising network of twenty-three agencies?"

"No."

Everyone looked shocked by her response.

"And that's why, if I'm elected chairwoman, things won't change."

Rasmussen frowned. "But how is that possible?"

"Because I would ask Evan to function as *de facto* CEO until he retires. He would collaborate with me only on major economic decisions. In brief, you would continue working with Evan as you have been. Business as usual. I would appoint Carswell immediately and ask for your consent on that appointment."

Many directors breathed out in relief, knowing they could continue reporting to Carswell.

"Any more discussion?" Carswell asked.

Madison girded herself for new attacks on her inexperience, but, amazingly, none came.

"In that case," Carswell said, "let's vote on my motion, namely that Madison McKean be named chairperson of Turner Advertising. All those in favor please raise your right hand."

Madison watched six directors raise their hands: Evan Carswell, Alison Whitaker, plus the Corporate Counsel, and three others.

"And those opposed?"

She watched four directors – Karla Rasmussen, Leland Merry-weather, Inga Kruger and Dana Williams - raise their hands.

Silence filled the room.

"Congratulations, Madam Chairwoman," Carswell said, grinning at her.

"Thank you. I'm honored." *And scared as hell.* "I'm sure you all have questions and concerns. I know I would. So later this morning, say at 11:30, let's reconvene so we can discuss any concerns you may have. If you can't make that meeting, just see me at your convenience. But right now, please excuse me. I have to make an important phone call."

Madison stood, feeling elated.

And terrified.

And wondering if she'd walked into a snake pit.

* * *

The Executive Vice President watched Daddy's Little Princess open the boardroom door and walk out.

Sorry, Madison, but your tenure here will be short-lived.

After all, you were only elected because Daddy left you his 79 percent voting share. But then, Daddy McKean has given you nothing but silver spoons your entire coddled life.

By the way, when Daddy told you about the e-mail he received, did he also indicate who he thought might have sent it? Did he tell you what he accidentally saw in my office? Did he leave you a note about all this, a note you haven't found yet?

Whatever the case, Madison, I can't take that risk.

Six

M adison hurried from the boardroom, checking for an empty cubicle with a phone. She had to call John DuMaurier, CEO of
her Boston agency, and tell him she was resigning *before* he got blind-
sided by the news via the industry's warp-speed grapevine. She dreaded
telling John, her longtime friend and mentor at the agency.

She sat in an empty cubicle and called his cell phone. He picked
up and again offered his condolences for her father. Then she began explaining what had just happened in the board meeting, realizing sadly
that it would be a long time before she saw John's friendly smile again.
When she finished, he remained silent for so long, she thought the line
had disconnected.

"John?"

"Yeah...?"

"What's wrong?"

"Your knife in my heart!"

"You were my best boss ever, John!"

"I was your *only* boss ever!"

They discussed the transition of her Boston clients to other executives for several minutes, and promised to keep in touch with each other.

After hanging up, she walked from the cubicle, already missing John and her agency pals and feeling increasingly alone. She also felt overwhelmed. Had she been foolish to accept the enormous responsibility of managing gigantic Turner Advertising? Would some clients take their business away because she lacked big league experience? Would some refuse to work with a woman CEO?

Would the employees accept her? Was she risking their jobs? And everything her father had worked so long for?

I have about as much experience to run a $2.4 billion dollar global ad network as Saddam Hussein had to run a charm school. Still, despite her self-doubts, she had to try. Her father would have wanted her to.

Her throat felt like she'd swallowed chalk dust. Remembering a coffee machine on the seventh floor, she entered a nearby elevator and headed down.

The elevator door whooshed open. She hurried out and bumped smack into a tall young man, scattering his stack of videotapes and DVDs across the green carpet.

"Oh crap, excuse me," she said, scooping up some of his tapes. "I was hurrying to the coffee machine."

"Actually, it's down on five, where I'm going," he said, picking up the rest of the tapes and brushing his dark auburn hair away from very blue eyes. "I can show you."

"Only if I can carry these tapes for you."

"Deal."

They entered the elevator and he pushed five.

"Are you new here?"

"Yes."

"When did you start?"

She checked her watch. "About eleven minutes ago."

"So by now, you know all the ins and outs."

"Except for the elevators."

He smiled a very nice smile.

"Where will you be working?"

She hesitated to tell him who she was. "In various departments to start with."

The elevator opened and he led her around a corner to a cafeteria-like room with wall-to-wall vending machines. She was relieved to see they contained the four important food groups: Hershey bars, Cheez-Its, Almond Joys and Walnettos.

"How do you like your coffee?" he asked.

"Black, please."

He dropped coins in the slot, came away with two coffees and handed her one.

"Thank you."

"Welcome to Turner Advertising. I'm Kevin, the Creative Director."

"I'm Madison, the new girl."

"Those videotapes you're kindly now carrying are going to my office just around the corner, where I have been known to bestow upon neophytes, not unlike yourself, my highly esteemed, Creative-Guy's-Five-Minute-Overview of our glorious agency. Interested?"

"Yes, bestow away."

As she followed him, she realized that as Creative Director, Kevin would have known her father well and may have thoughts about who wanted to oust him. They walked past rows of cubicles and entered Kevin's spacious, high-walled cubicle. He sat behind his desk and she settled into a nearby director's chair with *Kevin Jordan* embossed in white letters.

She looked around his office. Typical creative guy. On one wall hung a toy moose's head, its furry pink tongue dangling out. Beneath the tongue was an old Gibson guitar, some TV commercial storyboards and a Nerf basketball with a big chunk missing. On the back wall were some highly-coveted advertising awards: Clios, a *Lion D'or*, and some Effies. Kevin Jordan was obviously a talented professional.

He was also a handsome, early-thirties guy with no wedding band

and a smile that clearly contributed to global warming.

For the next five minutes, he showed her some excellent ads and answered all her questions. When he finished, she thanked him.

"Kevin, can I ask you one more question?"

"Sure."

She smiled. "Did you know Mark McKean well?"

Kevin's eyes saddened fast. "I sure did. He was a terrific man. He often helped me sell innovative ads to timid clients. I considered him a great boss, a teacher and a friend."

"I heard a rumor about him."

"What rumor?"

"That someone here was out to get him."

Kevin frowned. "As far as I know, everybody liked McKean."

"I heard he was being framed."

His thick, auburn eyebrows rose. "Really?"

She nodded.

"I heard nothing about that."

Again, Madison studied him closely. His honest sadness at the mention of her father's death and the obvious admiration suggested she might confide in Kevin. Her instincts told her she *could* trust him. But then her instincts had been wrong before, especially when it came to men.

Madison put down her coffee and looked at him.

"Kevin, I have a little secret."

He waited.

"Mark McKean is my father."

Kevin's mouth opened wide enough to catch a line drive. "You're ... *that* Madison?"

"The very one."

"Jesus H...."

"Can I tell you something in confidence?"

Still looking shell-shocked, he nodded.

"Dad called me the day he died. Someone here accused him of misappropriating $8.7 million from company funds and was forcing him to resign."

Never taking his eyes from hers, Kevin stood up and paced back and forth. "I don't buy it. No way your father would take company money. He *was* the company! And he didn't need money."

"I agree. But there's also a note in his handwriting ... a suicide note."

Kevin dropped back into his chair and stared at her. "Your father would *never* have taken his own life, Madison. He was the original cockeyed optimist! You *know* that!"

She nodded. "I think someone *forced* him to write the note."

"That makes more sense."

"And then murdered him and made it look like a suicide," she added.

"What do the police say?"

"Suicide. Based on the note. And without the body, they won't investigate further.'

Kevin nodded and stared out the window.

"Any idea who might have accused him?" she asked.

His eyes took on a strange, faraway look for several moments, then he faced her. "Sorry, Madison, but no one comes to mind."

"Are you sure?"

He closed his eyes and seemed to search his memory. "Well, I heard that about nine years ago, before I got here, a couple of EVPs disliked him, but I don't know who."

Madison wondered if they were still on the board.

"How can I help you, Madison?"

She looked at his computer. "I'd like to see the anonymous e-mail memo that accused my father. But my dad's secretary, Christine, couldn't find it in his e-mail files."

"Should be a copy in the backup files," he said. "But we'll need authorization to get into them."

"I'm authorized."

"How'd *you* get authorized so fast?"

She paused. "I have another little secret."

"What's that?"

"I was just elected chairwoman of Turner Advertising." Saying the words felt awkward, like she'd tried on a dress ten sizes too big.

Kevin's jaw dropped open again, then an enormous smile spread across his face. He reached over and shook her hand like he was pumping water from a spigot.

"This is just terrific, Madison! Congratulations!"

"Thank you, Kevin."

She looked back at his computer. "I wish we could access Dad's backup e-mails without anyone here knowing what we're doing."

He closed his eyes a moment, then grabbed his phone. "Dean!"

"Who's Dean?"

"My pal, a computer whiz. He's an outsider and I'm sure he'll help if he's in town." He punched in a number, nodded at her when Dean picked up, explained what he needed and a minute later hung up.

"Seven o'clock tonight. I'll meet you at Dean's. I've got a client meeting before, or I'd drive you over." He wrote down Dean's address and handed it to her.

"Thank you, Kevin" she said, standing and walking over to the door.

"Madison...."

"Yes?"

"Two things I know for sure."

"What's that?"

"One, your dad would never misappropriate funds. Two, he'd never take his own life."

"It's nice to find another believer."

"It's nice to have a McKean running the agency."

Not into the ground, she hoped, as she headed back to the elevator. After all, she'd run some things into the ground before.

Like relationships.

Seven

For the first time, Madison settled in at her father's desk. She took a deep breath and told herself she could do the job. It would be stressful and overwhelming at times, but she'd rely heavily on Evan Carswell to teach her everything about the company. She'd also rely on Evan to help her identify her father's accuser.

Earlier, she'd asked Evan to set up some get-acquainted meetings with clients, and he'd already arranged lunch today with the CEO of an important client, Mason Funds. By then, Madison wanted to have at least a basic understanding of the man's vast banking and investment business.

"Madison...?"

It was Christine Higgins, hurrying into Madison's office.
Christine, her father's secretary for twenty-six years, was a smart, trim fifty-two-year-old. She'd recently run the New York Marathon faster than many women half her age. Madison's father had called Christine the secret behind his success, and for sure she'd played a huge role. She was organized, efficient and cheerful.

But right now Christine looked anything but cheerful.

"Evan Carswell wants to see you. It's urgent!"

"OK."

As Christine walked out, Evan hurried in. He plopped down in the chair opposite her desk with a concerned look. His jaw muscles looked hard as marbles.

She closed the Mason Funds file.

"Nat-Care just called me," he said.

Nat-Care was their health care client, a national, managed health care plan that she knew represented about seven percent of the agency's revenue.

"They already know about my appointment?"

He nodded.

"And...?"

Evan looked down at the carpet and shook his head.

"They've dropped us, Madison."

She felt like she'd been kicked in the stomach. A major client pulls out one hour after she's named chairperson?

"Because of me?" she whispered.

Carswell blinked. "No. They said they've been planning to switch agencies now for a few months."

"Why?"

"They claim they want a smaller agency that specializes in non-traditional media. You know, social media, consumer-generated media, customers blogging about their products on the Internet."

"But we already handle some consumer-generated media for them!"

"I reminded them."

"And...?"

"They didn't elaborate."

Madison shook her head in amazement. "What's really behind their decision, Evan?"

He paused, ran his fingers over his face and shrugged. "I wish to hell I knew."

"Did they get along with my father?"

"Yes. They greatly respected his advice."

And apparently weren't interested in mine....

"Who are they moving their advertising to?" Her heart was pounding in her ears.

"Kearns & Marcotte."

A damn good agency, she knew. "They do a ton of consumer-generated media."

"We do it as well. And our awards prove it."

She nodded.

"Here's what really pisses me off," he said, his face red. "We've increased Nat-Care's new customer enrollment by over 58 percent in the last three years. Second highest HMO growth rate in the nation. And this is our thanks?"

Evan was taking this hard. She understood. Every ad person, sooner or later, experiences the pain of losing a client for whom they'd created highly effective advertising.

"I saw no hint of this coming, Madison."

"I understand." She knew that clients often switched their ad assignment to another agency when a CEO left. *Or when a young, inexperienced CEO like me is brought in....*

"They've given us the basic three-month notice."

She nodded at the standard release time in most agency agreements. "At least we'll have Nat-Care's revenue for three more months."

"During which time I'm going to find us another health care client."

"I'll help," she promised. "My college friend is with a Los Angeles-based HMO."

"Good." He shook his head and looked out the window. "I'm sorry, Madison. This is a hell of blow for your first day."

My first hour....

And despite what the client told Evan, she knew why Nat-Care left.

They left because I was elected chairperson!

Eight

"They're all in the small conference room now," Christine Higgins said.

"Do they know about Nat-Care?" Madison asked.

"Yes."

Madison had called the follow-up meeting of the directors to get a closer look at each individual in the hopes that her father's nemesis might reveal himself or herself inadvertently.

She stood up and headed toward the smaller conference room near her office. The directors were seated around a polished walnut table with yellow legal pads and pens in front of them. As she walked in, the directors stopped whispering and looked at her.

Clearly, they knew about the loss of Nat-Care. Some eyes seemed to suggest that Nat-Care left because of her appointment.

She sat down and said, "As you probably know, Nat-Care just gave us three months' notice."

Everyone nodded.

"They said their decision to go with Kearns & Marcotte was made some time ago."

A few nods.

"I would like to thank all of you who worked hard on the account. And be assured, we'll work hard to get a new health care client in the agency as soon as possible."

"Did Nat-Care say why they left us?" Leland Merryweather asked, his unpatched eye riveted on her.

"They told Evan they wanted a smaller agency that specialized in social media and consumer-generated communications. Evan told them we're winning awards doing that, but they weren't specific about what they really wanted. He'll try to find out more." She sipped some water.

"Meanwhile, as you know, I called this meeting to answer any concerns or questions you might have. So please, ask away."

Karla Rasmussen raised her hand.

"As you know, Madison, the big ComGlobe merger vote is coming up soon. ComGlobe has made a very generous offer to Turner Advertising. We directors have been firmly divided, five for and five against, not counting your father. But just recently he said he planned to cast the deciding vote *against* the merger. Do you know yet how you will vote?"

Madison knew that Rasmussen was her father's most vocal critic on the ComGlobe merger.

"Like my father, Karla. Against the merger. Just two weeks ago, he told me that ComGlobe had sweetened their offer price for Turner. They'd also promised him much more stock and an initial public offering which would have greatly increased the value of his holdings. But still, he planned to vote against the merger."

Rasmussen's jaw line tightened. "Did he say why?"

"He said the merger would require us to resign four of our long-standing clients due to conflicts with ComGlobe's clients."

"But two of those clients are small," Rasmussen said with a dismissive wave of her hand.

"Size wasn't his main concern. Loyalty to clients was."

Karla Rasmussen frowned as though loyalty was an Aesop fable.

"Why should we be loyal to clients? They drop us like used Kleenex. Like Nat-Care!"

"Yes, but it's *their* money."

"But in today's mergers, it's quite common for agencies to resign clients' accounts where there are brand conflicts."

"I know. But he said *these* four clients helped Turner grow large over the last thirty years. Releasing them, after all they've done for us, he felt, was betraying them."

Rasmussen's expression suggested that betrayal was standard business practice.

"My father was even more concerned about loyalty to our own employees. He'd seen what ComGlobe did after other mergers, like the Hartzell merger. ComGlobe executives rolled out champagne and fat bonuses for themselves, while Hartzell rolled out three hundred forty-six heads."

The room was silent for several seconds.

"Are there any more comments?" Madison asked, cracking her knuckles, something she did when nervous.

Leland Merryweather raised his hand. "I must say that this merger makes good financial sense for our company. Especially now! Look at our industry. Consolidation, buyouts and mergers. Why? Simple. Our business is a numbers game. Agency mergers result in more media buying power, and more media buying power means lower media rates, and lower media rates means more ads and happier clients."

"I couldn't agree more, " Madison said. "But my father's view, and mine, is that there is a better merger candidate for us than ComGlobe. Maybe Interpublic, WPP, Publicis or others."

Merryweather shook her head. "But an offer on the table is worth two that don't exist."

"Point taken, Leland. And clearly, we need to discuss this merger much more. Let's meet tomorrow. Christine will set up the best time for everyone."

Heads nodded.

Madison wanted to ask *her* big question and see how each director reacted.

"I have just one question." Madison sipped some water and took a deep breath. "The day my father passed away, he phoned me in Boston. He told me someone here at the agency had accused him in an anonymous e-mail of misappropriating company funds."

Several people gasped. Merryweather's gold pen banged onto the floor.

"His accuser demanded that he retire immediately."

Silence.

"Does anyone know anything about this?"

Silence.

Madison studied them closely, looking for any hint of guilt, or anyone averting her eyes or using defensive body language. Only blank, stunned faces looked back at her.

Is one of you that good an actor? Apparently so.

"My door is open if anyone wants to talk about this in private."

No one looked like they did.

* * *

After the meeting, Leland Merryweather sat in his office, toying with his eyepatch as he brooded over Madison's decision to vote against the ComGlobe merger. Her decision was bad news for him, especially in light of his broker's warning that the stock market would not rebound for several months.

Merryweather needed money now. Both his stock money *and* the ComGlobe merger money.

His private cell phone rang. He fished it from his briefcase, saw 'Jarvis Smythe' on Caller ID. Merryweather knew why the man was calling from London.

"Hello, Jarvis."

"I hear Madison McKean is your new CEO?"

Merryweather was amazed that Jarvis already knew.

"Not for long, Jarvis. And don't worry, your money is coming."

"But I hear she plans to vote against the merger."

"Don't worry, Jarvis."

"I am worried. And don't forget, I've got two other prospective investors over here begging me to let them buy into our agency. And they've got the money *now*."

Smythe was talking about the hottest new agency in London, Smythe-O'Rourke. Jarvis Smythe and Liam O'Rourke wanted a third, equal partner, an American who might bring them some big U.S. multinational clients. They wanted Leland Merryweather and his lucrative clients, plain and simple.

And Merryweather wanted to buy into their fast-growing agency.

"Remember, Jarvis, I have one thing your other prospects don't have."

"What's that?"

"Two big international clients who'll follow me from Turner to your agency. They'll make us all wealthy."

"I hope so, Leland. But you've got two weeks. I've promised the other prospects an answer by then."

"You'll have the money."

They hung up.

Merryweather sat back and looked out the window at the Manhattan skyline. He wasn't worried. The ComGlobe merger would pass.

Like her father before her, Madison McKean would go away.

Nine

Still shell-shocked over the loss of the agency's Nat-Care client, Madison walked with Evan Carswell under the canopy of the famous '21' Club for their lunch with the CEO of Mason Funds, Ltd., a global investment company.

Inside, the maitre'd greeted Evan like an old friend and led them through the crowded lounge area to a table in the exclusive Bar Room. The Bar Room was everything she'd heard it was. Corporate heavy-hitters hunched over delicious smelling meals on tables covered with red and white checkerboard tablecloths. The ceiling was unique – like someone's attic had exploded and a bunch of model planes, trucks, footballs, tennis rackets, phones, ice skates, ballet slippers and more got stuck up there.

Madison found herself seated directly under a New Orleans Saints football helmet which would bounce off her head any second the way her luck was going today.

"President Nixon often sat at this table," Evan said to her.

"And look what happened to him!"

Evan managed a weak smile. "You're doing fine, Madison, honestly. You had nothing to do with Nat-Care."

Then why didn't they drop us last week? she wondered.

"Evan, about my father...."

Evan waited.

"Any more thoughts yet on who might have accused him?"

"Madison, I've racked my brain again and again and still came up with no one. Hell, several board members, including me, have had serious professional disagreements with him over the years, but nothing serious enough to accuse him like that. I loved the man!"

Suddenly, Carswell jumped up as the waiter led a tall, thin executive in his late fifties toward them. The man had steel-gray hair combed straight back above half-rimmed, tortoise-shell glasses that gave him a distinguished look. His charcoal suit looked custom tailored, his navy blue silk tie looked expensive. Tucked beside his gold Rolex was *The Wall Street Journal*.

"Madison, meet Daryl Hanson. My favorite client."

"You say that to all your clients!"

"And I mean it."

Hanson laughed, shook hands with her and sat down. "Madison, it's nice to meet you. And please accept my condolences. Your father was a very good friend. I will miss him dearly."

"That's very kind of you to say, Mr. Hanson."

"Daryl, please."

The waiter took their drink orders and handed them luncheon menus. They chatted a minute and ordered. Seconds later, the waiter brought the two men their scotches, neat, and Madison her Chardonnay, chilled.

"I valued your father's counsel greatly."

She nodded. "Thank you. Evan is acting CEO and overseeing your business."

"That's very assuring. By the way, how is Dan Davies doing in Afghanistan?"

Davies had been the Turner account director on Mason Funds,

handling the day-to-day activities for years until six months ago when his National Guard unit sent him as a major to Afghanistan.

"Dan's fine," Evan said. "He's east of Kabul, near the Pakistan border. Our prayers are with him,"

"Ours too," Hanson said. "By the way, my marketing people tell me that Dan's replacement, Scott Breen, is a good guy and works hard." Hanson paused and sipped his scotch. "But, they say he doesn't yet have the all-around Mason Funds knowledge and expertise that Dan had. They miss that expertise."

There it was. A subtle but real complaint, Madison realized. Hanson's people were complaining about Scott Breen. Her stomach began to tighten.

Madison leaned forward. "Why don't Evan and I talk with your marketing people and decide how best to give them the additional expertise they want."

"Sounds like a good idea."

"Other than that," she asked, "are we handling your ad business satisfactorily?"

He sipped more scotch, then nodded slowly. "You are from my perspective."

But not from someone else's, she heard.

"I'll be frank. My new marketing director tells me he and his team are being seriously courted by a strong competitor of yours."

Madison's mouth went dry.

"This other agency says we should be spending much more money in ads for the new technologies because the Internet's accessible virtually everywhere today. They recommend we drastically cut our spending in traditional media, like TV, magazines and newspapers."

"Who's the agency?" she asked.

"Anthony & Longo."

Madison's stomach tightened. A & L was an excellent, fast-growing agency, specializing in creating ads for BlackBerrys, cell phones, iPods and the like.

"Well, my understanding is that your primary audience is skewed toward people forty to seventy-five."

"Right. But we have some younger customers."

She nodded. "May I suggest that we review your audiences in much more detail, then develop a new proposal that reaches your older audience *and* your younger tech-oriented buyers. We'll also look at new ways Mason Funds can benefit from these new technologies."

He nodded. "When can you show us your proposal?"

"Is next Thursday okay?"

Hanson checked his Blackberry and frowned. "Anthony & Longo are presenting to us on Thursday."

Her stomach did another flip. "Could we present Wednesday?"

He checked his screen, then looked back at her. "How's 7:00-8:00 in the morning?"

"We'll be there."

He nodded and sipped his scotch. "Good."

Beneath the table, she wiped her damp hands on the tablecloth.

The waiter placed their meals on the table. Her Ahi Tuna tartare and crab cakes looked delicious, but her stomach was thinking Maalox. She'd have to make a show of eating.

Madison looked around the Bar Room and saw a group of men leaving. Behind them in the far corner, she noticed an attractive woman holding hands with a handsome man. The woman was Dana Williams, one of her Turner Executive VPs. Dana managed some very large Turner clients.

What concerned Madison was *whom* Dana was holding hands with. Lamar Brownlee, CEO of Griffen-Girard, a large, well-respected ad agency. Was their lunch just romantic?

Or were they also discussing business? Turner business maybe. The more she watched them, the more concerned she grew.

The waiter handed Evan's American Express card back to him and smiled.

As they left '21' she thought, *What a day! One client leaves us, another is being courted by a very good agency, and one of my EVPs looks like she might be sleeping with the enemy.*

And I've still got the afternoon left....

* * *

When the fat man at the next table burst out laughing, Dana Williams turned around. She was surprised to see Madison McKean and Evan Carswell with Daryl Hanson of Mason Funds leaving the Bar Room.

Had Madison or Carswell seen her?

Dana scooted her chair around quickly so they couldn't see her face. If they had seen her with Lamar Brownlee, they'd worry. Frankly, they should worry. Because Dana was looking out for herself.

All she wanted was her fair share of the money she deserved in this crazy business. She'd contributed to the success of Turner Advertising over the last seventeen years. She'd brought in new business, kept clients happy, even slept with a couple to bring their accounts into the agency.

But the company hadn't compensated her adequately.

And Mark McKean hadn't treated her fairly. When Dana had again made it clear that she cared for him a few months ago, he treated her like a high school girl with a crush. She'd been enraged.

But now he was gone.

And his daughter soon would be.

Ten

Harry Burkett watched Madison McKean's yellow cab roll to a stop next to some trees near West Seventy-Ninth Street. She looked around, probably checking for creeps the way women do before they get out of a car. She couldn't possibly know he'd followed her. His military training had taught him to avoid detection.

He pulled out his silver flask, and took a long hard pull of the Norwegian aquavit. The strong liquor burrowed a nice warm feeling down to his gut.

Like the warm feeling he'd have when Madison was no longer a problem.

* * *

"It's down there," the cab driver said, pointing toward a thick cluster of maples.

"Down where?" Madison said, squinting through the trees.

"On the *river!*"

Dean Dryden lives on a boat?

Madison bent down and saw dozens of yachts strung out along the pier jutting into the Hudson River. She hoped Dryden, Kevin's friend, could access the agency's backup e-mail that accused her father.

As she stepped from the cab, she turned to see if the dark Lincoln that had followed her taxi was nearby. She saw no Lincolns, but still had the odd feeling she was being watched.

She walked into the shady wooded area, heading down toward the water. Across the river, the dark sky hung low over the New Jersey shoreline. Suddenly, two squirrels scampered past her and disappeared into the bushes. Behind her, movement. *More squirrels?*

No. Footsteps....

Footsteps snapping twigs.

She walked much faster.

So did the footsteps. Then they *ran ... toward her.*

Her heart pounding, she spun around and glimpsed a tall man hurrying through the thickset trees, rushing toward her! Seconds later, he pushed through a leafy branch in front of her.

"Jesus, you walk fast!" Kevin Jordan said, huffing.

She breathed out and smiled. "A girl needs her aerobics." She decided not to tell him she'd only been seconds from sprinting away.

"So tell me about your friend, Dean."

"My friend the CEO."

"A CEO like me?"

He smiled. "Well, yeah, but there's one big difference."

"What's that?"

"I can't say."

"Why not?"

"It's uh ... politically incorrect."

"Tell me anyway."

"You'll fire me."

"Say it!"

"You're cuter."

"You're fired!"

"I meant *smarter!*"

"What, I'm *NOT* cuter?"

He laughed. "You're cuter *and* smarter!"

"In that case, Mr. Jordan, you're rehired and promoted." *And, oh yeah,* she thought, *I'm pleased you think I'm cute.*

They stepped over a rain puddle.

"So Dean can afford a big expensive yacht?"

"Yep. He's rich. Self-made. He worked his way through NYU by repairing computers, then joined a small dotcom in Palo Alto and quadrupled their business in seven months. Later, he bought into three small dotcom startups that rocketed in value in the mid-90s. Then he somehow sensed the dotcom rockets were about to fizzle out and sold his stock five weeks before they actually did."

"Sounds smart."

"Over 70 million dollars smart."

"Computers are his life?"

"Yep. But something else tickles his gigabytes."

"What's her name?"

"Hacking."

"What's her *first* name."

"Computer."

She smiled. "Hacking into computers is against the law."

"Not if the law asks you to. The FBI and Pentagon have asked Dean to try to hack into their sensitive computer networks and make them more secure."

They stepped onto the dock of the West Seventy-Ninth Street Boat Basin. She saw about fifty vessels, sailboats, motorboats and yachts strung out along the piers. Kevin gave his name to a security guard who gestured for them to proceed. They walked up to Dean's yacht, eighty feet of sleek, gleaming white fiberglass with tinted panoramic windows and satellite communication dishes on the bridge. She smiled at the name on the yacht's deck: *The Mad Hatteras.*

"Yo, Dean, it's Kevin and Madison."

"Come aboard, mates."

They stepped down into the salon and Madison found herself surrounded by beautiful teak paneling, stainless steel trim, several large flat-screen computer monitors and a lot of very sophisticated-looking communications equipment. The fifty-inch TV looked as thin as a credit card.

In the middle of the room, a red-haired, ruddy-complected man flailed away on a keyboard. He wore a faded NYU sweatshirt, tattered jeans, Nikes, and tiny headphones. Tufts of hair stuck out in back.

He stood up, at least six-feet-four-inches of him, lean to the point of skinny, and high-fived Kevin.

"Madison, meet Dean Dryden."

She shook his hand. "Thank you, Dean, for offering to help."

"Glad to." He brushed back his curly red hair, sat back at his computer and smiled at her. "So, Madison, Kevin said you're looking for a company back-up e-mail?"

"Yes."

"Then pardon my pun, but let's get crackin'." He spun around and tapped away on a keyboard. Kevin handed him his personal Turner username and password to access the company's internal computer network. In the darkened room, Dean's fingers flew over the keyboard like a concert pianist's. Within thirty seconds, he was accessing agency files and memos.

He tried entering the e-mail backup files, but was password-blocked. He immediately shifted to a software program that searched for passwords and ways around them.

"This may take some time," Dean said. "Anybody for a snack?"

Kevin and Madison both nodded.

From a small refrigerator, Dean took out a prepared tray of brie, crackers, thinly sliced salmon, cream cheese and mini bagels.

Madison still had no appetite, thanks to losing the Nat-Care business in the morning, possibly losing the Mason Funds Ltd. account at lunch, and seeing her EVP Dana Williams holding hands with the CEO of a competitive agency. But she put some salmon on a bagel and nibbled anyway. It tasted great.

Suddenly, a trumpet blast erupted from Dean's computer.

"Wow!" Dean said. "We're in already! Let's search for documents with key words like 'misappropriation,' 'Mark McKean,' and 'resign'." He typed in the words, hit 'search' and sat back. Within seconds a memo popped up on the screen. *The* memo, she realized. Her heart pounded as she began to read.

In view of compelling evidence now in the possession of this Turner Advertising executive, it has been demonstrated that Mark J. McKean has over the last sixteen years misappropriated company funds totaling 8.7 million dollars from various company accounts; and that on April 9 of this year, he deposited the entire sum in his name to an offshore account, #0632-AQ-54330 in the Caribe National Bank in St. Kitts-Nevis.

Mr. McKean will immediately wire transfer the aforementioned funds from the Caribe National Bank account back to the appropriate Turner Advertising RSQ-#6A Citibank account. In addition, Mr. McKean will resign as Chairman of Turner Advertising and leave the agency, effective tomorrow.

In consideration of Mr. McKean returning the aforementioned funds, resigning from Turner Advertising, selling his Turner Advertising stock at a forty percent discounted rate, and agreeing to never discuss this matter with anyone, Turner Advertising will, on its part, drop all charges that might have been brought against Mr. McKean in this matter. This settlement is offered for the express purpose of avoiding potentially negative and unfair publicity detrimental to Turner Advertising's image and that of their distinguished clients."

"The smoking gun...." Kevin said, staring at the memo.

"Can you determine who sent this e-mail?" Madison asked.

Dryden tapped in a few more commands, and moments later shook his head.

"What's wrong?" she asked.

"The sender used a proxy IP address, one of many available on the Internet. The proxy IP hides the identity of the sender. Could be anybody."

Her frustration growing, Madison looked outside at the New Jersey shore. The dark gray clouds now looked like dirty balled-up sweat socks rolling across the river toward her. It was getting late.

Dean Dryden slid his finger along the keyboard. "Tomorrow, I'll work on identifying the person behind the proxy IP. I'll also enter your agency's financial records to determine whether any money was in fact misappropriated. And if it was, I'll then try to access the Caribe National Bank records to see if the money is still there. But the bank records might be impregnable. These offshore banks have firewalls behind firewalls."

"Thank you, Dean," she said, realizing that he'd uncovered as much as he could in one night. "I really appreciate your help."

"Happy to, Madison."

Madison and Kevin left *The Mad Hatteras* and walked down the long pier toward shore. The scent of roasted garlic drifted over from the nearby Boat Basin Café. She looked around for the dark Lincoln she thought had followed her earlier and didn't see it. Still, she had the odd sense she was being watched.

A strong river breeze hit her and she shivered.

"You going to your father's apartment now?" Kevin asked.

"Yes."

"I'll drop you off."

"I can grab a taxi. You said you live way up near the Triborough Bridge."

"Yes, but I'm heading back to the office for a casting session and to prepare for a client meeting tomorrow. Your dad's place is right on the way."

"OK," she said, happy for the ride. They walked a while, then she turned and smiled at him. "Kevin ...?"

"Yeah?"

"If you're trying to impress the new boss by working late, you're impressing her."

"Hey, I'm just trying to not look like a doofus in front of our client tomorrow."

You'll never look like a doofus, she thought, *not with those blue eyes....*

Eleven

As Kevin helped Madison down into the passenger seat of his Chevy Impala, he couldn't help but notice her long, shapely legs. She told him she'd run cross-country at Wellesley and still jogged a few times a week. Maybe he should offer to take her running in Central Park in the next few days to help ease the stress she was bound to be feeling.

He *should* help her. After all, she was his boss. But she was also a good person who'd had a lot of pain and responsibility thrown at her in the last few days. Considering everything, she seemed to be holding up well.

But beneath her controlled surface he sensed a certain vulnerability, probably because her friends were in Boston and her brother had flown back to Paris. She was all alone in Manhattan.

Kevin got behind the wheel and they drove off toward her father's apartment.

"Your folks live in New York, Kevin?"

"Mom does. Dad died several years ago."

"Oh, I'm sorry."

He nodded. "Fortunately, it was pretty fast. Cancer."

She nodded. "Where'd you grow up?"

He paused, unsure how much to reveal. "Down in Camden...."

They drove in silence for a bit and he wondered if she sensed his reticence to talk about his family background. He decided to shift the focus to her.

"You have any friends in New York City, Madison?"

"My college roommate. Linda Langstrom. She's like a sister. But she's in London on business for two more days. We've been talking a lot since Dad...."

He nodded. "Talking helps."

"It does. I have one other friend here."

"Who's that?"

"I'm talking to him."

He smiled. "Hey, I gotta be your friend, *boss!*"

She laughed as her cell phone rang. She answered. "Hi, Linda. I was just talking about you."

As they talked, Kevin wondered what Madison really thought of him personally? He had no clue. Nor should he concern himself. A personal relationship with her was out of the question. She was his chairman. And she came from an elite, rarified social stratum well above the one he'd come from. Madison's parents had risen from middleclass to considerable affluence on the strength of Mark McKean's skill and drive.

Kevin's parents, Casimir and Anna Jowarski, had risen from the poverty of a one-room shack in Stoczek, a village near Warsaw. They'd arrived in New York thirty-eight years ago, carrying all their belongings in one suitcase and all their money, seventy-six dollars, in his mother's bra. They spoke very little English.

Their sponsor, Kevin's Uncle Jakub, a pediatrician in Albany, advised his father to anglicize his name to get work. His father grudgingly agreed, and Casimir Jowarski became Cassie Jordan.

Two days later, Cassie was hired as a stevedore on the Camden docks. Anna began cleaning offices. They saved every dime and soon moved into a small rental house. "*Five* rooms!" they bragged. And two years later, they bought the house because it was only two blocks from St. Joseph's Polish Catholic Church.

Growing up Polish, Kevin often found himself the butt of jokes and slurs. In sixth grade, two eighth grade bullies, Karl and Drew, beat up 'the dumb Polack' badly. As he lay in the muddy field, wiping blood from his lips, Karl said, "Hey, Drew, how many Kevins does it take to change a light bulb?"

"How many, Karl?"

"None."

"Why?"

"Cuz Kevin's Polack house ain't got no electricity!"

Which was true at the time, since New Jersey Power and Light had turned off their electricity when the bill wasn't paid during Cassie's dock strike. When Kevin got home that night, his father taught him to box.

Two years later, when Karl and Drew picked another fight with him, Kevin left them both lying in the alley moaning behind Thompson's grocery store – the same store where the clerk told him, "No more credit for you Polacks! Cash only!" Kevin's face had turned red and he'd run home, embarrassed.

Over time, Kevin learned to roll with most of the insults.

Suddenly, his phone vibrated in his pocket. Caller ID read *Lonnie Ray,* his basketball buddy.

* * *

As she hung up from talking with Linda, Madison saw Kevin talking on his cell phone. Moments ago, she'd sensed he was reluctant to talk about his family and where he grown up. She wondered if his early life been difficult.

At a red light, she noticed a young couple holding hands as they walked down the street. It had been a long time since she'd held hands like that. So many years ago.

Brace Brenner and she were sophomores; he at Harvard, she at nearby Wellesley. They'd met in their freshman year and fallen in love.

Then came the raucous, hard-drinking, exams-are-over party. They drank too much. So much, in fact, she forgot to take her birth control pill. Five weeks later, she looked down at the results window of her Clearblue test and read – *PREGNANT*. Panicked, she hurried over to Brace's apartment and told him. He smiled and pulled her into his arms.

"This is wonderful, Madison."

"No –"

"Don't worry. We'll manage."

"But Brace, I've got school, you've got med school, how can we –"

"Trust me, we'll manage."

She was shocked by his response. She'd been certain Brace would want to do the only reasonable thing in view of all the circumstances: an abortion. Instead, he seemed like he couldn't wait to be a father.

She also wanted children, but not at nineteen, not with school and a career ahead, and especially not with traces of the cocaine she'd tried a couple of times last week still in her blood. Cocaine could have injured the fetus!

"I can't do this, Brace. I'm just not ready. We're in school. All the responsibility."

"We can handle it."

"I can't! I'm very sorry!"

With tears spilling from her eyes and her emotions spinning out of control, she ran to her dorm where her roommate, Linda Langstrom, listened to her story. Linda then called her uncle, an M.D. The following morning, she drove Madison to the WomensMed Institute in Boston. Brace didn't come because he didn't agree with Madison's decision to have the abortion.

The morning after the procedure, she woke up depressed, dazed and regretting what she'd done. She remained in her dorm room for the next four days, cutting classes, not eating, not talking to friends, staring out the window. Gradually, she returned to her regular routine. But Brace called rarely and acted cooler toward her, distancing himself.

Two months later, he started dating an old girlfriend.

The following summer, he married her.

Now, as Kevin pulled up to her father's apartment, she wondered if she'd ever love anyone as deeply as she'd loved Brace Brenner.

* * *

In his black Lincoln Town Car, Harry Burkett watched Kevin Jordan park his Corvette in front of the apartment building. Madison got out and walked inside.

Burkett looked down at his expensive laser-eavesdropping device on the passenger seat.

"What a piece of shit!"

The eavesdropper hadn't picked up one damn word of their conversation inside Dean Dryden's yacht, even though he'd aimed the device at the proper angle against the windows. Dryden had either coated his windows with Teflon to prevent eavesdropping, or he'd installed some kind of sophisticated, electronic shield-like helmet over his yacht.

Burkett had no idea what they'd discussed in the yacht.

That would drive his Executive VP boss ballistic.

But the EVP would calm down in an hour or so ... when Harry reported that Madison McKean was dead.

Twelve

The Executive Vice President sipped the twenty-five year old Glen-fiddich. It went down smoothly. The office phone rang and Harry Burkett's name popped up on Caller ID.

"Yes...?"

"Madison McKean just visited some guy on a big yacht over at the Seventy-Ninth Street Boat Basin. Kevin Jordan was with her."

"Jordan?"

"Uh-huh."

"Why was he with her?"

"I don't know."

"Whose yacht?"

"Guy named Dean Dryden."

"What'd they talk about?"

Burkett paused, then sighed heavily. "Uh...I don't know. My eaves-dropping equipment didn't work. This Dryden guy has some kinda advanced anti-listening shield."

The Executive VP's frustration rose. "Where is McKean now?"

"At her dad's apartment. Jordan just dropped her off."

"Is she alone?"

"Yeah."

Then my problems are over, the EVP thought. "Keep an eye on Jordan."

"OK."

The EVP hung up and leaned back. The name Dean Dryden sounded familiar. A quick Google search brought up several hundred *Dean Dryden* references. Dryden was a computer guru, a dotcom multimillionaire who on occasion did computer freelance work for various Federal government organizations.

Did Madison ask Dryden to break into our company's computer files? Why ask him? As CEO, she could demand access to any file in the company. It made no sense, unless she didn't want anyone to know she was searching the company files. Which could only mean one thing: She was searching for the e-mail accusing her father. Waste of time. Harry Burkett had deleted the memo.

But had he deleted the backup file copy?

The Executive VP grabbed the phone and called Burkett.

The fool couldn't remember if he'd deleted the backup or not. Idiot!

The EVP directed him to delete it fast if he hadn't already.

Harry Burkett. One more person I can't rely on.

Fortunately, I won't have to much longer.

Thirteen

In the basement of Mark McKean's apartment, Eugene P. Smith pushed up the sleeves of his RCN Cable repairman's uniform. On his hand-sized TV monitor he watched Madison enter the apartment. He waited a few moments, then walked over to the phone control room and quickly disconnected her alarm system and telephone.

Earlier that morning, he'd searched her apartment thoroughly and found no indication that Mark McKean had left his daughter any written clue about who had accused him of misappropriating the $8.7 million. The problem was, he might have told her something. And she might tell the police.

That could not happen.

* * *

Madison dead-bolted the door, set the alarm and looked into the apartment's dark, tomblike silence. She felt the overwhelming, gnawing absence of her father, yet also his presence. Each chair, each room,

69

even the shadowy hallway rekindled a warm memory, like the scent of his pipe tobacco, the shuffle of his slippers, the echo of his laugh.

Sadness washed over her again and she closed her eyes.

She kicked off her shoes, padded into the kitchen, poured a glass of Merlot and sipped some. She knew she'd been drinking too much in the last few days, trying to numb the pain. She took the glass into the bathroom, turned the tub faucet to hot, poured in a glop of bubble bath and breathed in its fresh lavender fragrance.

She removed the rest of her clothes, hung them behind the door and walked back toward the tub. Passing the mirror, she noticed that her stomach was flatter. For good reason. She'd been eating little.

As she eased herself down into the hot water, the steam warmed her face. She began to relax and soon realized this was the most serene she'd felt in days.

Sipping more wine, she watched the rich, soapy bubbles rise almost to her neck. She slid deeper into the silky water, exhaled slowly and began to drift into a kind of dreamy calm.

Moments later, an odd breeze fluttered across her face. Had she left a window open? No. She'd locked them all this morning. And she'd just locked the front door and set the alarm.

Relax girl, relax....

* * *

Eugene P. Smith rode the elevator up to the fourth floor and walked down the hall toward McKean's apartment.

At the door, he stopped and listened. He heard nothing. From his tool kit, he removed his new MagnaQuench device. He placed the rare-earth-metal magnet flat against the door, set the dial on "9" and pushed the button. Slowly, the powerful MagnaQuench magnet pulled the deadbolt back into its door slot.

He then took out his diamond lock pick and inserted it into the simple tumbler lock. Within seconds, the tumblers fell into place.

Smith eased the door open and stepped inside the apartment. He saw Madison's purse on a table and her red high heels nearby on the floor. Then he smelled lavender – bath oil, maybe – and heard the gentle trickle of water.

He pulled the black ski mask down over his face, then fixed the silencer on his Beretta 92FS. He moved the safety to off and stepped silently along the carpeted hallway toward the bathroom.

This morning, when he'd looked around the apartment for a plausible deadly "accident," he'd found one. Luckily enough, the "accident" – a hair dryer – was in the very bathroom where she was now cleansing her firm, young body. The hair dryer was perched precariously on a ledge above the bathtub. Hair dryers fall into bathtubs and electrocute people all the time.

Smith paused and considered the irony of this assignment. The EVP paying him handsomely for this job had no idea that he would have handled Madison for free. Smith had a very personal reason for handling her, one that involved Mark McKean.

* * *

Madison's eyelids grew heavy and she felt herself dozing off in the hot, luxurious water.

Then she heard something....

The creak of a floorboard in the hall. Not the creak of dry wood, but a *snap*. The same snap caused by her father when he stepped on a certain wooden plank down at the end of the hallway.

Someone was out there.

She stepped from the tub, locked the bathroom door, threw on her bathrobe and listened.

Another loud creak. Much closer.

Someone was on the other side of the door.

* * *

Kevin Jordan walked toward the entrance of Turner Advertising, his concern for Madison's safety growing with each step. When she told the board of directors she would vote against the ComGlobe merger, she'd unintentionally made herself a target of those people who wanted the merger at *any* cost.

Like certain directors at Turner and at ComGlobe. After all, billions of dollars were involved. Billions, year after year. And to control that much money, certain individuals would stop at nothing. They would even arrange Mark McKean's fake suicide – and his daughter's death if she got in their way. Which is exactly what Madison had done.

As he entered the agency lobby, he dialed her father's apartment to warn her, even though she'd probably think he was overreacting. The phone did not ring. He dialed again, but still got nothing. Was his cell phone acting weird again? Or was it her phone? He didn't know her cell phone number.

He shrugged and decided to try again later.

* * *

Where's my cell phone?

In the kitchen, Madison remembered. She looked for something to defend herself with, but saw nothing.

Someone turned the bathroom door knob and discovered it was locked. The door knob rattled hard. Her heart pounded.

"I know you're in there." Deep, male voice.

The man lunged against the door and it loosened.

Then she saw it. The red alarm button next to the tub. Did the old alarm still work? Madison ran over and hit the button.

Nothing!

Then, two seconds later, a loud, shrill alarm wailed throughout the apartment.

The door banged open.

The hall light cast a man's shadow onto the white bathroom floor. A tall, thin man wearing a RCN Cable repairman's uniform and a black ski mask stepped in, holding a gun with a silencer.

She grabbed a pair of scissors from behind the Kleenex box.

The man's black mask bent in a smile, revealing perfect but tiny white teeth. "Well done, Madison. But it's so noisy, we'll just have to meet later. Soon. I promise."

He hurried away and seconds later, she heard the apartment door slam shut.

Her heart pounding, she ran into the foyer. She locked the door, dead-bolted it again, and tried to set the alarm, but it wasn't working. She pulled over a hall chair and wedged it under the door knob.

Then she grabbed the desk phone and dialed 911.

The line was dead.

She hurried over to her father's desk, grabbed her cell phone and called Detective Loomis. He said he'd be there in minutes.

After hanging up, she sat in her father's chair and closed her eyes. An armed man had just broken into the apartment. The man had walked past her purse but taken no money or anything of value. Why hadn't he simply shot her?

He'd called her by name and promised to see her again soon. Somehow the man was connected to her father's death.

She took several deep breaths, calming herself.

Minutes later, as she stood to go recheck the front door, she accidentally nudged her father's hickory pipe stand, causing a pipe to tumble off. She picked it up. The same old briarwood, looking exactly like it did on the night she borrowed it many years ago.

She thought back to that night. She was seventeen, a chubby, C-minus student, unhappy with her looks and filled with teenage doubts, certain she could never measure up to what her parents expected of her, or match her brainy brother's high grades. And that afternoon, her boyfriend had asked a tall, shapely blonde, not her, to go to the junior prom.

Overwhelmed, depressed and fat, she took the briarwood pipe to the basement, stuffed it with the marijuana her friend Marilyn had given her, and started puffing away behind the furnace. Within seconds, the ventilation system carried the sweet, unmistakable scent up to her father's study. A minute later he was standing beside her.

"Problems?" he asked.

"No...."

"So tell me about them."

So she did. For over an hour, she told him. Tearfully, she complained about everything. He listened patiently, asking questions now and then. Finally, he hugged her and confessed that at her age, he too had been a chubby, so-so student, certain he'd never measure up to his demanding father.

"Obviously, you overcame your doubts. How?"

"I faked confidence. Coach Reiber, my high school baseball coach, taught me how. We had this big game. The opposing pitcher liked to throw 85-90 mph fastballs high and inside. Coach told me to *fake* confidence, stand in the batter's box like a .400 hitter."

"Were you?"

"No. I was lousy. Anyway, I stepped up to the plate, stuck my chest out and pointed my bat right at the pitcher – shook it at him!"

"What happened?"

"As expected, he threw a fastball high and inside. I hit it for a triple that won the game." From then on, I started *acting* confident all the time. Soon it was a habit."

Her father's message hit home. The next day, Madison began faking confidence, reading confidence-building, self-esteem books, listening to tapes, and jogging. Within a year, she'd slimmed down, run a marathon, raised her grade average to A-minus and her confidence level to maybe a B.

And over the years, her professional confidence had grown with each promotion.

Her personal life was another story.

* * *

Eugene P. Smith was a little embarrassed. He'd noticed the old red alarm buttons earlier that day, but assumed he'd disconnected them when he disabled the main apartment alarm.

He'd *assumed.*

Unforgivable in his line of work.

He was slipping. Years ago, as a CIA operative, he never would have made the mistake.

There was a word for operatives who assumed.

Dead.

Fourteen

Madison bolted upright in bed, her heart slamming against her rib cage. She watched the bedroom door, ... knowing her attacker was back ... knowing he'd burst into the room any moment. Seconds passed ... more seconds ... then a minute ... she heard nothing.

Just another nightmare, she realized. Not *real.* Not like last night.

Detective Pete Loomis had arrived shortly after she'd been attacked. She told him about the incident and he confirmed that the building surveillance camera showed a tall, ski-masked man in a dark green RCN Cable repairman's uniform hurrying down her hallway.

She also told Loomis that her assailant said, "I'll see you soon."

Loomis said he understood her fear, but their precinct was shorthanded and therefore he had no one to guard her. He suggested Secur-US, a private bodyguard company. She phoned them and they sent over a muscular ex-Navy SEAL named Neal Nelson. Neal was outside now, guarding her apartment, and would drive her to work.

She looked at the bedside clock: 5:32 a.m.

She rubbed sleep from her eyes, got out of bed, stretched and realized her leg muscles felt as stiff as coiled springs. She needed a good run. But jogging in Central Park was out of the question with her attacker still out there. So she laced up her Nikes, started running in place and turned on the television.

A silver-haired WNBC anchorman was speaking about a big new corporate merger in which the merger management team got 'fat cat' bonuses and thousands of mergees got pink slips.

Is that ComGlobe's plan? she wondered. Merge with us, cut jobs, then stuff fat bonuses into their pockets? ComGlobe had done it often before. But not this time, she hoped.

Thirty minutes later, Neal Nelson drove her toward the office. As they drove, she thought about her day ahead. First, she wanted to ask some directors about whom they thought might be her father's accuser.

Then she had to act like a CEO. Hopefully today would be better than yesterday: one client resigned, another was being hotly pursued by another agency, and EVP Dana Williams was holding hands with the CEO of a major competitive agency.

Neal Nelson's Chevy TrailBlazer suddenly crawled to a stop in traffic. They were blocked due to road construction. Some people were leaving their taxis and walking.

"We're stuck here for a while," Nelson said.

"I can walk from here."

"Bad idea."

"It's only a block and a half."

"Bad idea."

"I'll stay real close to people."

"Close to the bad guy maybe!"

Nelson was right, of course. But looking around, she saw no tall, thin body shapes even remotely similar to her attacker. Then she saw a tall body shape she did recognize. She rolled down her window and shouted, "Kevin!"

Kevin Jordan, walking down the street with a Starbucks coffee, waved back.

"He's going to the agency. I can walk with him."

Nelson stared at Kevin, then at the crowds and said, "I'll walk you both to the agency." He pulled into a No Parking zone, placed a *Homeland Security* sign in the windshield and they got out.

She introduced Kevin to Nelson and they all started walking down Fifth Avenue, Nelson trailing behind them.

"A bodyguard?" Kevin said.

"It's a long story."

He nodded. "By the way, I tried to call you last night, but your phone was dead."

"Me too ... almost."

Kevin stopped walking and stared at her.

"A man broke into my apartment. He had a gun."

"Jesus, Madison...."

As she explained everything, the color drained from his face.

"I *knew* you were in trouble!"

"Why'd you think that?"

"The ComGlobe merger. I began to think someone might try to stop you from voting against it. Like they stopped your father."

They reached Turner Advertising. Neal Nelson explained he'd be back to drive her home from work and left. She and Kevin walked into the dark, empty lobby of Turner Advertising, greeted the guard, and took an elevator up.

Kevin exited on the fifth floor and she continued up to the tenth, the executive floor. The elevator doors slid open and she stepped out into almost total darkness. She had no idea where the light switches were.

Behind her, the elevator hissed shut. She started feeling her way down the long shadowy hall and stopped cold. She was staring at a brochure: *RCN Cable News,* resting on a table. On the cover was a RCN service man wearing a uniform like her intruder's!

She didn't recall seeing the brochure there yesterday.

Had her attacker placed it there this morning to frighten her? Did he persuade the lobby guard that he had to check the RCN Internet cables before employees came to work? Was he hiding in the black shadows ahead, or in one of the offices along the hall?

Panic seized her and she tried to calm herself.

She knew her imagination was in overdrive. *Play it safe*, she told herself. Go down and ask the guard to come up and check out the floor.

She started back toward the elevator and suddenly remembered that Christine told her service personnel had to get a signed work order before they could enter the building. There was no way her attacker could have obtained a work order during the night.

Steeling herself, she turned around and hurried back down the shadowy hall. She made it to her office alive, flicked on the lights and couldn't believe her eyes.

The office was cleared out. Her father's desk was bare. The walls were stripped of his photos and awards. His desk drawers and large armoire were empty. Even his treasured 1902 Oliver typewriter was gone from the corner.

Shocked, she slumped down in his chair.

Then she heard someone behind her.

Spinning around, she looked into the face of Karla Rasmussen standing a few feet away, staring at her with dark, icy eyes. No, envious eyes, as though she felt *she* should be sitting where Madison was.

"You're in early," Rasmussen said.

"Not early enough to stop someone from clearing out my father's things."

"Christine and I thought it would be easier this way for you to decorate. But if you want some things back, just tell Christine."

"Just a few things. By the way, do you know where my father kept his recent, active files?"

"In those cabinets." Rasmussen pointed toward the small adjoining room filled with tall gray file cabinets.

"Is that where his ComGlobe file is?"

Rasmussen's eyes darkened at the mention of ComGlobe. "Christine keeps all his files in there."

"I'd like to read it," Madison said, standing up.

"Of course." Rasmussen seemed caught off guard by the request. They walked into the file room. Rasmussen reached behind a row of thick *Advertising Red Books* and took out a set of keys. She slid a key into a cabinet labeled *Cars – Drug Companies,* opened the drawer and gestured for Madison to look.

As Madison fingered through the files, Rasmussen stood slightly behind her, ramrod straight and silent. Madison reached a file labeled *Communications* and saw a two-inch gap.

"The ComGlobe file is not here," Madison said.

Rasmussen did not seem the least bit surprised that the file was missing.

"Where else might he have kept the file?"

"On his desk."

"But wouldn't Christine have filed it back here?"

Reamussen gave a slow nod.

"Let's ask her." Madison said, walking back to her desk. She dialed Christine's home number. Christine answered and explained that she'd placed the ComGlobe file back in the cabinet around four o'clock yesterday afternoon.

Madison hung up and explained what Christine said.

Rasmussen shrugged.

"Well, the file's missing. Any idea who has it?"

Karla's cheek muscle twitched. "No...."

Madison sensed the woman knew more than she was saying or was flat-out lying.

"Well, I'm sure you have a lot to do," Rasmussen said, walking to the door. "So I'll leave you to it."

Madison nodded and watched her go. There was something cold and unsettling about the woman. Why wasn't she surprised that the ComGlobe file was missing? Was it because she'd *taken* it? Perhaps because my father wrote something in it that incriminated her?

What does Kevin think of Rasmussen? Madison wondered. She started to phone him, than realized that Rasmussen might be nearby, listening.

Madison left her office and walked down to the elevators. Two minutes later she walked into Kevin's office, carrying two cups of coffee.

"I owe you caffeine." She handed him a cup.

"Thanks. I need it."

His smile hit her like a sonic boom. She nearly forget what she'd come for.

"What's up?"

"Karla Rasmussen."

"What about her?"

"How'd she get along with my dad?"

He paused a moment. "Better with him than with most people. But recently, she was quite upset with him."

"Because he planned to vote against the ComGlobe merger?"

"Yeah. Karla wants the merger, probably because it would greatly increase the value of her company stock."

"For her, money comes first?"

"Second and third, too. If the merger passes, the IPO would net her a five or six times stock split. Maybe more! I'm guessing she'd pocket tens of million of dollars."

That's strong motivation, Madison thought.

"So when you told the board *you* plan to vote against the merger, you made her very unhappy."

"She practically hissed. What about you? Do you favor the merger?"

"No."

"Why?"

"Because ComGlobe treats the mergee employees like the bankruptcies treated auto workers."

"Like crap!"

"Yeah, it's merge, purge and outsource. Nine million good-paying American jobs have been outsourced forever. Congress sees nothing wrong with that!"

"Maybe we should outsource Congress!"

Kevin smiled. "Like Mark Twain said, 'Suppose you were an idiot. And suppose you were a member of Congress. Ah .. but I repeat myself.'"

They laughed. She liked the sound of his laughter.

Madison decided to ask him the big question. "So, do you think Rasmussen is capable of arranging my dad's fake suicide so the merger would pass?"

As Kevin considered the question, Madison looked out the window as a fiery red Manhattan morning sun burned off the night sky. Two white gulls rode the wind currents between the buildings then turned and glided off toward the East River ... the river where her father....

"Karla is tough, Madison, even ruthless sometimes. But *that* ruthless? I just don't know."

She nodded and stood up. "Thanks, Kevin. I really appreciate your thoughts."

"Any time."

As she walked away from his office, she again wondered whether Rasmussen was behind the plot to oust her father. The woman had motive. He was blocking the merger that would give her the two things she wanted most: money and power.

And speaking of power, Kevin's eyes were like powerful beacons that seemed to draw her in. And if, as those poets say, the eyes mirror the soul, his soul was in great shape, not unlike the rest of him.

But, she cautioned herself, *you were seduced by blue eyes in handsome faces once before and paid dearly for it.*

Ease up, woman! Now!

Fifteen

Karla Rasmussen sat at her desk, thinking about Madison's surprise when she discovered the ComGlobe folder was missing from the file cabinet.

Obviously, Madison wanted to search the folder for any clue her father had left about his accuser.

It's also obvious, Rasmussen thought, *that she suspects I'm the accuser. Maybe that I staged his suicide.*

Sorry, Madison, but you won't find any incriminating notes against me in the ComGlobe file.

Because you won't find it.

And, you won't find enough votes to stop the ComGlobe merger.

Like her father, Madison didn't realize how many directors wanted the money from the merger now!

Directors like me. *Unlike you, Madison, I've paid my dues! And the ComGlobe merger money is my payback.*

Rasmussen thought ahead to the IPO sale of her Turner stock after the merger. Her stock could bring her as much as nineteen million dollars. A most pleasing sum.

She leaned back in her leather chair, smoothed out her red scarf and thought back to when she first discussed the ComGlobe merger with Mark McKean. He flat out refused to merge.

"We'll have to resign some clients and dismiss a lot of employees..."

"It's just business," she'd said. "All other industries are experiencing consolidation. AOL grabbed Time Warner, Rupert Murdoch's News Corp grabbed *The New York Times*. Macy's gobbled up Marshall Field's and Filine's. Consolidation is inevitable."

But no, his mind was made up. He refused to reconsider his decision. That enraged her. Business was war. Mark McKean simply didn't get that.

So she'd decided that he was no longer competent to run the company in the years ahead. The job required someone with vision, someone who saw the big picture and was tough enough to steward the company in the future. Someone who understood the necessity of the ComGlobe merger.

Mark McKean had been her roadblock.

Now his daughter was.

Her phone rang. Caller ID said, *Harry Burkett.*

Sixteen

Madison watched Karla Rasmussen cross her arms over her chest and frown with obvious contempt at the document in front of her. "It's very weak!"

"It's strong and balanced," said Alison Whitaker, the Director of Account Services. "Exactly the media plan this new DietRxx product needs."

Madison tended to agree with Whitaker, whose olive blouse complemented her pale-blue eyes and brown hair. Madison had come to the meeting to learn more about DietRxx, a new weight-loss pill, but also to get a closer look at Karla Rasmussen.

They sat at a lacquered rosewood conference table along with the agency team working on the DietRxx business.

"We need more television," Rasmussen said, "to build awareness of DietRxx!"

"We already have a heavy television schedule," Whitaker shot back.

"Says who?"

"Says outside research! The same research that says we need direct marketing to crank up early sales fast!"

Madison knew that both women presented valid arguments. The question always was: which medium would give the client the most sales bang for their advertising buck? Was it big network television? Cable? Direct Marketing? Newspapers? Radio? Magazines? Internet? Social media? The answer, Madison knew, was usually a smart mix of media.

But *smart* often was decided by the most dominant person in the group. A person like Karla Rasmussen.

"Chop 40 percent off direct marketing and dump that money into TV!" Rasmussen said.

"Too late," Whitaker said.

"It's *never* too late!"

"Meg's already committed her media budgets."

"She can un-commit them!"

Whitaker took a deep breath and let it out. "She can't, Karla! She's signed the media buys last week."

Red-faced, Rasmussen slammed her thick day planner down on the table. "Meg can goddammed well un-sign them!"

Whitaker rolled her eyes as though she was talking to a four-year-old.

Madison sensed this was not the first time these two determined women had locked horns. Nor did it appear to be the first time Karla had entertained this group with a hissy-fit tantrum.

Alison turned and smiled at Madison. "Madam Chairwoman, it must comfort you to know that all your executives think alike."

Everyone smiled except Rasmussen.

"It comforts me that you *don't* think alike," Madison said.

"I agree. But do you feel familiar enough with this plan to share your perspective with us?" Whitaker asked.

"No. But that's never stopped me before."

More smiles.

"Based on my ad experience with Pfizer," Madison said, "this media mix seems pretty well-balanced. My only suggestion is to see if the client can scrape up some extra money from non-marketing budgets to buy a bit more TV *and* direct marketing."

"Makes sense," Whitaker said, checking her watch. "But right now we have to give up this conference room. There's a client meeting in here in five minutes."

Everyone stood and filed out of the room.

In the hallway, Madison saw Whitaker walking toward the elevator. Whitaker had known her father a long time and Madison wondered if she had any thoughts about who'd accused him.

"Alison, do you have a moment?"

Whitaker turned and smiled. "Sure. Actually, I was wondering if you had some free time today?"

"I have some now."

Moments later, they entered Madison's office and settled themselves into two beige leather chairs facing a table covered with issues of *Advertising Age, ADWEEK* and *The Wall Street Journal*. Madison was delighted to see her father's family photo back on his desk. She was also pleased to see his 1902 Oliver typewriter, a treasured gift from his grandfather, back in its rightful place in the corner. Having her father's things nearby comforted her ... made her feel like he was close by ... watching over her.

"Your dad would have been proud of you in yesterday's board meeting," Whitaker said, brushing back her thick brown hair.

"Thank you, Alison." Madison appreciated the compliment from someone with Whitaker's credentials.

"You looked calm, but I sensed you were a little nervous."

"Arrid doesn't make enough deodorant."

Whitaker smiled, but then her eyes grew serious. "Actually, I wanted to discuss something you mentioned in our follow-up board meeting."

Madison hoped she meant the e-mail accusing her father.

"The ComGlobe merger," Whitaker said. "Last night, I changed my mind. I've decided to vote like you, against the ComGlobe merger."

Madison was delighted. "Thank you. But what changed your mind?"

"Your father's arguments. The more I thought about them, the more sense they made. Like him, I think we can find a better merger candidate than ComGlobe."

"I agree. And your vote now gives us a more comfortable margin of two."

Whitaker looked down at the carpet. "Not any more."

Madison felt her chest tighten.

"Inga Kruger changed her mind."

"She's going to vote for the merger?"

Whitaker nodded.

"So our margin's down to one again."

Again, Whitaker looked away, then slowly shook her head.

Madison didn't want to hear this.

"Someone else," Whitaker said, "who's been against the merger is apparently going to vote for it."

"My God, the merger could pass! Who is it?"

"I don't know."

"But how'd you learn this?"

"I received an anonymous e-mail two hours ago. I tried to trace it, but the sender used one of those proxy addresses they get from the Internet."

Just like the proxy e-mail sent to my father, Madison thought.

"Sorry to bring you such bad news."

"Better now, while we still might be able do something."

Madison felt nauseated. "But even if the directors tell me they're voting against the merger, there's no guarantee they will. As you know, our corporate bylaw says major decisions affecting the future owner-ship of the company will be decided by a majority of the directors' votes, whose votes shall be unsigned."

Whitaker nodded. "Your father wanted directors to vote their hon-est preference, without undue influence by him or others."

"Yes, he told me that."

"So, if a director tells us they're voting against the merger, they can easily vote for it and we won't know if he or she did."

Madison nodded and looked out the window a few moments.

"Well, Madison," Whitaker glanced at her watch. "I'm late for a World Motors meeting. Let's continue this discussion later."

"Just give me a call."

As Madison watched her leave, the phone rang and she picked up. Christine said, "I have Kevin Jordan on the line for you."

She picked up. "Hi Kevin. What's up?"

"Dean Dryden just called. He was able to get into our company financial files and search for the missing $8.7 million."

"What'd he say?"

"That we had to see him right away."

"Why?"

"He started to tell me, but then his phone went dead."

* * *

From the lobby, Harry Burkett watched Madison and Kevin eat chili dogs they'd bought from a street vendor, then grab a taxi and drive off.

Burkett flipped open his untraceable cell phone and dialed a number. It rang several times and he was tossed into voice mail.

He left a message saying that McKean and Jordan were heading back to the yacht at the Seventy-Ninth Street Boat Basin.

Then he hung up and remembered that Eugene P. Smith had said he might visit the yacht.

Perhaps he already had.

Seventeen

Madison and Kevin sat on frayed seat covers in the old Yellow Cab heading toward Dean Dryden's yacht. She found herself overwhelmed by the scent of garlic reeking from three fat salami rolls hanging from the rearview mirror. She cracked her window to breathe fresh air, but got bus fumes.

Several minutes later, the taxi pulled to a stop near the Seventy-Ninth Street Boat Basin and they got out. As they walked down the pier toward the yacht, she wondered why Dean had wanted to see them so urgently. Had he found the missing $8.7 million? And why hadn't he called back after his phone disconnected? Kevin had phoned him twice but got nothing, not even voicemail.

As they stepped onto the deck of *The Mad Hatteras,* Kevin leaned into the main cabin and shouted, "Dean!"

No response.

"Yo, *DEAN!*"

Still no response. They entered the cabin and she saw Dean's four large computer screens glowing in the dark, but no sign of Dean. The haunting melody of *Bolero* flowed from small Bose speakers.

"I'll check the staterooms," Kevin said, heading down the stairs.

Madison walked behind the computers and stepped further into the shadows. Her heart rate kicked up a notch when she noticed magazines scattered on the floor, a wastebasket tipped over, and steam swirling from a coffee cup.

"Hey, Dean...?"

Nothing.

Bolera was reaching its crescendo ... and so were her nerves. Then, in the shadowy corner she saw a man in a camouflage jacket lying on the floor.

She hurried over....

Only a duffle bag, for crissakes!

She breathed out.

Suddenly, behind her ... footsteps.

She spun around and saw blue tennis shoes hit the rear deck. Dean.

He walked inside with a grocery bag, took out a large pastry box and opened it.

"Anyone for Cinnabons?"

Madison smiled. "Cinnabons. My secret weapon! I had an impossible client who never bought anything. One day, I brought Cinnabons to the meeting. He scarfed down three, turned pink and bought every ad we put in front of him. Tried to buy our wall painting!"

Dean laughed as Kevin stepped back into the main cabin.

"Hey, why didn't you call me right back?"

"Couldn't. My phone bounced off the deck into the river when I was talking to you."

"Klutz!"

"Yeah, but *this* is what I was so hot to show you guys." Dean hurried them over to a computer.

Madison stared at a screen filled with numbers.

"You're looking at Turner Advertising's financial records for this fiscal year," Dean said. "I studied them five ways from Sunday."

"And?" Kevin said.

"Absolutely nothing's out of the ordinary."

"No misappropriated money?" Madison asked.

"Not a dime."

"Did you check the company 401K funds?"

"Yep. No money missing."

"What about previous years?"

Dean nodded. "I went back over the last twelve years with the help of two numbers geeks who work for me. We used some new sophisticated accounting software that we helped develop for the U.S. military's General Accounting Office. Again, we found no hint of missing money. No funny numbers. Nothing!"

Relieved, Madison scanned the maze of numbers. "But how can you be so certain?"

"We're not talking intricate Enron-type-cooking-the-books games here. As Kevin explained to me, most ad agencies today work with their clients on an hourly fee basis, or on performance-based compensation. But some big agencies, like Turner Advertising, still work with your large clients on the traditional commission-based compensation. For example, Turner tells NBC to run a commercial for your World Motors client. So NBC runs the commercial, then sends a bill for the commercial time to World Motors. When World Motors pays the bill, NBC sends a commission check to you at Turner Advertising. That all figures out to the penny."

"What about our hourly fee-based clients?" Madison asked.

"They also checked out."

Madison felt another wave of relief wash through her.

"So that's your revenue," Dryden said, pointing to another screen. "And here's how your agency spends it. Fifty-five percent goes to employee and management salaries; twenty percent to rent, facilities and maintenance; twenty-two percent to profit and three percent to new business development. That's what happened. The numbers vary slightly from year to year, but they balance out."

"So how could they accuse my father of misappropriating $8.7 million?"

"Good question," Dryden said.

"And where did the $8.7 million deposited in his name into Caribe National come from?"

"Even better question."

"Was the $8.7 transferred back to the Turner's RSQ Citibank account like the e-mailer demanded?"

"No."

"So the money may still be in the Caribe National Bank?"

"It may."

Madison stared at the screen in silence for several moments. "I'm going to visit the bank and find out who the *real* depositor was."

"Won't be easy," Dryden said. "Most of these offshore bankers would eat their firstborn before divulging information about a protected account. But the account is in your father's name and you are his surviving daughter. So who knows, you might persuade a Caribe National banker to share some information with you."

"That's my plan. Last night I booked a flight to St. Kitts."

"Makes sense," Dryden said.

Kevin didn't appear to agree.

They thanked Dean again, left *The Mad Hatteras* and walked outside. The sun warmed Madison's face and she breathed in crisp river air. She looked over at the Boat Basin Café and saw two young boys tossing bread crumbs to some seagulls.

"When are you flying down to the Caribe National Bank?" Kevin asked.

"Tomorrow afternoon."

Kevin's eyes narrowed.

"What's wrong?"

"Your attacker."

She appreciated Kevin's concern, but she had a plan.

"*I* ... won't be flying down."

"What?"

"Tonight I'm staying in a Manhattan hotel under an assumed name. My bodyguard, Neal, will be there. And I've booked the flight under my assumed name, Shae Stuart. Tomorrow, I'll wear a disguise to the airport. My attacker will never even know I've left Manhattan."

Kevin nodded, but didn't seem convinced. "Let's hope he doesn't. Tomorrow I'm driving my mom up to Albany for her semi-annual get-together with my uncle. I could reschedule her trip and come with you."

Madison's heart did a little dance. "That's very kind, Kevin, but not necessary. I'm certain your mom's get-together is very important to her. But thanks for offering to come."

"You're sure?"

"Positive."

As Kevin flagged down a taxi, Madison was surprised at how pleased she'd been at the prospect of Kevin traveling with her to St. Kitts. No, she'd been more than pleased. She'd been excited about being with him.

Quickly, she reminded herself to cool it.

You have more pressing things on your mind, not the least of which is running a two billion dollar company, and trying to keep more clients from walking out the door.

And so far you've done a lousy job at both.

* * *

In his parked Lexus, Eugene P. Smith focused his powerful binoculars on the faces of Madison McKean and Kevin Jordan as they got into the taxi.

Smith had lip-read their conversation as they walked down the pier toward him. *So, Madison, you plan to stay in a hotel tonight and fly to St. Kitts tomorrow....*

See you soon....

Eighteen

Madison and Kevin stepped from the cab. She noticed something was bothering him as they walked toward the agency.

"Your chili dog acting up?" she asked.

"No. A mean, motivated moron is."

"There's a word for people like that."

"What?"

"Client."

Kevin forced a smile. "Actually, he is a client, and I've got a meeting with him now. I just can't seem to work well with him. None of us can."

Madison couldn't imagine anyone who couldn't work well with Kevin. "Who's the client?"

"Maurice Dwarck, ad director for FACE UP Cosmetics."

"FACE UP is a good brand."

"Good brand, lousy client. He redesigns and rewrites every ad."

"So why'd he hire our agency?"

"Good question."

The ad industry was filled with stories of corporations who spent a hundred grand or more finding the right agency, then told the winning agency exactly how to design and write each ad. Sort of like choosing the best heart surgeon and then telling him how to do your quadruple bypass.

"His budget's twenty million a year, but we're losing money on the account."

"Why?"

"We present three, four, five tested campaigns. He tosses them all out for no valid reason." Kevin's face reddened. "And, the guy's a scumbag!"

"Why?"

"Dwarck believes his agency relationship entitles him to a physical relationship with any woman in our agency. At a recent sales convention, he groped one of our young copywriters and promised to get her promoted if she spent the night with him. When she said no, the bastard pinned her against a parked van and fondled her. Fortunately her friends walked by and he backed off. But he tried the same thing with one of our art directors the next night."

What a pig! Madison thought, realizing it was time for her to act like the CEO. "I'll attend the meeting."

"Great! Hopefully your presence will keep Maurice in line."

"Actually, I'd rather he didn't know my title."

* * *

Madison and Kevin walked into the conference room where everyone was settling in around the table. She identified Maurice Dwarck immediately. He was bragging loudly about some arm-twisting deal he'd made. Dwarck, about forty, was a huge, bull-shouldered man with flushed jowls and thinning black hair combed straight back. Thick, large eyebrows hung over brooding eyes that were the strangest shade of gray she'd ever seen. Gorilla hands, thick and matted with hair, stuck out from his monogrammed french cuffs.

Beside Dwarck sat a short blonde with large breasts that appeared to be erupting from the low-cut bodice of her cherry-red shiny leather dress. Kevin whispered that she was Soozie Bender, Dwarck's personal assistant in all ways. Soozie seemed entranced by the wood grain in the conference table.

Madison signaled her colleagues that she didn't want to be introduced.

Maurice Dwarck finished his bragging, turned around and acknowledged Kevin, then eyeballed Madison, his gaze sliding from her face to her blouse.

"Let's get this thing over with," Dwarck said, slurping his coffee.

Tess Jennings, the agency's attractive FACE UP account director, explained that the meeting was called to review a FACE UP lipstick advertisement for *Cosmopolitan* and *Oprah* magazines. She then presented the ad layout and placed it in front of Dwarck. The ad's Asian model was stunning, and her lipstick and make-up worked beautifully with her tawny skin. Madison thought the ad looked terrific.

"This ad," Tess said, "tested thirty-nine percent higher than Revlon's ad, and over forty-seven percent higher than L'Oréal and three other competitive ads. These are terrific figures!"

Dwarck was looking at Tess's terrific figure.

Tess finished and everyone waited for Dwarck's reaction. He sat still as a statue, apparently savoring his absolute power, then grabbed the ad and frowned as though searching for something to criticize.

"Where the hell's my FACE UP logo?" Dwarck demanded.

About three inches from your nose! Madison wanted to say.

Tess pointed to the logo in the lower right corner of the ad.

"You call *that* a logo?" He slammed the ad back down on the table and folded his arms.

"That logo size is exactly appropriate for a full page advertisement," Tess said. "If we make the logo bigger, it makes the ad less inviting to the reader."

"Well, *this* reader wants it much bigger!" Dwarck said.

Kevin leaned forward. "Maurice...?"

"Yeah?"

"We researched this ad with a larger logo. It turned people off so fast, they flipped the page and missed the product message."

"Yeah, well here's my message: *Bigger logo!* A bigger logo sticks in their minds! Right, Soozie?"

Hearing her master's voice, Soozie Bender stopped doodling with her Bic pen. "That's right, Mr. Dwarck!"

"But the logo cannot stick, if they don't even look at the page!" Kevin persisted.

Maurice snorted. "Look, here's the way it is. First, you will double the size of my FACE UP logo. And second, you will stick my big double-sized logo right up in the headline where no one will miss the goddammed thing!"

From bad ... to worse, Madison realized, her anger welling up fast.

"Does anyone have a problem with that?" Dwarck said, jutting his jaw out defiantly.

The room was silent for several seconds.

"I do," Madison said.

Dwarck actually chuckled. "You? Why don't you stick to pouring coffee or whatever else you do around here."

Madison forced herself to remain calm. "Mr. Dwarck, all we do at this agency is create ads. We do that ten, twelve hours or more a day. We know how to make people stop and read your ads. This research proves that. And you know more about FACE UP products than we ever will. So if we've written something factually wrong, we'll gladly change it. But if it's a question of style, like the size and location of the logo, well, that's our expertise."

"So...?"

"So, Mr. Dwarck, we won't change it."

Dwarck's mouth fell open. "Just who the hell do you think you are? You're just a gofer!"

She paused. "I have other responsibilities as well."

"Are you actually saying the agency won't make my logo bigger and stick it in the headline?"

"That's what I'm saying."

The room went graveyard quiet.

Dwarck blinked rapidly, as though he was having trouble believing what she'd said. His jaw muscles bunched up. "Listen, Toots, no one talks to Maurice Dwarck like that. Either this agency makes my logo bigger, or I take my business elsewhere."

All eyes shifted back to her.

"Perhaps your suggestion makes sense."

"Damn right my bigger logo makes sense!"

"No. Taking your business elsewhere."

Dwarck looked like he'd been whacked upside the head with a two-by-four. "I've had enough of your fucking insolence! I'm speaking to your new CEO!"

"You are," she said.

"Damn right I am!

"No ... you *ARE* speaking to her."

Maurice Dwarck's eyes actually bulged from their sockets. He turned to Tess for verification. Tess nodded.

Enraged, Dwarck stood and yanked Soozie Bender to her feet, causing her BIC pen to flop deeply into her cleavage where it disappeared from sight.

"This is grounds for firing your agency," Dwarck sputtered.

"That won't be necessary, Mr. Dwarck," Madison said. "Our agency hereby officially resigns your business. Our resignation is effective immediately. We'll confirm it in writing this afternoon, and of course, we'll handle your work with complete professionalism until you've selected another agency."

Dwarck's neck arteries bulged above his collar. "You wanna play rough, lady, I'll show you rough! *Advertising Age* is going to run a big article next week about how rudely Turner Advertising's new CEO treated me, a good and decent client."

Madison nearly choked on *good and decent*. All eyes in the room swung back to her.

"If they run that article, the same issue will run an article that the good and decent Maurice Dwarck, and his bosses, won't like."

"What article?"

"About two Turner female employees who are considering filing criminal complaints of sexual harassment against their lecherous FACE UP client, one Maurice Dwarck."

Dwarck's face turned dark purple. His mouth opened, but nothing came out. Abruptly, he stormed from the room, Soozie following close enough to be his fanny pack. Madison heard him cursing loudly as they stormed to the elevator.

She looked back at her colleagues. They were grinning.

She grinned back. "So how does everyone think the meeting went?"

Nineteen

Harry Burkett sat at the computer in his basement office, deep in the bowels of Turner Advertising, savoring the afterglow of lunch: a slab of juicy prime rib, Caesar salad, oven browned potatoes and three double martinis. His old man had called martinis 'razorblade soup,' and they'd hurt like razor blades when the bastard began forcing them down Harry's throat at the age of six, thinking Harry wouldn't remember what happened next.

But Harry did remember ... the old man's liquor breath, the sweat, the perverted sex. Harry remembered it all with shame ... and hatred.

But he'd overcome all that through hard work and reading self-esteem books. Today he had a decent job, lots of Gulf War medals, even officer status in his elite white supremacists group. He was a solid American, a normal guy.

Burkett turned to his computer and clicked onto his favorite new porn Web site, *PrePubies,* featuring pre-teen girls.

He sighed at the photos a few moments, then had to force himself back to work. He entered the agency's internal computer network and began his midday check of the company's departmental networks. All systems were functioning well. He then scanned outside log-ons to the company network and saw a typical number of employees logged on from their home computers.

Then he saw something that felt like a kick in the gut.

Kevin Jordan was logged on with an outside IP address. Impossible! Jordan had walked by his office thirty seconds ago! Some outsider was using Jordan's username and password to enter the company files.

Which files?

His heart pounding, Burkett quickly tracked the intruder's meandering pathway through the company's private network and one minute later he had the answer.

The financial files!

SHIT! Cold sweat trickled down Burkett's neck. *Did the hacker change our numbers?* Burkett's mind reeled with the potential damage to the company, and him!

He yanked open his bottom desk drawer, grabbed his silver flask and chugged down more aquavit.

Quickly, he ran a special software program that highlighted any modifications made to the financial files in the last seventy-two hours. As he waited, he stood and paced back and forth, biting his nails, afraid to look at the screen, knowing he would be drawn and quartered if the hacker had altered any numbers.

Two minutes later, the computer beeped. Burkett forced himself to look at the screen.

Documents Un-modified.

Burkett collapsed in relief into his chair. Then, slowly, his hands curled into fists. He grabbed the phone and called CyberMan, an e-mail tracking wizard he often used. Burkett gave CyberMan the outsider's IP address and demanded he get back with the hacker's name and location fast. With the location, Burkett would go have a gun-to-head meeting with the sonofabitch!

Suddenly, he wondered whether the hacker was the same guy who hacked into the memo accusing Mark McKean of stealing $8.7 million dollars from the company?

Burkett scrolled through yesterday's outside log-ons. Seconds later, his eyes froze on the *same IP address*!

He swallowed, knowing he now had to report these system incursions to the EVP. He'd rather disarm a ticking time bomb.

He sat back and closed his eyes. All of a sudden, the aquavit and prime rib and potatoes and salad and double martinis began to slosh around in his gut. He belched, and felt like he might vomit. But he forced himself to take control.

Like he did at seventeen when he beat the shit out of his old man. And like he did in Desert Storm where he had a license to kill and used it greasing Iraqi soldiers. After Iraq, the military sent him to computer school at Fort Gordon, Georgia.

But two years later, he realized his computer skills would earn him three times more money in the real world. So he quit the Army and got a job in Information Technology at Turner Advertising.

He liked the job, but he wouldn't have it much longer if he didn't stop the hacker.

Forty minutes later, CyberMan phoned.

"The hacker's name is Dean Dryden."

The guy on the yacht, Harry knew.

He stood and hurried toward the door.

Twenty

The Executive Vice President sipped black coffee as Harry Burkett walked in and plopped down in the chair opposite the desk. Burkett's plum-red cheeks and gleaming eyes suggested he had consumed yet another martini lunch. As a man, Burkett left much to be desired. But his skill with computers and handling the less savory tasks in life, unencumbered as he was by moral restraints, had proven indispensable over the years.

And Harry's secret little sexual perversion gave the EVP excellent control of the man.

"I just heard back from CyberMan," Burkett said. "He found out who hacked into our financial systems."

"Who?"

"Dean Dryden. The guy McKean and Jordan went to see on the yacht."

The Executive VP had suspected it was Dryden. "Destroy his computers."

"Him, too?"

The EVP paused. "Only if it's necessary."

Burkett's grin suggested he felt it was necessary.

"Did you hear back from Eugene P. Smith?"

"Yeah. He's handling Madison. Don't worry!"

"Do I look worried?"

Burkett blinked and looked down. "No."

"I pay you and Eugene P. Smith to worry for me, right?"

"Right."

The EVP picked up *The Wall Street Journal,* letting Harry know their meeting was finished. Burkett sprang to his feet and hurried from the office.

Leaning back, the EVP realized that Dean Dryden's incursions into the agency financial files would only lead to a dead end. So would his attempt to trace the 8.7 million dollars, since the name of the original depositor was a fake name.

Only Mark McKean knew the person behind the name. And he was dead.

Soon to be joined by his lovely daughter.

* * *

Madison entered the restroom where she saw Alison Whitaker brushing her hair in front of the mirror. Whitaker turned and smiled.

"Hi, Alison." Madison walked over beside her, noticing they were alone in the restroom. "How'd your World Motors' meeting go?"

"It's *Rebate-A-Rama* time!"

"In Boston, we called it RID time," Madison said.

"RID?"

"Yeah, R-I-D. Rebates, Incentives, Discounting. Anything to get *RID* of the new cars, especially after the car company bankruptcies. Buyers are addicted to these deals, and pounce on them."

"Damn," Whitaker said.

"What?"

"You could have saved us sixty thousand dollars. The research firm just came up with the same findings."

Madison smiled, made sure they were still alone, then faced Whitaker. "Alison, you knew my dad a long time..."

Whitaker's eyes saddened as she brushed a spec of lint from her sleeve. "About nineteen terrific years."

"As I mentioned yesterday, someone here accused him of misappropriating $8.7 million from the company."

Whitaker shook her head. "Your father would never steal money from anyone. Never!"

"I know. And our financial books just confirmed that. No company money is, or has been missing. But still, someone accused him."

"Did he give you any indication who?"

"No. He remembered seeing the $8.7 figure somewhere in the agency, but by the time I got to Manhattan, he was already...." Her stomach churned at the reminder of her father's death. Suddenly, her eyes welled up again. She paused and took a deep breath.

Whitaker reached over and placed a comforting hand on her shoulder. "Time will help, Madison."

Madison nodded, then leaned close to the mirror and saw her eyes were bloodshot from a lack of sleep. "Do you recall anyone who was having a serious problem with my father?"

Whitaker appeared to search her memory. "Not really, but as you know, Karla Rasmussen is quite unhappy over your father's intention to vote against the ComGlobe merger."

"Enraged, I hear. Anyone else?"

Whitaker paused, then seemed to remember something. "Well, Leland Merryweather and Finley Weaver both want the merger. And they seem to be up to something. Today, when I walked into a conference room, they stopped whispering and looked suspicious."

"What are they like?"

"Finley is a gifted direct marketer. But he complains about not having enough money ever since his wealthy wife stopped covering his gambling losses. And Merryweather ... well, he's a solid international ad man. He wanted Evan Carswell's job and never forgave your father for not giving it to him."

Are Weaver and Merryweather behind everything? Madison wondered.

"Anyone else unhappy with my father?"

"Well, now that I think of it, Dana Williams had a big argument with your father a couple of weeks ago. I heard she was quite angry. I have no idea why. Which is strange, because they'd been good friends."

Madison wondered why Dana Williams was so angry with him. And why was Dana holding hands with the CEO of a competitive agency at the '21' Club yesterday?

"Dana favors the ComGlobe merger, right?"

"Right."

"Maybe Dana was upset because Dad was against the merger."

Whitaker shrugged. "My sense is it was something else. Maybe even something personal. Let me think about this a while and get back to you. But right now I'm late for another meeting."

"Thanks, Alison. I'm out of the office for a couple of days, but if you learn anything, just leave me a voicemail."

"Will do."

As she left, Madison leaned back and took a deep breath. People said her father was well liked by everybody, but clearly his decision to vote against the ComGlobe merger had created a nest of enemies.

Including a murderer.

Twenty One

Madison sat in the conference room listening to the MedPharms client compliment the agency's creative team on the new television commercial storyboards. Next to the client sat Dana Williams, EVP of Strategic Planning, whom Alison Whitaker said had recently been extremely upset with Madison's father. Why was she upset? And why was Dana holding hands with Lamar Brownlee, CEO of Griffen-Girard at the '21' Club? Was it strictly romantic – or were they talking about business? Specifically *Turner* business?

Williams' Strategic Planning group developed research and advertising strategies for the agency clients. According to Kevin, Williams had an uncanny ability to identify precisely what it was that made customers buy a product, as evidenced by her string of highly successful advertising campaigns.

Madison studied Williams, a very attractive, trim woman in her late thirties. Her thick blonde hair framed large light-brown eyes and delicate, high cheekbones, a face that hinted at a previous nip and tuck. Kevin had said that Williams, a former model, was intelligent, organized, focused, and at times a control freak.

There were even rumors that she could be ruthless. Years ago, when a CEO at a rival agency tried to steal one of Dana's clients, she'd reportedly mailed the CEO photos of himself in bed with two twelve-year-old Thai girls. The accompanying note warned that if he ever talked to her client again, his wife and the police would see the photos within an hour. The CEO never contacted her client again, and apparently retired months later.

The MedPharms meeting ended and everyone herded out into the hallway, where Madison caught up to Williams.

"Dana?"

Williams turned and smiled. "Oh, hi, Madison. Good client meeting...."

"Very good."

So ... how's your agency learning curve going?"

"Like a shuttle launch. Straight up!"

Another smile. "I'm still learning, too."

"You've been here quite a few years, right?"

Dana ran her manicured fingers through her hair. "This August, it will be, let's see ... seventeen years."

"So you knew my father quite well?"

Dana's eyes seemed to freeze, then go dark. "Yes. We worked together on many successful new business pitches."

Madison leaned close so no one could overhear them. "Dana, do you have any idea who might have accused him of taking company money?"

Dana's cheek muscle twitched a couple of times. "No, and frankly I was shocked when you mentioned that in yesterday's board meeting. I can't imagine anyone accusing him of any financial wrongdoing." She inched toward the elevator.

"Dana ...?"

"Yes?"

"May I ask you about a rumor?"

Williams hesitated, then nodded.

"I heard that recently you were quite upset with my father."

Dana's notepad fell to the floor and she picked it up. "Did Karla Rasmussen tell you that?"

"No. But I'd rather not say who did."

Williams' cheeks flushed and she averted Madison's eyes. "Well, it was nothing. Your father and I simply had a heated disagreement over a strategy for World Motors. That's all. Nothing more."

But Madison sensed there was more. Like the truth.

"Listen, Madison, I'm late for a client conference call. Can we continue this later?" She hurried toward the elevator.

"Sure. Come and see me when you get a chance. I have a couple of other questions."

* * *

And I've got questions, too, Dana Williams thought as the elevator doors closed. *Like, what do you know about your father's death? Do you believe he committed suicide? Do you believe he was murdered?*

Do you suspect me?

And, yesterday at '21', did you see me with Lamar Brownlee?

Twenty Two

B ack in her office, Madison settled in at her desk and began working through a stack of memos. Minutes later, she sensed someone
nearby. Looking up, she saw Karla Rasmussen staring at her from the
door. How long had she been lurking there?

"How'd the MedPharms meeting go?" Rasmussen asked, fingering
her thick gold necklace.

"The client loved the media plan and the TV commercials."

"Good." She stepped into the office. "But Alison Whitaker thinks
we pay too much for our MedPharms TV time at National Media."

"Really? What do you think?"

"I think we get a very good rate."

"Maybe I can find out," Madison said.

"How?"

"I have a very close friend at National Media. I'll ask her to compare our MedPharms rates."

"Who's your friend?"

"Linda Langstrom."

Rasmussen's nod suggested she knew Langstrom. "Let me know what she tells you."

"I will."

Rasmussen opened her mouth to say something further, paused, started to speak again, then simply turned and walked away.

What did Rasmussen start to say? *Strange woman....*

Madison remembered something Kevin had mentioned about Karla. The woman always funneled an inordinately large share of client money to televison advertising at National Media. Was it because she honestly believed that TV advertising was the smartest way to spend a client's money? Or was there a more personal, more nefarious reason?

Madison glanced at her watch. It was time to leave for the airport and her flight to St. Kitts.

"Guess what I have?"

Madison looked up and saw Christine holding something behind her back.

"My future husband?"

Christine laughed and held up a thick, red file. "The missing Com-Globe Merger file."

"You found it!"

"The cleaners did."

"Where?"

Christine looked toward the door, then walked over and whispered, "Didn't Karla just tell you?"

"Tell me what?"

"They found it behind *her* credenza."

Madison slumped in her chair. "She told me she didn't have it."

Christine nodded.

"What's her excuse?"

"She has no idea how it got there."

"Here's a thought – maybe *she* put it there," Madison said, her pulse increasing with her suspicion of Rasmussen. Madison placed the file in her briefcase, then grabbed her suitcase and headed toward the door.

"Madison...?"

"Yes?"

"Be careful and have a safe trip."

Christine sounded wonderfully maternal, reminding her of all the times her mother had uttered those same comforting words as she headed off somewhere.

"I will, Christine. And I'll call you."

On the elevator, she decided to stop off and tell Kevin that the MedPharms client really liked his new commercials. She walked into his office and saw him on the phone. He mouthed "Hi" and waved her to a chair.

As she sat down, she noticed an old family photo on a file cabinet. Kevin, and probably his sister, stood beside an old blue Chevy Nova with a rusted fender. Kevin looked about six in the photo and had tufts of windblown brown hair, a swath of freckles over sunburned cheeks and a big smile minus some front teeth. His sister, about nine, had a cute face dominated by dimples and a cherubic smile. They wore red and green Polish costumes similar to those worn by children Madison had seen dancing at South Boston's Polish Festival.

She saw no photos of beautiful young women. Was he dating anyone special? Young women seemed to constantly sashay past his office like runway models auditioning to be his significant other. His quick smile and light blue eyes were as seductive as his sense of humor and easy way with people. All that, plus his creative talent, explained why Evan Carswell and others considered Kevin a fast-tracker at Turner.

"What brings you to my bailiwick?" he asked, hanging up.

"I just wanted to tell you the MedPharms client loved your television commercials."

Kevin smiled big. "That's great! And thanks for letting me know."

"Sure."

"So, you're off to St. Kitts now?"

"This very minute."

"What about your disguise?"

She pointed to her suitcase.

"You're going as a *suitcase?*"

She laughed and stood up.

His face grew serious. "Madison...?"

"Yes?"

"Be careful."

"I will."

She realized that a lot of people were warning her to "be careful." She was being careful! She was wearing a disguise, flying under an alias, and staying at a hotel booked under the same alias. Only Christine and Kevin knew where she'd be.

Kevin handed her his business card with his various phone numbers.

As she walked out, he said, "Call and tell me how it went at the bank. I'll worry until I hear from you...."

She nodded, then remembered something.

I'll worry until I hear from you,' Grant Hartwell's exact words three years ago as she'd left on a business trip.

She'd been attracted to Grant, a Boston Brahmin lawyer, to his breezy outgoing charm, keen legal mind and stunning good looks. He was the first man she'd really cared for after Brace Brenner dumped her in college and married his ex-girlfriend.

She was infatuated with Grant. He'd even mentioned marriage. She remembered the wonderful weekend on Cape Cod during which he'd repeatedly professed his love for her. Three heavenly days.

Followed by the night from hell. That evening, after wrapping up a Gillette commercial, she stopped by Grant's Boston law office. As she approached his office, she saw a "Vacation Day" sign on the desk of his secretary, Tanya, whom his law partners referred to as The Treasure Chest.

Grant's office door was closed, but Mantovani's music seeped out. She knocked but got no response.

She opened the door and her life ended.

Fifteen feet away on the sofa, Grant was making love to Tanya. Tanya's smile suggested that she and Grant had vacationed often on the sofa.

Even now, Madison felt the sharp, searing, heart-crushing betrayal of that moment.

Grant had turned and saw her. "Madison, this ... just happened...."

She tried to speak, but couldn't.

"Really, I can explain at dinner!"

"Forget dinner! And forget me!" she shouted as she stormed down the hall and back outside into a hard rain. She got drenched as she walked faster and faster, turning corner after corner, going nowhere, feeling lost and injured. Why hadn't she believed her friends who warned her that Grant had a reputation as a womanizer?

Simple. She thought she could change him. Thought she *had* changed him. But she was wrong. So pathetically wrong.

Now she looked back on the whole Grant Hartwell affair as yet another painful lesson: The *packaging-is-sometimes-better-than-the-product lesson.* She was president of the Smitten and Bitten Club and it would be a long time again before she gave her heart away to anyone.

Besides, these days, she had no time for affairs of the heart. She had to focus on her new responsibilities.

She left, and took the elevator down to the area near the garage. She entered a small restroom and locked the door. She opened her suitcase and took out the frizzy blonde wig and put it on. Next, she squeezed into a tight red leather jacket, applied flaming red gloss to her lips, and clipped on some fake gold banana earrings. She topped it off with large gold-rimmed sunglasses. She looked in the mirror and marveled at the brazen hussy grinning back at her.

She walked into the agency garage where Neal Nelson, her body-guard, smiled at her.

"Nice disguise," he said, opening the passenger-side door to his TrailBlazer.

She got in and they drove out of the building. As they headed up Madison Avenue, she decided to check the side mirror to see if a car was following them. She gave up when all she saw were yellow cabs.

Forty minutes later, she passed through JFK Airport security and headed down toward the departure area to board her American Airlines non-stop flight to St. Kitts.

* * *

Eugene P. Smith followed Madison McKean toward their departure gate. The tiny spy cam he'd placed in her underground garage had given him a clear view of her getting into the TrailBlazer. Her disguise was ridiculous. She had on the same slacks she'd worn to work and carried the same expensive COACH briefcase. Amateur mistakes. She might as well have stenciled MADISON across the back of her red jacket.

Although, he had to give her some credit. Last night she'd ditched him by changing hotels at the last moment. But he'd been given her flight number and was waiting for her at JFK.

She continued walking down the long runway past the departure gates. He liked how she walked. Long, shapely legs. Fast, no-nonsense stride. Clearly she was on a mission.

Me too, Madison.

Smith flipped open his cell phone and called Harry Burkett.

"She's about to get on the flight to St. Kitts."

"She's going to the bank!" Burkett said nervously.

"So it would appear."

"Don't let her learn anything."

"Sorry, but she will learn something."

"What?" Burkett asked, panic-stricken.

"What dying feels like."

Twenty Three

Madison felt her American Airlines 737 bank hard right. Her three-and-a-half-hour direct flight from JFK had been smooth and uneventful.

"If you look out the right side of the aircraft," the pilot announced, "you can see St. Kitts and Nevis."

Madison glanced out at both islands and some smaller ones, sparkling out like an emerald necklace on the blue Caribbean. She loved the islands. Their peaceful hills, ocean breezes and sunny beaches always seemed to melt away the stress she picked up in congested, horn-honking, brake-squealing cities.

But she wasn't here for the sunny beaches. She was here to get a tight-lipped banker to cough up some information about $8.7 million deposited in her father's name. And even though the banker might not divulge anything about the deposit, he might inadvertently reveal something about the depositor.

She looked down at the ComGlobe file in her lap. During the flight, she'd scrutinized each page, but found no hint of who her father suspected. Of course, any hint easily could have been removed from the file by Karla Rasmussen, who'd apparently hidden the file behind her office credenza.

Madison felt a hard jolt as the landing gear locked into place. Moments later, they touched down at Robert L. Bradshaw International Airport. She breezed though customs and the crowded Arrivals Hall, then stepped outside into a warm, humid night. She took a deep breath and was rewarded with the sweet, honey-like scent of jacaranda flowers.

"Taxi, ma'am?"

She turned and saw a tiny old man with snow-white hair and a weathered brown face. His wrinkled hands looked like they'd been microwaved.

"Yes, please."

Smiling, he placed her luggage in the trunk.

"And where would you be stayin', ma'am?" he asked with a lilting Caribbean accent as he drove off.

"Ottley's Inn."

"'tis a lovely place."

"So is St. Kitts," she said, as his headlights illuminated brilliant crimson flowers, and a row of majestic palm trees swaying in the breeze.

"Mighty nice of you to say, ma'am."

Soon she saw pedestrians in various hues of black, brown, tan and white, strolling beside tin-roofed homes tucked into the lush hills. A giant mountain loomed to the north, the last rays of the sun painting its summit orange-red.

"What's that mountain?"

"Mount Liamuiga."

"It's huge!"

"A *volcano* too," he said, looking back at her with a grin.

"Really? When did it last erupt?"

"Way back when I was just a kid."

"Which year?"

"1843." He giggled and slapped his thigh.

His giggle made her laugh, and the laughing felt good.

"Liamuiga's about 4,000 feet high. Crater's a mile wide. Nelly, that's my niece, she takes tours up there. Beautiful orchids in the rain forest. Green monkeys, too. More monkeys than people on St. Kitts."

"I'd love a tour if I can find some time."

He handed her his card over the seat. "Just call me. Name's Fletcher."

"Okay, Fletcher."

Minutes later, he pulled into a driveway that curved into Ottley's Inn, a magnificent old estate with a sprawling yellow main house and several cottages. She'd read that back in the 1700s it had been a major sugar plantation. Today, it was a luxurious resort nestled among thirty-five acres of manicured lawns, rolling hills and lush tropical gardens. It looked peaceful, romantic.

In the bright, attractive lobby, she signed in quickly. As she headed toward her room, she noticed a tall man in a dark business suit step from a taxi and stroll toward the lobby. He looked familiar.

Was he on my flight? she wondered. She seemed to recall him sitting in first class.

"This way, ma'am," the bellhop said, leading her down a hallway. Her room was charming: carved mahogany and wicker furniture, a queen-sized bed, lovely paintings, colorful plants and the tart scent of tiger lilies thanks to the slow-rotating ceiling fan. Out her window, the Atlantic rolled gently toward the shore.

She tipped the bellhop, hung up her clothes, then took out her new RangeRoamer international phone, which she'd been assured worked in over eighty countries. She searched its "phonebook" feature and found Linda Langstrom's number. Linda, her best friend, had been her roommate at Wellesley College for four years, and over that time became the sister Madison always wanted.

After graduation, Linda joined National Media and was promoted rapidly. Today, she and her team negotiated the advertising rates for prime time cable programs. National Media purchased billions of dollars of television and radio commercial time for ad agencies' clients over the years.

Madison dialed Linda's cell phone and Linda picked up on the first ring.

"Hey, Maddy. How's it going today?"

"A little better, Lin."

"I'll come stay with you."

"No, I'm OK."

"Really?"

"Really. But thanks for offering. Actually, I called you on behalf of one of our Executive Vice Presidents. She wondered whether our Med-Pharms client is paying you greedy guys at National Media too much for television time?"

"You can *never* pay us too much," Linda said with a chuckle. "But let me look into it. I'll compare MedPharms rates to other companies with similar spending levels on the same programming. By the way, which EVP is asking?"

"Karla Rasmussen."

"Ah, yes ... Karla the Cannibal."

Madison smiled.

"The woman chews up our young planners and spits 'em out."

"Doesn't surprise me."

"She chews up our time, too, Maddy. Extra reports. Media research. Comparisons. Analysis. If you don't mind my saying it, she's a piece of work. On the other hand, I shouldn't complain."

"Why's that?"

"The woman sends us a ton of advertising money."

"So I've heard."

"Where can I reach you, Madison?"

"This cell phone is best for the next few days."

"I'll have something for you by tomorrow afternoon."

"Thanks, Lin."

They hung up.

As Madison turned she nudged her purse and Kevin Jordan's business card fell out. She picked it up and smiled.

Kevin ... the best thing that happened to her since she'd come to New York. *Before* New York, too. He was considerate without faking it, smart without flaunting it, and passionate about work without being obsessive about it.

But how does he feel about me? she wondered. He was obviously concerned because she'd lost her father, and because she'd been attacked. But it was probably just concern.

She walked to the window and looked out at the stars hovering over the black moonlit sea. In the distance, a cruise ship lit up like a floating Christmas tree, inching its way south. She felt like she was watching the Travel Channel....

She also felt tired. She yawned, took a hot bath, and minutes later was sound asleep in bed.

* * *

Two rooms away, Eugene P. Smith was wide awake. He poured Bowmore single malt scotch into a large glass tumbler, marveling at how the 25-year-old amber liquid danced over and around the ice cubes. He sipped the velvet liquid onto his tongue, savoring the cultivated taste.

He leaned back in his chair and scrolled the television channels to a rerun of *Fawlty Towers*, a BBC comedy he got hooked on when the CIA posted him in London. Without taking his eyes off the television, he began to assemble the pieces of his plastic Glock handgun. He'd packed each piece in a separate location, and once again each piece had sailed through airport security undetected.

Sipping more scotch, he flipped open his cell phone and dialed Harry Burkett's home phone. Burkett picked up on the first ring.

"Jennifer...?" Burkett said in a high, zippy voice.

Sounding young for your underage girls, Harry? Smith thought.

"It's Eugene."

"Oh...." An octave lower. "You there already?"

"Yes."

"Is she?"

"Yeah."

"She's gonna tell the banker she's Mark McKean's daughter and demand the account information!" Burkett, as usual, sounded on the verge of panic.

"Harry...?"

"Yeah?"

"The bank has written instructions not to reveal any information on the account to anyone, right?"

"Yeah."

"Even to family members, right?"

"Right, but– "

"Relax, Harry!"

"Gimme one good reason why I should relax?"

Smith paused. "Her room is fifty feet away from mine."

Two hours later, Smith left his room and walked toward Madison's. As he turned the corner, he was surprised to see a large, uniformed guard sitting behind a desk at the end of the hall, about thirty feet from Madison's room. A walkie-talkie sat on the desk. The security guard, who obviously lifted weights, looked settled in for the night.

Time for Plan B, Smith thought. He walked down to the reception area, went outside and strolled around to the back of the resort. He looked up at her window. Too high and too well illuminated. And the roof was too far above it.

Time for Plan C. Tomorrow. Smith returned to his room.

His CIA training had taught him that there was always another way. Like with Barzin Tura, an Iranian attaché stationed in London years ago.

CIA Intelligence in Langley had told Smith that Tura possessed highly classified information about Iran's nuclear reactors in Bushehr and the uranium enrichment facilities at Natanz. The information was vital to Middle East security, and therefore America's. Smith arranged through a Belgian diplomat to be casually introduced to Tura at a cocktail party. At the party, Smith posed as an automotive parts supplier. He chatted with Tura, a chubby, bald man, about the former General Motors-Iran operation in Teheran. Tura bragged that his uncle's eleven-year-old, Iran-built GM-Opel still was climbing the steep mountains north of Teheran. Smith smiled appropriately and suggested they meet for coffee and discuss setting up a lucrative spare parts distributorship for Tura in Teheran. Barzin Tura quickly agreed, obviously envisioning juicy revenues filling his coffers.

They met at a Starbucks near Marble Arch. After a few minutes of car talk, Smith cut to the chase. He offered Tura $200,000 for information about the Bushehr and Natanz plants' radar and anti-aircraft gun security capabilities. Tura refused. Smith bumped the offer to $300,000. Again, Tura refused.

But Smith knew that every contact has a vulnerable spot. Smith found Tura's two days later.

His daughter, Alish.

Alish was dying from Batten disease, a very rare neurodegenerative disorder that was slowly stealing the young girl's ability to see, move and think. There was no treatment. Tura and his wife could look forward to watching their daughter wither away and die, probably in her teens. Smith asked the CIA medical staff in D.C. to check for any experimental treatments for the disease. A week later they told him that University of Rochester researchers recently had discovered a new drug therapy that offered some hope for Batten sufferers.

Smith told Tura, and promised to bring Alish to the USA for the potentially life-saving new treatment - if Tura gave him the secret information.

Barzin hesitated, but four days later he e-mailed Smith an encrypted document detailing the security installations surrounding the Bushehr plant, plus an Iranian research site and a new uranium enrichment facility.

Alish was immediately flown to the U.S. and began treatment. Within weeks she began responding well, feeling a little better each day.

Nine months later Smith met Tura at a coffee shop near Teheran's Hotel Naderi.

"My daughter is doing much better thanks to you."

"I'm happy for you."

Tura leaned forward and whispered, "And if you asked me today for the secret information I e-mailed you, I would give it to you for free!"

Smith was shocked. "Why?"

"Because our diminutive, loudmouth president is leading my country into a devastating war with Israel and the United States, a war we will surely lose."

Barzin Tura would never know if war broke out. The next day, Iranian State Security arrested him and threw him into notorious Evin Prison. A fellow diplomat had discovered his secret e-mail to Smith. That same night, Tura was beheaded.

With Tura's death, the CIA stopped paying Alish's medical bills. Angered by their decision, Smith continued paying her bills out of a clandestine operations budget only he had access to. And he still visited Alish when he could.

A year later, Smith visited the Iranian diplomat who ratted Tura out. The next day the diplomat was found dead from a broken neck on a ski slope north of Teheran.

Exciting times, Smith thought. He missed them.

Twenty Four

Dana Williams lie nude and physically spent beside Lamar Brownlee on the luxurious black silk sheets of the massive bed in his company's executive apartment on Park Avenue.

"You remind me of my favorite country song," he whispered.

"Which is...?"

"If I said you had a beautiful body would you hold it against me?"

Laughing, she held it against him. Her mind drifted back to four months ago when she set her sights on Lamar Brownlee. She read in *Ad Age* that Brownlee, the CEO of Griffen-Girard Advertising, had left Kentucky twenty-seven years ago with a fast brain, good looks, and an easy Southern charm that swooped up clients like a Hoover vacuum cleaner. And he'd grown Griffen-Girard into a large, highly profitable agency ... but an agency that lacked clients in two major product categories.

It just so happened that Turner Advertising had clients in those two categories. And Dana Williams managed them.

That presented her with a lucrative business opportunity – to move them over to Griffen-Girard.

So she asked a friend to introduce her to Lamar Brownlee at a Time Inc. media party. At the party, Dana gave Brownlee her undivided attention, laughed at his jokes, gushed over his successes, shamelessly brushed her new breast implants against him a few times.

And, bingo – like most men, Brownlee fell for her charms.

After the *Time* party, the handsome, sandy-haired, fifty-year-old took her back to the Park Avenue apartment. He phoned his trophy wife in Greenwich and told her that his workload forced him to stay overnight in the apartment. Then Lamar spent the night making love to Dana like a prison escapee.

Now, weeks later, as she ran her fingers through his curly blond chest hair, she was pleased that her plan was right on track.

She was also pleased he thought she had a beautiful body. And frankly, she did. After all, she'd been a top model, and still worked out five times a week at her exclusive Trump Tower spa. People said she looked twenty-five, not thirty-nine, thanks to some judicious tucks by Hollywood's world famous cosmetic surgeon, Dr. Robert Kotler, MD.

But one man had not succumbed to her beauty: Mark McKean. After his wife died, she politely waited a full year, then tried to start a relationship with him. He clearly wasn't ready. So she waited another year. Again, he gently put her off. Then just a few months ago, she gave him one more chance, and once again, unbelievably, he refused her. She was furious.

She hated rejection by men, in part, she knew, because of her father's abandonment when she was five. But the lesson was clear: reject before you're rejected.

And above all, always control the relationship with a man.

That is why she took control of Lamar by telling him she could bring two big Turner clients over to his agency. Two clients who billed a total of one-hundred-eighty million dollars annually. Lamar's eyes lit up like halogen bulbs.

"These clients will absolutely follow you to Griffen-Girard?"

"Yes."

"Why?"

"They trust me." *And,* she thought, *because one client enjoys my sexual favors, while the other knows his account will be resigned by Turner due to a ComGlobe merger business conflict.*

"If you bring me the clients, Dana, I'll deposit a million dollars in a Belize numbered account. Sound good?"

"Sounds most generous."

"When can you bring them into my agency?"

"Right after the ComGlobe merger."

"Why not now?"

"My Turner stock. After the ComGlobe-Turner IPO stock deal, I'll walk out with millions."

He nodded and smiled at her. "I prefer well-heeled lovers."

Don't we all...?

"So, how's Madison McKean working out?"

"Badly."

"Why?"

"She's lost our Nat-Care client. The next day she resigned our FACE UP cosmetics business, and I hear Mason Funds is shaky. And ... frankly, it doesn't really matter."

"Why not?"

"Madison won't be around much longer."

Twenty Five

I t's just too damn beautiful!" Kevin said, signaling his producer to replay the roughcut version of a TV commercial they were editing for their client, Sea & Sand CruiseLines.

"It's *supposed* to be beautiful!" the producer, Kirk Beauregard, said.

"But that's the problem. It's beautiful like every other cruise line commercial is beautiful."

"Huh?"

Beauregard frowned and ran his fingers through his long blond hair. "Are you saying the viewer can't tell one beautiful cruise line commercial from another, and therefore won't remember our beautiful cruise line commercial?"

"Yep."

"So what do we do?"

Kevin stood and paced in front of the large AVID editing console, knowing that the first job of any commercial was to grab the viewer's attention. Research said you had five seconds to hook 'em or lose 'em.

"So we do an opening so different, original, or even outrageous, they *have* to watch."

"But how? Cruise ship commercials *have* to show yummy food, romantic dancing, sexy singers, silver-haired captains, exotic destinations, stuff like-"

"That's it!" Kevin said.

"What's it?"

"Exotic destinations."

"I'm not following you."

"Remember that strange island that only Sea & Sand docks at?"

Beauregard closed his eyes and grinned. "Maria Elena...."

"Right!"

"That's a different *planet!*"

"Yeah. The waterfall spills into the lagoon with the green mist?"

"And those bug-eating plants."

"And the little yellow birds that walk funny?" Kevin said.

"Like they got hemorrhoids!"

Kevin laughed. "And *only* Sea & Sand can show them to you because...?"

"... *only* Sea & Sand sails to Maria Elena!"

Beauregard took a bow, then spun around to search the film archives for the Maria Elena footage. He tapped in a few time-code commands on the AVID and sixty seconds later they were looking at the breathtaking footage of the island.

"Let's plug in the hemorrhoid birds at the beginning," Kevin said, "the waterfall in the middle, and those blue herons soaring over the forest at the end."

"You got it."

"Can you make the music soar when the herons do?"

"Soar can!"

Kevin rolled his eyes.

As Beauregard began editing in the scenes of the exotic Caribbean island, Kevin thought of another Caribbean island – St. Kitts, where Madison was now. He hoped she'd arrived safely. Tomorrow, he'd call her to see if she learned anything about the $8.7 million deposit at the bank.

Kevin found himself thinking of Madison more each day. She was smart, honest, gutsy and fun to work with. He'd been attracted to her from the moment he bumped into her at the elevator. And, as he got to know her, he'd grown more attracted.

He liked how she really listened to people, even though they were sometimes talking nonsense. And how she tackled her new CEO responsibilities, even though she felt unprepared. And how she resigned the cosmetic business of lecherous Maurice Dwarck, even though it reduced her agency's revenue. And how she pursued the truth behind her father's death, even though she was risking her life.

Mostly though, he liked how her smile and large green eyes gave his heart an aerobic workout – which worried him. Because another adwoman had made his heart beat fast once, and then left it in pieces.

Alexis Weatherly. A smart, terrific-looking young account executive with thick brown hair and large eyes the color of dark blue sapphires. Her quirky sense of humor and slightly outrageous spirit won him over fast. They began dating and growing more serious each week.

Then came the invitation he wish he'd thrown out! It was to a VIP Park Avenue party. Show biz celebrities and ad agency heavy breathers would be there. Kevin was about to decline when the CEO of a respected agency asked him to attend and talk about an important job offer.

Alexis begged Kevin to take her, which was a problem. The last party he'd attended in this same apartment had drugs available. Alexis had a history with pot and cocaine use a year earlier. Once they started dating, she stopped using and was doing well.

Still, he worried the party atmosphere and drugs might prove too tempting for her. But she continued to beg him, and finally he caved in.

As they walked into the party, Kevin saw the CEO waving him over. Kevin told Alexis he'd be out on the balcony with the CEO. She said she'd be schmoozing with the celebrities.

Thirty-five minutes later, after accepting CEO Mark McKean's very generous offer to become associate creative director of Turner Advertising, Kevin raced back inside to tell Alexis the great news. He found her in a small back bedroom that reeked of pot. She stood between an anorexic woman in black and a goateed man wearing thick gold chains around his neck.

"I've got the job!" he whispered in her ear.

"Awe ... some!" Alexis said, turning around to face him.

He knew instantly. Her pinpoint pupils, thousand-yard stare and slow movements told him Alexis was *very* high, maybe on heroin.

He led her from the apartment and took her home. There, he put her in her bed and sat nearby, watching her during the night for any adverse reactions.

The morning sun awakened her. She opened her eyes and stared at him.

"You OK?"

She nodded, but looked as though she couldn't remember going to bed.

"I tried heroin."

He nodded.

"Just to see what it was like."

"Now you know."

"Yeah...."

"I hope it's your last time, Alexis."

"It is."

It wasn't. Six days later, the man who gave her heroin gave it to her again. Then he continued to supply her with heroin and cocaine over the next few weeks. Kevin knew. Her dazed eyes, slurred words and cold, moist skin were giveaways to her addiction.

Two months later, she hit bottom.

He got her into rehab. Twenty-eight days later, she was released and stayed clean, getting stronger week by week.

Then he flew out to California to film some car commercials in the Mojave Desert. Two days later, a friend called him at 2:23 a.m. and said that Alexis's body was found in an alley behind a seedy nightclub in Jersey City. A drug overdose.

Even now, Kevin felt some guilt. He'd known her history. Yet he'd taken Alexis to the VIP party.

Her death devastated him. To forget, he poured himself into his drug of choice – work. It helped soothe problems of the heart and left little time to brood about a loss.

After her death, he dated infrequently. A stockbroker, a journalist, an attorney. Terrific, beautiful women. But when the relationships heated up, he hit the brakes.

With Madison, however, the brakes didn't seem to be working.

How did she feel about him? he wondered. Did she see him as friend, or only a helpful employee schmoozing the big boss? Or maybe even as a sleazeball, lusting after her money and body?

It didn't matter. She was his boss. It was crazy to even think about a personal relationship with his CEO. Human resource experts condemned such incestuous corporate relationships. Employee tongues would wag about how she helped him at the expense of others.

"Take a look!" Beauregard said as he ran the revised commercial. Kevin watched the funny new opening with the hemorrhoidal-strutting birds and couldn't help but laugh.

They high-fived each other, and moments later Kevin left the studio.

He stepped outside into the cool night air and flagged down a taxi.

As they drove up Third Avenue, his thoughts drifted to Madison's father. Kevin was convinced that someone had faked his suicide to eliminate his vote against the ComGlobe merger ... the same someone who'd hired the man who almost killed Madison ... a man who told her he was coming after her again. Soon.

Fortunately, she'd worn a disguise to the airport and traveled under an alias.

But had the man somehow discovered she was in St. Kitts?

Twenty Six

M adison felt heat moving up her face....
She opened her eyes and saw it was brilliant sunshine flooding through the lace curtains onto her and the flowery chintz bedspread.

Yawning, she got up, pulled back the curtains, looked outside and smiled. Mother Nature was strutting her stuff.

The blue Atlantic glistened under a fiery sun. Whitecaps curled toward the sandy shore. A thick green rain forest swept up the slopes of the huge volcano. The sweet fragrance of flowers and fresh-cut grass drifted into the room. And somewhere nearby, tennis balls thumped.

I'm in paradise to visit a bank? she thought. *How crazy is that?*

Thirty minutes later, after breakfast, she put on a lightweight blue suit and headed down to the lobby.

"Taxi, ma'am?" the desk manager asked.

"Yes, please."

Seconds later, she got into the roomy back seat of *Leonard's Luxury Limo,* a Toyota van. The driver was Leonard. On his right shoulder sat a beautiful blue and red parrot. The bird seemed to be searching for something in Leonard's Afro.

"The ferry to Nevis, please," she said.

"Straightaway, ma'am." Leonard gave her a gold-toothed smile.

In Nevis, she would visit the Caribe National Bank and try to find out who deposited the money using her father's name, and whether the money was still there or was transferred back to Turner's Citibank account as the e-mail demanded. She'd also try to see if the man who opened the account bore any resemblance to her father.

Nevis, she'd read, was fast becoming one of the world's most preferred offshore banking centers. The reason was simple: Nevis bankers were pit bulls when it came to guarding the confidentiality of their depositors.

Her plan was simple: play the grieving daughter in hopes they might give her a morsel of helpful information.

As the taxi hugged the narrow, winding roads, she saw sugarcane fields in the distance. She'd read that sugar production had been the island's number one industry for centuries, and was astonished to learn that in 1660, little St. Kitts, only five miles by eighteen miles, had produced sugar profits greater than the combined profits of the original thirteen U.S. colonies.

They drove past a beautiful, twin-spired church, the Immaculate Conception, and Independence Square lined with charming, pastel-colored houses, a business district, and finally the market area, already bustling with locals and tourists.

Moments later, Leonard stopped next to the ferry, the *Islander*. Madison bought her ticket and watched several people step off a bus and walk toward the boat where dozens more were boarding. Most men wore Bermudas and short-sleeve shirts. Women wore colorful, flowery dresses.

Everyone walked a leisurely pace.

Rush hour without the rush.

As a breeze cooled her face, she boarded with a young couple and three small children, some elderly couples, and a bunch of noisy tourists wearing gaudy shirts.

To get a better view of the harbor, she stepped behind a big blue *LABOUR DAY PARTY* banner and walked over to the rear deck. As she leaned against the railing, two five-year-old boys, identical twins, scampered past her, one boy trying to grab a GameBoy away from the other. She smiled and watched them disappear into the passenger cabin.

She noticed dark clouds pushing in from the west. The wind kicked up and large waves began to rock the ferry.

She leaned over the railing and stared down into the churning aquamarine water.

* * *

Eugene P. Smith couldn't believe his good luck. The woman had foolishly separated herself from the other passengers. Everyone was inside the cabin. No one knew she was out here except the two small boys.

And, of course, him.

Even more helpful, the large blue banner blocked everyone from seeing her ... and what he was about to do to her.

As the *Islander* chugged out of Basseterre Bay, he watched her lean further over the railing, obviously mesmerized by the foaming wake.

How fortunate for me, Smith thought. Although he'd meticulously planned a credible "accident" for her on Nevis, experience had taught him to seize a fortuitous opportunity like this. And now that he thought about it, this "accident" would work out better. Even the windy weather was cooperating.

A large wave slapped against the side of the boat, rocking it hard. The wind was gusting to about twenty-five miles per hour now. Inside the cabin, people were sitting down and talking or reading.

In his coat pocket, Smith ran his fingers along the familiar hardcover case. The syringe inside brimmed with potassium cyanide. The poison would incapacitate her in seconds, kill her within two minutes. He'd simply ease her body into the churning water. The splash would be drowned out by the wind and engine noise.

Days later, her body, or rather the chunks the sharks hadn't eaten, would wash ashore ... just another careless tourist who'd fallen into the sea and drowned.

Drowned like her poor daddy.

How fitting, Eugene P. Smith thought.

Twenty Seven

L eaning over the rear deck railing, Madison watched the blue-green waves churn and swirl higher and higher as the *Islander* rocked its way toward Nevis. The spray dampened her face as the boat slapped down into a deep swell. The turbulent sea was beautiful, so hypnotic she couldn't seem to pull her eyes away. But she'd have to. She had to think about ways to persuade the banker to reveal information about the account in her father's name.

"Ma'am!"

A man's voice behind her.

She turned and saw an *Islander* attendant signaling her and a tall gray-haired man with a Yankees baseball cap and sunglasses standing a few feet behind her.

"Sea's too rough. Captain wants everyone inside, please."

She nodded, then she and the tall man, who seemed upset that he had to go inside, followed the attendant into the passenger cabin where she sat down. For some reason, she sensed the tall man was still staring at her, but when she looked back, he had disappeared.

She took out her phone, called Christine and learned that everything was going well at the agency. Relieved, she hung up and looked
around the cabin.

Most passengers were reading papers or dozing in the morning sun.
The woman across from her was reading *Star* magazine. On the cover
was Roger Corman's newest masked slasher jamming an ice pick into
a creature's eye. The slasher's mask suddenly reminded her of her attacker's mask. Her skin began to crawl.

Relax, she told herself. *Only Christine and Kevin know you're here.*

She'd purchased her airline ticket under the name Shae Stuart,
reserved the Ottley's Inn room using that name, traveled to JFK Airport in disguise, and hadn't used any credit cards. He couldn't possibly
know she was in St. Kitts.

Sit back, enjoy the view.

Thirty minutes later, the ferry docked at Charlestown harbor on
Nevis. The island town looked small, but big on charm. Her map indicated she could walk to the bank in minutes ... and in beautiful
weather.

She strolled into the picturesque town, passing a row of ginger-
bread-trimmed houses with ornate, second-floor balconies where people sipped their morning coffee. A warm breeze carried the aroma of
fresh-baked bread. On Main Street, she walked along with a group of
tourists past some interesting shops, a row of quaint houses, and the
Nevis Customs House where two goats were munching on grass.

She turned onto Prince William Street and saw a rum shop doing
a brisk duty-free business with tourists.

All of a sudden, she sensed someone watching her. She looked back,
but saw only an old man in a wheelchair and some kids.

She shrugged it off and three minutes later arrived at the Caribe
National Bank, a two-story gray stone building with large, street-level
windows and a statue of a blue dolphin at the entrance. Stepping inside, she felt a blanket of cool, refreshing air wrap around her.

"May I help you?" asked a receptionist with a Halle Berry smile.

"Yes. Could I please speak with a bank officer about a protected account."

"Of course, just have a seat."

Madison settled into a beige leather chair and looked around the plush lobby. Colorful paintings of island scenes hung on the walls, including a gold-framed, signed Chagall print. Expensive art objects sat on pedestals, and a large Persian carpet graced the polished oak floor. Not all the bank's money was in the vault.

Moments later, a short, obese man in his mid-thirties lumbered toward her wearing a snug linen suit and a trust-me smile. Wisps of fine, blond hair were draped intriguingly over a head that seemed too small for his large, pear-shaped body.

"Bradford Tipleton. Welcome to the Caribe National Bank."

She introduced herself, shook hands and followed him into an immaculate office dominated by a large desk and thin-screen computer. His big window overlooked an outdoor café a few feet away where tourists drank coffee. One tourist, she noticed, was the man from the rear deck of the ferry, the gray-bearded man with the Yankees baseball cap. He was reading a newspaper.

"Coffee?" Tipleton asked, settling in behind his desk.

"No thanks."

"Cookies, maybe?" He tapped a Pooh Bear cookie jar on his credenza and smiled.

"No thank you, Mr. Tipleton."

His eyes dimmed a bit, like maybe he'd hoped to munch cookies with her.

"How may I help you?"

"I'd like to learn more about an offshore account."

Big smile. "A very smart way to protect your hard-earned dollars. You sound American."

She nodded.

"Great country, but your IRS can be rather, ah ... consumptive, dare I say?" He gave her a knowing wink.

"Well, yes, taxes are high, but I'm actually interested in an existing account here."

He crossed his arms. "I see...."

"The account's in my father's name. Mark McKean."

"Did he list you on the bank account?"

"I'm not sure."

"Hmmm...."

"He died last week in New York."

Tipleton's banker eyes softened. "Oh, I'm sorry. Please accept my condolences." He glanced toward the large photo of an elderly woman on his credenza. "Mother left me three years ago next Thursday. Stroke. We were quite close."

"I'm sorry for your loss, Mr. Tipleton."

"Thank you," he said, turning back to Madison. "Now, the account was in the name of your father, Mark McKean?"

"Yes. It had $8.7 million in it last week. He was going to transfer the money back to a CitiBank account in New York. I wondered if he did."

"Do you know the account number here?"

"Yes." She gave him the number Dean Dryden had taken from her father's e-mail.

"Are you his sole surviving family member?"

"My brother, Thaddeus, and I are. But this notarized letter authorizes me to represent him here today." She handed Tipleton the letter.

He read it and nodded.

"And here is my father's death certificate, plus my birth certificate and passport."

He studied each document carefully.

"You understand that everything will depend on your father's specific instructions."

She nodded.

He tapped the number into his computer, then turned the screen so that she couldn't see it. A strand of blond hair drooped down over his eyes. He fingered it back up to his scalp where it clung miraculously to another strand.

"Please excuse me a moment," he said, hoisting himself up and hurrying down the hall.

Madison looked over at the photo of Tipleton's mother, who seemed nearly as obese as Tipleton. The woman was smiling proudly at an enormous cheesecake smothered in cherries and cream. Beside the desk in Tipleton's wastebasket was a large pastry box smeared with chocolate.

Bradford Tipleton waddled back into the room carrying a blue folder and sat down.

"Well," he said, "the account clearly stipulates here that no information may be released. I'm quite sorry."

"But he's my father."

"Yes, but he made a specific written request that the account balance and disposition of the money therein be kept in strictest confidence. And he further stipulated, 'even in the event of my demise, and even from my family members.'"

Madison knew her father would never stipulate that.

"Did he open the account here in person?"

Tipleton bit his upper lip. "Well, since you know his account number, I can tell you, yes, he opened it here in person."

"Did you assist him?"

"No."

"May I speak to the person who did?"

"He's not here today."

"Is the $8.7 million still here?"

He frowned. "Again, Ms. McKean, please understand that I'm not at liberty to discuss the disposition of these funds."

As her brother predicted, the banker was digging in. Madison felt her frustration mounting.

"As his banker we are obliged to respect his wishes. You understand our position."

"Yes. But as his daughter, you understand mine."

He nodded, but gave her the old my-hands-are-tied shrug.

Clearly, she would learn nothing more from Tipleton today. She stood and thanked him for his time.

———

Stepping back outside, she took out the phone number of the local lawyer, Peter Parsons, that her brother Thad had recommended. Thad had spoken to Parsons and said the man sometimes worked miracles in getting local banks to release information. She had tried to phone Parsons yesterday, but he was in court. Now, she dialed his firm again.

A young woman answered. "Brooks, Kelly, Parsons and Phipps, Barristers at Law."

"This is Madison McKean. Could I please speak with Mr. Parsons?"

"Oh, Miss McKean, I've been expecting your call. Mr. Parsons wanted me to tell you that he had to fly unexpectedly to London this morning. He asked me to apologize for his absence and to tell you that he'll return in a fortnight."

"Two weeks?"

"Yes."

Crap! Madison thought, breathing out slowly. "Would you please let him know that I called, and that I'll try to reach him again."

"Yes, of course."

Madison left her number and hung up. No luck with the banker. No luck with the attorney.

The trip was turning into a dead end, she realized, as she started walking back into town.

Twenty Eight

Walking down Prince William Street, Madison realized she had some time before taking the ferry back to St. Kitts. Enough time to make some phone calls at the quaint restaurant she'd seen beside the dock. She began window-shopping down the street, when suddenly she sensed someone was following her. She turned, but saw only a nun walking with an elderly woman and some kids. Madison shrugged it off and continued walking with some tourists toward the dock.

Minutes later, she entered Unella's, a charming restaurant overlooking the bay. She sat at a small table in the corner and breathed in the delicious aromas of freshly-grilled fish and curry. She ordered lunch and looked out at the harbor. Boats sparkled like polished gems in the sun-dappled water.

Nearby, a large pelican dove into the water, scooped out a small fish and swallowed it.

Her phone rang. Kevin, maybe?

She answered.

"Madison, it's Linda."

"Hey, Lin. What's up?"

"Not the media rates you asked about. Your agency pays about two percent *less* for MedPharms TV commercials than what other clients with comparable budgets pay."

"That's good news."

"Yeah. But I stumbled onto something that's not."

"What?"

"An odd fee."

"Why odd?"

"Because it seems to be hidden in our Turner Advertising records."

Madison didn't like the sound of "hidden." "What type of fee?"

"A consulting fee."

"Our agency uses consultants."

"Yeah, but this fee seems ... wrong."

"Why?"

"For one thing, I can't find anything on the consulting firm's name, MensaPlan."

"MensaPlan ... I've never heard of it either."

"And it looks like the fee has been paid for maybe fifteen years or more."

Madison leaned forward. "Paid to someone at Turner?"

"No way to tell."

"You said it's in the *Turner* Advertising records?"

"Yeah."

"Maybe it's related to our media commissions?"

"No. That checks out to the penny."

Madison tried, but couldn't make sense of the weird consulting fee. "So what now, Lin?"

"I'll dig into it some more, ask my boss about it. But the fact that it's been paid to a consulting company I've never heard of scares me."

"The fact that it's hidden in our Turner records scares me!"

"I'll phone you when I know more."

"Thanks, Linda."

After hanging up, Madison looked back at the shimmering bay.

What the hell was going on? Was someone at National Media skimming money? If so, for themselves? Or for someone at Turner Advertising?

Then it dawned on her. The MensaPlan fee had been paid for more than fifteen years – and the anonymous e-mail accused her father of misappropriating money for sixteen years and depositing it in the Caribe National Bank. Did the multi-year fee accumulate to the $8.7 million in the bank?

$8.7 million wasn't much compared to the billions of dollars Turner Advertising spent with National Media over the last sixteen years.

National Media, like other large media companies, was under increasing pressure to hang onto their large, but shrinking share of traditional-media advertising dollars: the money spent to place ads in TV, cable, radio, magazine, newspaper. The problem was that many small upstart agencies were developing advertising expertise in the new tech-driven media, like the Internet, BlackBerry, blogger sites, iPods, social communications, Twitter and more. And these upstarts were chomping off big chunks of money that used to go to the big traditional-media companies.

Was someone at National Media so driven to hang onto their big fat traditional budgets that they paid the secret fee to someone at Turner in return for keeping those big ad budgets? Someone like Karla Rasmussen? As the Executive Vice President of Media Services, Karla had steered hundreds of millions of dollars, maybe even billions, into National's coffers over the last sixteen years. Was the MensaPlan fee some kind of kickback to Karla?

Kickbacks and gifts were no less common with media companies than with other industries.

You scratch my back, I'll put mink on yours.

Madison sipped her iced tea, phoned her brother and left a long voice message updating him. Then she dialed Kevin's number, but it didn't ring. She tried again and still got nothing. Looking down, she saw why: the red light on her phone suggested the battery was dead.

Perfect day, she thought. A banker who won't disclose any information. A local attorney who's en route to London where he'll be for two weeks. A secret fee that could ruin her company's image. And now, a fancy phone that won't work.

"Bon appetite," her waitress said, setting down her lunch. The red snapper had been marinaded in herbs and spices, chopped scallions and mushrooms and smelled delicious.

She took a bite. It tasted wonderful. She realized this might be the best part of her day.

* * *

Eugene P. Smith repeated the last words of Madison McKean's phone conversation with someone named Linda into his palm-sized recorder. He'd also recorded her conversation with the fat banker.

Smith's ability to read lips, the result of partial deafness from childhood viral meningitis, had over the years paid off for him. Surgery had restored over seventy percent of his hearing. And what he couldn't hear with his ears, he heard with his eyes.

Smith dialed Harry Burkett.

"What did the banker tell her?" Burkett demanded.

"Nothing about the money."

"How can you be so sure?"

"I lip-read their conversation."

"Good."

"Yeah, but you got trouble, Harry."

"Why?"

"She just got a phone call from somebody named Linda at National Media. Madison got all worked up about a consulting fee this Linda found."

Burkett sputtered. "A consulting fee?"

"A hidden consulting fee to a company called MensaPlan."

"Jesus...."

"Bad news?"

"Yeah. Hang on, I'll call you right back."

"Make it quick. We're boarding the ferry to St. Kitts."

Eugene P. Smith watched Madison stroll down the dock toward the ferry. Drop-dead good looks, shapely figure, thick brown hair, natural athletic poise. Very sexy lady. Nobody said he couldn't mix pleasure with work.

He tossed down the rest of his scotch, left money on the bar, and followed her. Two minutes later, his phone rang and he answered.

"She needs to have the accident there. The sooner the better."

"Done."

Twenty Nine

B ack in St. Kitts, Madison strolled through Basseterre, reading bits of local history from a tourist leaflet she picked up on the *Islander* ferry. She learned that Christopher Columbus discovered the small island in 1493 on his second trip to the Americas. He'd sailed along the island's southwest coast, right past where she was standing now. The Great Discoverer would have pointed up at the lush, emerald hills and towering volcano and been in awe, like she was.

But old Chris would have missed seeing *Kate's Designs,* the intriguing art store that she was walking into.

Madison looked around at the colorful, multi-hued paintings of local inhabitants, who themselves, she noted, were also multi-hued. The artwork reflected their English, French, African and Indian cultures. One painting, *Sugar Train,* showed workers loading sugarcane onto railway boxcars. Another, that she really loved, showed chiseled, ebony-skinned men slashing cane in a field. She paid cash for it to avoid leaving a credit card trail, and had the painting shipped to her father's apartment.

Back outside, she stopped and looked out at the harbor where small tenders were ferrying passengers to and from the massive Sun Princess cruise ship, anchored in the water like a 14-story floating hotel. She looked over at the tall, Lord Berkeley Memorial Clock, which reminded her it was time to get back to Ottley's Inn and phone the office. She wanted to update Kevin and also ask Alison Whitaker if she'd learned anything about who'd accused her father.

But finding a taxi would be tough. Earlier, they'd all been stuffed with cruise ship passengers. She took a few steps and couldn't believe it: An empty blue taxi was rolling toward her. Quickly, she flagged it over and got in.

"Ottley's Inn, please."

"Yes, ma'am," said the driver. He wore a wide-rimmed straw hat, purple flowered island shirt and wraparound reflective sunglasses.

As they drove up the winding road, she found her eyes drawn to the scarlet-red hibiscus surrounding many homes. Beside one home, young children played kickball in a field. She smiled at a beautiful, wide-eyed girl with pigtails who waved and smiled back. The girl was about six or seven.

Madison swallowed, and thought back to her college abortion. The nurse had told her the fetus was female. Even today, the abortion, the lowest point of her life, saddened and haunted her.

What about now? Would she ever have children? Would her new responsibilities allow her to give them the time they'd need? Would she repeat her father's mistake?

The driver headed up a road that wound through sprawling sugar-cane fields. Above the fields, the land sloped upward to Mount Liamuiga. The slopes were dense with trees and soon she saw fewer tin-roof homes poking up through the green vegetation.

Moments later she realized they were driving up a road she didn't recall.

"Is this a different route?"

"Yes, ma'am. Banana truck tipped over, blockin' the road to Ottley's. We come from de back way in." He adjusted his large sunglasses.

149

His accent was odd, not quite East Indies, not quite English, not quite anything. And his skin was too pale, especially for a white man in such a sunny climate. Further up the mountain, they passed trailbikers coasting downhill.

The rich, green scenery took her breath away and soon, so did the road. The taxi hit every rut as they bounced along, heading northwest according to the dashboard compass, away from Ottley's Inn.

"How much farther?" she asked.

"Be there soon. Just over that hill we start back down toward Ottley's."

Definitely not a St. Kitt's accent, she realized.

He steered down a narrow pathway, hitting even deeper ruts. The forest closed in on them and soon the trees hunched over the road, blocking out most daylight. He skirted along the edge of a deep ravine, rousting a flock of white egrets from their trees. The foliage was now too thick to see through and soon he slowed to less than five miles an hour. He'd obviously taken the wrong path.

A few yards farther, the taxi crept to a stop.

"Wrong turn?" she asked.

"No, ma'am."

"What's the problem?"

He smiled in the mirror.

She froze as she recognized the small white teeth of the masked man in her apartment.

Thirty

K evin checked his cell phone messages again. Still none from Madison. He was standing in the backyard of his Uncle Jakub Jowarski's charming old Victorian home north of Albany. He walked past the squeaky red swing where he'd played as a kid, and the large blue birdbath where he'd watched robins splash in the water. For Kevin this backyard and the surrounding forest was his only summer camp.

Uncle Jakub, a soft-spoken widower, had helped bring Kevin's parents over from Poland thirty-eight years ago. He'd recently retired from the Albany Medical Center after four decades as a pediatric surgeon. He and Kevin's mom were in the kitchen listening to Frankie Yankovic's polka hits and laughing their way down memory lane with a little help from Chopin Wódka.

Kevin walked out to the rear of the property and stared into the thick, evergreen forest. Even today, years later, the dark forest sent a cold shiver through him. He thought back to that day, back when he was six, standing in this same spot. He'd heard a woman's high-pitched cry from deep in the forest. Frightened, he'd raced back to the house and told his aunt. She assured him it was only the Canada geese squawking on the nearby lake. But he'd been sure it was a woman, and that something bad had happened to her. The next day, he overheard his aunt whispering to a neighbor that a woman had been raped in the woods.

Since then, he trusted his feelings.

Like his feeling a few nights ago when a man almost killed Madison in her apartment. And the growing feeling *right now* that she might be in danger two thousand miles away in St. Kitts.

After all, the armed man had promised to see her soon.

And even though she'd worn a disguise to the airport and flown incognito, Kevin knew that any man who could circumvent her building's sophisticated alarm system was a professional criminal. Pros knew how to find anyone, or knew people who could.

And why hadn't Madison called him as she promised to?

He flipped open his cell phone and checked his office messages again. Still no calls from her. He phoned his home. No message there. Finally, he dialed her cell phone and was again bounced into voicemail. He left another voice message. He then called international information for St. Kitts and got the number for Ottley's Inn. The operator dialed it for him.

"Ottley's Inn."

"Miss McKean's room, please."

"Sorry, sir, we have no one listed under that name."

Then he remembered. "Oh, I meant Shae Stuart."

"Yes, she's listed. Just a moment, sir."

The phone rang several times, then clicked into voicemail. He left a message asking her how things went at the bank, then switched back to the front desk manager.

"Have you seen her today?"

"Early this morning, sir. But not since."

"Please let her know I called." He left his name and number, hung up and stared at the phone.

Maybe she's still at the bank....

He called information again and they dialed the Caribe National Bank for him. He waited for the inevitable tape recorded greeting and was amazed when a pleasant, living human being answered in a lilting East Indies accent.

"Is Madison McKean still there?"

"No sir. She left a few hours ago."

He hung up and stared into the dark forest. His concern for her grew. Thick dark charcoal clouds had muscled in from the west. Wind whipsawed the tall pines and carried the smell of rain.

Where was she? Why hasn't she called?

Overhead, a flock of geese streaked toward the forest. Their shrieks sounded like human cries for help.

Does Madison need help?

Thirty One

This isn't happening, Madison kept telling herself.

The gun in her back proved otherwise. The tall, armed man also carried a large shopping bag as he pushed her deeper into the jungle rainforest. She pushed through thick palm fronds and stringy vines that clung like cobwebs to her hair.

He's going to kill me, she knew.

She searched for a possible escape route, but saw none. To her left, she heard water rushing through a ravine. To her right, monkeys screeched as though warning her. Cold sweat dampened every inch of her skin as they climbed up the rocky slope of the volcano.

How had he tracked her to St. Kitts? Only Christine and Kevin knew her destination, and she'd traveled under an alias. Obviously, someone in the agency had informed him.

"Walk faster!" He shoved her forward.

She quickened her pace, weaving through foliage so dense she could see only a few feet ahead. As they walked around a large boulder, she glimpsed the red fender of a mountain bike behind some bushes.

Was the rider nearby? If she screamed, would the rider hear her?

Or would a bullet rip into her back?

Soon the jungle grew thicker and more treacherous. She wriggled through some black, stringy vines that stuck to her sweaty face. She stepped onto a pile of dark gray rocks. One rock suddenly morphed into a lizard that crawled onto her ankle. Gasping, she shook it off and paused to catch her breath.

The tall man shoved her forward.

Everywhere she looked, the rainforest was teeming with life ... and death.

Soon, the narrow path ended at a ten-foot wide clearing. She took a few more steps and saw she was standing on a cliff.

"Walk to the edge!"

She hesitated, her lifelong fear of heights paralyzing her.

"Walk!"

She inched her way over to the cliff's edge and glanced down. The slope dropped off steeply and was covered with small shrubs and partly exposed roots. The ravine floor, thirty-five feet down, was a carpet of sharp volcanic rocks.

"What's this all about?" She knew it was about the $8.7 million, but she wanted him to talk so she could plan an escape.

"Your unfortunate hiking accident."

"Like my bathroom incident almost was?"

Anger flashed in his eyes, and she realized she shouldn't have mentioned his earlier failure.

"This time it's different," he said.

"Why?"

"You have no red emergency button to hit."

"But I have money - "

"Me, too."

"If you have money, why are you doing this?"

He smiled, and she realized that for him, killing her produced the same moral angst as stepping on an ant.

"Mostly for Lori."

"Who's Lori?"

"Long story involving your irresponsible old man."

"What do you mean?"

"No time now."

She wondered what he was talking about .

He took another step toward her and she moved back, just inches from the cliff's edge. She was blocked in by him, the thirty-five foot drop-off, and a tree with long, thick branches.

He tossed the shopping bag in front of her.

"What's in the bag?"

"Look."

She opened it and saw a brown outdoor shirt, a pair of tan hiking shorts, some boots and a camera with a strap.

"Put them on." He grinned, his teeth like little white pearls in the jungle darkness.

"Why?"

"One doesn't have a hiking accident in a blue business suit, does one? So put them on *now,* or I'll put them on later. Actually that could be kinda fun."

She wouldn't give the bastard the pleasure.

His eyes narrowed as though he was already undressing her. She shivered, but realized that putting on the hiking clothes would at least give her time to think. Slowly, she began unbuttoning her jacket.

"Hurry along, Ms. McKean."

Stall him!

"Just tell me one thing," she said, placing her jacket on the grass beside the tree.

"What's that?"

"Did you kill my father?"

"Suicide killed your father."

"Did you assist with his suicide?"

"Like Dr. Kevorkian?"

"No, like a cold-blooded *murderer?*"

He smiled and pleasure registered in his eyes.

For the first time in her life she felt like killing another human being.

"Hurry, or I'll help."

She undid the blouse, took it off and placed it on her jacket.

His dark, brooding eyes focused on her breasts in the semi-transparent bra. Quickly, she put the hiking shirt on and buttoned it. Then, unzipping her dress, she stumbled a bit and steadied herself on a nearby branch. The branch, she realized, was strong – and amazingly flexible. *Maybe* ... she thought ... *just maybe.*

Madison slid her dress off and bent over to grab the hiking shorts. She felt his gaze on her near-naked butt. Balancing herself on the branch again, she stepped into the shorts, pulled them up and buttoned them slowly.

"The boots! Hurry!"

She took off her shoe and grabbed the hiking boot. Leaning on the branch, she purposely pulled it back farther and started to put the boot on.

"They're too small," she said, pretending her foot wouldn't slide into the boot.

"I'll make it fit!"

He took a step closer.

She shoved her foot in, then took the other boot and pretended to struggle with it.

"*Hurry,* goddammit!" The veins in his neck bulged in anger. He stepped closer.

"Time's up!"

He lunged....

She let go of the branch. It whipsawed hard into his face, startling him and forcing him back.

She ran two steps - and felt his hand grab her wrist.

With amazing strength, he yanked her back and swung her over the side of the cliff – but without realizing that she'd grabbed his belt. Her weight was now pulling him over the cliff with her.

As they bounced down the slope, her shoulder landed hard on his chest, crushing the air from his lungs. His hands released her.

She reached for a passing shrub, missed. She grabbed another bush that slowed her just enough to lodge her boot on a protruding vine that stopped her fall.

Below, she heard a *THUD!*

Looking down, she saw he'd landed face down on a narrow stone ledge, still ten feet above the rocky ravine floor. He was sprawled out crucifixion style.

And he wasn't moving.

Suddenly, her boot began to slip off the vine. Looking up, she saw a root two feet above her. She grabbed it and muscled herself up.

Below her, he moaned.

Her sweaty fingers began to slide down the root. She stretched her other hand up, gripped a bush and slowly inched her body up to it. Her muscles were burning, her pulse pounding in her ears.

The man moaned louder. He was waking up.

She was still two feet below the ledge of the cliff.

He was moving around now.

Suddenly, the bush she held began loosening in the soft soil ... pulling out....

Mustering every ounce of energy, she reached up, grabbed a pencil-thin banyan vine and pulled herself up higher. Gulping air, she threw a knee over the ledge, clawed herself up onto it, and collapsed face down in the ground.

She lay there, sucking dirt and hot air into her mouth. Then she looked down into the ravine.

The man wasn't there.

Madison ran for her life.

Thirty Two

The EVP watched Harold Cummings walk into her office with his slight limp, smiling like always and chatting on his cell phone like the busy executive he was. He settled his gray, custom-tailored Armani suit into the chair opposite her desk and held up a finger to let her know he was winding up his call.

Cummings was a distinguished Turner Executive Vice President, a solid professional. He was smart, organized and dedicated to creating brilliant advertising for his clients. They respected him, his family adored him, and charities appreciated his generosity.

Even more impressive, he'd worked his way up from the mail room where he'd started twenty-four years ago. Today, he managed many of the agency's major clients with consummate skill. And his thick, silver hair, handsome face and relaxed confidence further explained why people liked him.

She even liked him.

But Harold was a problem. He planned to vote against the Com-Globe merger. And nothing, it seemed, could change his mind.

Except what she had in her desk drawer.

Cummings closed his cell phone and flashed his high-voltage smile at her. "So what's up?"

"The ComGlobe merger."

"Yeah. We vote in just a few days."

"The merger can make you a very wealthy man, Harold."

"True. But, as you know, I agree with Madison. ComGlobe is not the best merger fit for us."

"Because you'd have to resign some clients due to conflicts?"

He nodded. "These clients have helped us grow huge. They've been terrific clients, and loyal."

"Loyalty in advertising, Harold? Please...."

"Hey, it still exists with some clients."

She cut to the chase. "I'd like you to change your vote."

Harold's eyebrows rose. "Excuse me?"

"I want you to vote for the ComGlobe merger."

"No can do." The polite smile, a glance at his watch.

"Sure you can."

"Give me one good reason."

She waited until his eyes found hers. "Because I know, Harold."

He stared back. Cool, composed. "You know what?"

She continued to stare at him, letting her words sink in. "I know about your ... other life."

He acted puzzled, but recognition flickered in his eyes.

"What other life? Hell, I barely have time for this life." Another executive grin.

"But you always find time for your ... *exotic* life."

His body stiffened. "I have no idea what you're talking about." The red creeping up his neck suggested otherwise.

She reached in her desk drawer and pulled out a large envelope. He began to squirm. Tiny beads of sweat appeared on his upper lip. She enjoyed making men sweat. She reached into the envelope and pulled out several eight-by-ten photographs.

"I'm talking about these!" She slid the photos across the desk to him.

His face went rigid and he refused to look at them. Then slowly, he glanced down at the top one and his head jerked up as though someone had yanked his hair. Quickly, he flipped through all seven photos, his face growing redder with each one.

"Please understand, Harold, I don't like the fact that you screw underage girls. Maybe they need the money. But the law calls it a felony. Years in prison."

A droplet of sweat trickled down Cummings's neck onto his starched white collar.

"Imagine, Harold, the humiliation your wife and daughters would feel when they see these."

He stared at the photos.

"Imagine what our board members here at Turner would think."

Harold swallowed hard.

"Imagine what your fellow New York Athletic Club directors would whisper behind your back."

Cummings looked like something had been ripped from his chest cavity. He studied the photos for several moments, a crushed man. Then, all of a sudden, his eyes sparked to life and his confidence seemed to roar back. Angrily, he shoved the photos back across the desk.

"I'll say these are computer frauds! Our Macs can put any face on any body. Hell, our art directors here do it for fun all the time. These are fake photos. You've got nothing here!"

She smiled back at him.

He stood and turned toward the door.

"Sit down, Harold!"

"Screw you! I'll tell everyone they're fakes! They'll believe *me!*"

"No. They'll believe *this!*" She took a DVD from the drawer.

Harold slumped back down in the chair.

"I have three DVDs. Thirty minutes each. Digital quality. You and the twin Asian teens are my favorite."

His eyes locked on the DVD.

"And, you'll recognize these." She slid a stapled report over to him.

"All the porn sites you visited on your office computer this year. Who's a naughty boy?"

Harold Cummings closed his eyes for several moments, then whispered, "What do you want?"

"Your vote. You will continue to say you're voting against the merger, but on the day of the vote, you'll vote for the merger. If you do, I'll give you all this highly embarrassing material. If you do not, I'll give it to your wife. I'll also give it to our directors, the media and the Internet within an hour."

Dead, unblinking eyes stared back at her.

"Any questions, Harold?"

Silence.

"I'll plan on your vote."

Defeated, Cummings nodded. He stood, shoulders slumped, and slowly walked out of her office. She could trust him.

Unlike the bastard who gave me this! she realized, looking at her Montblanc pen. She thought back to when she'd been given the expensive gold pen, a farewell gift from National Media, where she first worked after college. The man who presented the pen to her was none other than T. Remus Burdine, National Media's debonair, charming, swashbuckling, empire-building, back-stabbing chairman.

She was twenty-two when she started at National Media. Within two years, she'd been promoted three times and Burdine had invited her to be his personal assistant. A month later, he invited her to his bed. She accepted. Soon, she grew infatuated with his massive power and wealth, estimated at nearly one billion dollars. And she'd grown infatuated with him, especially after he told her repeatedly that he loved her. A year later, when he asked her to abort their fetus, she'd done so willingly.

Then, four months later, everything changed. Burdine told her he'd fallen for someone younger in his Miami bureau. He also said he would not loan her the money he'd promised for her Aunt Sarah's life-saving heart surgery. Four weeks later, unable to afford the costly, insurance-denied surgery, her aunt died.

To avenge his cruelty, she set up a secret consultant's fee within National Media. Over the years, the fee had siphoned money from Burdine's various corporate coffers into her offshore bank accounts. Burdine's company had paid dearly.

And soon, Burdine would pay personally. She would send photos to Burdine's wife of him in bed with his latest mistress, along with DNA proof that the woman bore him two children. The insanely jealous wife would sue him for divorce, and Burdine would have to fork over half of his billion dollar estate.

Now, she looked down at the last copy of the e-mail sent to Mark McKean and fed it into her document shredder. Even if Madison and Kevin had read the e-mail back-up copy, they could never trace it back to her.

And only two other people had ever seen it. Harry Burkett. And Mark McKean, who was quite dead.

Like his lovely daughter soon would be.

Thirty Three

F eeling better this morning, ma'am?" the desk manager asked as Madison limped gingerly on her sore leg into the lobby of Ottley's Inn.

"Much better...." *Despite bouncing down a cliff.*

The manager nodded with obvious relief.

But she was still badly shaken by her near-death encounter with her tall attacker. After running from the cliff, she'd jumped on the red mountain bike she'd seen earlier and peddled furiously down bone-jarring jungle footpaths and roads for twenty minutes until she finally found Ottley's Inn.

A detective from the Royal St. Kitts Police had interviewed her at length and assured her they would pull out all the stops to apprehend her attacker. But, as of three minutes ago, the detective said her attacker was still at large.

And her attacker knew she was at Ottley's Inn, since she told him that in the taxi.

Last night, she considered switching to another hotel, but stayed when the manager placed an additional security guard near her room.

Madison heard a vehicle outside. Turning, she saw a dark blue taxi, identical to her attacker's, pull up near the entrance. A tall male, facing the other way, stepped out on the far side. She froze, telling herself that her attacker would never come here in broad daylight!

The tall man turned around and Madison's mouth fell open.

Kevin Jordan!

She couldn't believe her eyes. She also couldn't believe her heart. It was pounding like he'd come to ask her to the prom. Kevin walked into the lobby smiling, and greeted her with a hug.

"Just happen to be in the neighborhood?" she asked.

"Yep. I'm researching sea urchins for our cruise line client."

They both laughed.

"And to assist my favorite CEO," he said.

"In that case, you're promoted."

"To what?"

"Bodyguard."

His brow tightened as he apparently noticed the scab and bruise on her cheek. "Jesus, Madison, what happened?"

She led him over near the window where they sat in facing chairs. She explained how her Manhattan attacker had tried to kill her on Mount Luiguima. When she finished, Kevin shook his head.

"So he's still out there somewhere?"

"Yes."

"You described him to the police?"

"Well, sorta. But he looks different every time I see him. In the taxi he concealed his face with wraparound sunglasses, a mustache and a wide-rimmed straw hat. On the ferry, he wore different clothes, glasses, a baseball hat and maybe an brownish-red hairpiece. And in New York, he wore a mask."

Kevin nodded.

"All I know is he's tall and thin and has small teeth," Madison said, realizing how much more secure she felt with Kevin beside her. "Let's sign you in."

She led him over to the reception desk. When he finished, the bell-hop led them down to Kevin's room, which she was relieved to see was just a few rooms from hers. After he unpacked, they sat at his desk.

"So what's next?" he asked.

"Job One is to talk to the tight-lipped banker again. My brother suggests we tell him that the U.S. Senate Banking Committee and the Central Regional Bank here in the islands are considering looking into this account."

"There's another Job One."

"What?"

"Staying alive."

She agreed.

"We need some protection," he said.

"Yes, but the detective told me tourists can't buy firearms in St. Kitts."

"We can visit a fishing store."

"For what?"

"Knives," he said.

Better than nothing, she thought.

"And about that banker...," Kevin said.

"Yeah?"

"There might be a quicker way to loosen his tongue."

"How?"

"I'm thinking we might scare him with the possibility of a big, bad PR nightmare for his very private little bank."

She nodded and glanced at her watch. "I'm thinking we'll miss the ferry to Nevis unless we hurry."

* * *

In his rented Ford Escort, Eugene P. Smith put down his binoculars. Through the lobby window, he'd lip-read Madison McKean telling a tall, well-built man she referred to as Kevin about her escape yesterday. Now, Smith watched them get into a taxi and head off toward

Basseterre.

Hanging back several cars, Smith followed them. He tossed two more Tylenol #4s with codeine into his mouth and washed them down with Glenfiddich. That made ten Tylenol #4s since the bitch yanked him into the ravine. The pills had reduced his back pain.

But not his anger.

Smith hadn't been slammed that hard since he was a CIA operative years ago. He remembered the night well. He'd been waiting for his DGSE French Intelligence contact in a Marseille bar, when an anti-American drunk bashed him in the head with an empty Merlot bottle. Bleeding, he crawled back up off the floor and managed to wrestle the broken bottle away.

Later, after meeting his DGSE contact, Smith stayed at the bar. Near closing time, he lured the drunk into the back alley with the promise of free cocaine. In the alley, he jammed the jagged bottle into the drunk's gut, nearly disemboweling the bastard. Smith had no idea whether the man lived or died. It didn't matter. What did matter was enjoying how he moaned for help as Smith walked away.

Now, Smith parked his car and watched Madison and Kevin buy tickets for the *Islander,* then board the ferry.

So they're off to Nevis to see the fat banker again. Twist his flabby arm. Waste of time! Even if they learned something, it wouldn't matter.

Smith opened his theatrical case, took out a dark beard and matching ponytail hairpiece and put them on. He applied Instant Tan lotion to his face and hands, then pushed cotton padding into his cheeks. He donned his Royal St. Kitts Golf Course hat and reflective sunglasses and slung a Nikon Zoom 150 around his neck. He reached into his tourist bag beneath the Fugi film and flicked the Glock's safety off.

As he started to go buy a ferry ticket, something gave him pause. After yesterday's attack, Madison would be scrutinizing all tall male passengers. She knew he wore disguises. And even though he looked completely different today, there was a remote possibility that she might recognize his tall, thin profile. He didn't need the risk.

Besides, there were other ways to Nevis. Like the one advertised on his rental car's sun visor: LIAT Air Express. He phoned LIAT and chartered a flight. When Madison and Kevin arrived in Nevis, he would be waiting for them.

Smith phoned Harry Burkett.

"A man named Kevin just arrived here."

Burkett cursed under his breath. "He's Kevin Jordan, an employee."

"She told him everything."

"Shit! Hang on a second." Burkett put him on hold, obviously to tell the EVP. Moments later he came back on. "Handle Jordan, too."

"It'll cost extra."

"How much?"

"Fifty grand."

"Thirty."

"Fifty or forget it."

Burkett spewed out another stream of obscenities. "Okay, fifty."

"Wire it to my account at Bank Bruxelles Lambert in Brussels."

"Yeah, yeah."

Smith hung up, then watched the *Islander* chug out of Basseterre harbor. McKean and Jordan stood at the side rail, elbow to elbow, smiling at each other. *A little Love Boat romance going on there,* he thought. *Too bad it'll end so soon.*

Thirty Four

Please come in," Bradford Tipleton said, ushering Madison and Kevin into his office and over to the matching mauve Baker chairs in front of his immaculate mahogany desk.

The banker seemed surprised that she'd returned.

Madison saw another empty pastry box in his wastebasket. The box had smudges of chocolate, except for a thick smudge perched on Tipleton's fleshy upper lip.

She introduced Kevin and everyone sat down.

"So how are you today, Ms. McKean?"

"Still looking for answers."

"Of course. But as you know, our hands are still tied. Nothing has changed."

"Something has changed."

The banker stared back.

"Yesterday, a man followed me from your bank. He tried to kill me on Mount Liamuiga."

Tipleton's fleshy eyelids shot open. "Good Lord! Were you hurt?"

She turned the scab on her cheek toward him, then touched the bruises on her wrist and pretended to wince, hoping for a little sympathy.

"This is bloody awful!"

"And, almost fatal!"

Tipleton gasped. "Was he a local?"

"No."

Tipleton exhaled with obvious relief.

"I believe he's the same man who probably murdered my father."

"But your father's death certificate said ... suicide."

"My father would never take his own life."

"But...." Tipleton looked confused.

"And, I don't believe my father opened the 8.7 million dollar account here."

"But our records say that a Mark McKean with your father's Manhattan address and P.O. Box did open it."

"I believe a man posing as Mark McKean opened it."

Looking concerned, Tipleton ran his tongue along his upper lip where he discovered the smudge of chocolate and flicked it back inside.

"I saw a security camera in your lobby," she said.

Tipleton nodded.

"Could I view the video or DVD for the day he opened the account."

Tipleton checked his calendar. "It's video, but I'm afraid it's been recorded over several times."

Madison's hope dimmed. "Is the employee who assisted him here today?"

"Yes he is."

"May I speak with him?"

The banker fidgeted in his chair. "Well, as I mentioned yesterday, he's not at liberty to give you any details about the account or the depositor."

Madison had expected Tipleton to say no. "Even though my father's dead?"

"Yes. That's confidential information, protected under our country's banking laws." Tipleton took out a folded white handkerchief and patted perspiration from his chin.

Beside her, she sensed Kevin's growing frustration with the banker.

She leaned forward. "There's something else you should know, Mr. Tipleton."

"What's that?"

"The U.S. Senate Banking Committee may soon investigate this account. Maybe the FBI, too."

Concern flashed in Tipleton's eyes, then he crossed his arms. "We have great respect for your Senate Banking Committee and the important work they do in your country. But, as you know, all Nevis banks and our Central Regional Bank are outside the legal jurisdiction of U.S. banking laws. We are bound by our own commonwealth's banking privacy laws, and those laws are strictly enforced."

"But what if an account is directly linked to serious criminal activity? Wouldn't your bank then share information about the account?"

"It depends."

"On what?"

"On all the circumstances."

Kevin leaned forward and locked eyes with the banker. "Mr. Tipleton, all the circumstances surrounding this account are serious and criminal. Mark McKean, the man who allegedly deposited the $8.7 million in your bank, was most probably murdered. The New York police are investigating. His daughter here was almost murdered a few days ago by a man in New York. The same man followed her to Nevis, and then to your bank yesterday, and after she left, he again tried to kill her. There is an obvious link between Mark McKean's death, and the two attempts to murder Madison McKean ... and that link is the 8.7 million dollars in your bank."

Bradford Tipleton blinked anxiously, then stared at his cookie jar.

"Imagine," Kevin continued, "if the *Wall Street Journal,* or CNN, or your local newspaper, *The Democrat,* discovered that Mark McKean, a highly respected executive, had been murdered because of an $8.7

171

million account in your bank. Your customers will see headlines like *'Caribe National Bank Customer Murdered'* or *'Police Investigate Suspicious Millions at Caribe National Bank.'* The damage to your bank's excellent reputation could be irreparable. Customers would drag their money out of your bank like they did back in our 1930s banking nightmare!"

Tipleton looked like his customers already were dragging fat sacks of money out the door.

"I have a suggestion," Madison said.

"What is it?" Tipleton lurched forward as though grabbing a life preserver. The armpits of his blue shirt were dark with perspiration, despite the frigid air conditioning.

"Your regulation says *I* can't ask your colleague who opened the account, right?"

"That's right."

"What about you?"

"Me?"

"Yes. Does it also prevent you from asking him?"

Tipleton looked puzzled. "Well, no...."

Madison took a photo from her purse and handed it to him. "This is my father, Mark McKean. Would you please ask your colleague if he's ever seen this man?"

Tipleton took the photo. "I suppose my asking a colleague that question would not strictly violate our privacy laws."

Madison hoped it didn't, but frankly didn't care much if it did.

Tipleton hoisted his three hundred pounds onto surprisingly tiny feet encased in gray tasseled loafers, and scurried down the hall to another office.

Madison reached over and touched Kevin's arm. "Your big bad PR nightmare is working."

"Bad PR is like Ebola for a bank. Deadly."

Moments later, Bradford Tipleton came back and plopped down, whooshing air from his seat cushion. He handed the photo back to her.

"My colleague has never seen the man in this photo."

Madison breathed out in relief.

"He *has* met a man named Mark McKean who was twenty-five years younger, shorter and stockier with a brown buzz cut."

She couldn't think of anyone fitting that description. "Was the money wired back to a Turner Advertising Citibank account in New York?"

Tipleton paused. "No. It was not."

"So the money is still here?"

"No."

"Where is it now?"

Tipleton squirmed in his chair again, like he had a bad case of piles, then grabbed his cookie jar.

"Care for a pinwheel? Chocolate lowers your blood pressure."

Madison and Kevin declined.

Tipleton crammed a pinwheel cookie into his mouth and swallowed it quickly. Then he checked the doorway, leaned forward and whispered, "The money was transferred to Tradewinds Protected Investments, a bank in the Caymans."

"Do you know this bank?"

"I've heard of it."

"Is the money still there?"

"You'd have to ask them."

"Anything else you can tell us?" she asked.

"No, and let's all agree on one thing."

"What?"

"I didn't tell you anything!"

Madison and Kevin nodded.

"Thank you, Mr. Tipleton, Madison said, standing. "We appreciate your candor."

Stepping outside the bank, the warm breeze felt good, but nowhere near as good as the confirmation that her father had not deposited the money in the bank. Nor had he misappropriated money from Turner Advertising. Her father was innocent, as she'd known all along. But now she had proof.

Still, questions remained. Who deposited the money into the Caribe National Bank account in her father's name? And who transferred
the money to Tradewinds Protected Investments? And what about the
money itself? Was it connected to the strange MensaPlan consultant
fee her friend Linda had discovered at National Media?

One thing she did know – whoever was behind the money was also
behind the man trying to kill her.

* * *

Standing behind a clothing store sign, Eugene P. Smith repeated
the last words of McKean's and Tipleton's conversation into his tape
recorder. Once again, he'd sat at the café across from Tipleton's office
window, lip-reading the conversation between the banker, McKean
and Jordan.

Smith flipped open his cell phone and called Harry Burkett.

"The banker blabbed," Smith said.

"Bastard!"

"He told them the money was transferred to Tradewinds Protected
Investments. He also told them the man who opened the account did
not look like Mark McKean."

"Did he describe the man?" Burkett sounded anxious.

"Yes."

"How'd he describe him?"

"He described *you*, Harry."

"*The bastard!*" Burkett went ballistic for several moments. "Did he
give them the e-mail address the bank sent the statements to?"

"No."

"Eliminate that son of a bitch before he does."

"Sure, for a fee."

"But we're already paying you extra for Kevin Jordan."

"Harry...."

"Yeah?"

"No tickee, no laundry." Smith savored the agony he was giving

Burkett. "But I've got good news, Harry."

"What?"

"I'm running a special on fat bankers today. Just twenty-five grand."

Burkett mumbled something under his breath. "Your Brussels bank?"

"Yes."

They hung up.

Smith turned and looked through the window at Bradford Tipleton sitting in his office. The fat banker looked toward his door. Seeing no one, he reached into his desk, pulled out a Hostess Twinkie and crammed the whole thing into his mouth.

This little piggy may explode before he ever goes to market ... and before I earn my fee!

Thirty Five

The noon sun felt hot on Madison's face as she and Kevin walked down the long ferry dock toward the center of Basseterre.

"So how do we persuade someone at Tradewinds Investments to give us the account information?" she asked.

"We scare 'em with the fear of devastating PR for their bank."

"Like we scared Bradford Tipleton...."

"It worked."

Suddenly, Madison jumped back as two large goats bolted from an alley, chased by an angry chicken, squawking and flapping its wings.

"What's with all these chickens and goats?" Kevin asked.

"I read they're family pets who scrounge around town for food."

"Speaking of food, where's this Hullabaloo restaurant?"

"Ballahoo's. And it's just around the corner."

Suddenly, a dark blue taxi crept to a stop beside her. She felt every muscle in her body constrict. When she saw the driver was a woman, she relaxed, but still couldn't shake the real sense that the Tall Man was always nearby, watching her.

Kevin stopped walking and snapped his fingers.

"What?" she said.

"Craig Borden."

"Who's he?"

"My longtime pal. And an international banker over in Dominica. He visits banks all over the Caribbean. Maybe he knows someone at this Tradewinds Bank."

Kevin flipped open his cell phone and began searching for Craig's phone number. As he did, Madison couldn't help but notice how the sun brought out streaks of gold in his auburn hair and lightened the blue of his eyes.

They stepped into Ballahoo's restaurant and were met with the mouth-watering aromas of fresh seafood sandwiches and garlic-lemon chicken. A waitress led them past some window latticework and large hanging plants to a table overlooking the town square. A breeze eased through the open windows. They ordered lobster sandwiches with cole slaw and glasses of white wine.

Kevin dialed Craig's cell phone, and seconds later gave her a thumbs up that Craig had answered.

"Hey, man, it's Kevin. I need your help." He listened, smiled, then said, "No, you owe *me* for Drucilla."

Madison wondered who Drucilla was.

"Yeah, Drucilla is nice," Kevin said, "She's also six-three and wrestles professionally as *The HumVee*."

Madison smiled.

After catching up with Craig, Kevin quickly explained everything about the money and the banks. Moments later, he hung up.

"Craig is over on the island of Antigua. He's flying here this evening to attend a meeting tomorrow morning at the Royal Bank of Canada. He can meet us for dinner at Stonewalls tonight."

"Terrific. Does he know anyone at Tradewinds Investments?"

"No. But he knows a guy who dates a loan officer there." Kevin smiled.

Kevin's smile caught her off guard. Again. It always reminded her of his innate kindness. He'd been the friend she needed after her father's death. He'd asked his friends like Dean Dryden and now Craig Borden to help her. He'd made her laugh when she didn't think she could. He'd even flown down to St. Kitts to help protect her. *And, did I mention he's handsome?*

But despite his easygoing manner, Madison got the sense that Kevin was holding something back. Something personal that he wasn't ready to share, or maybe never would share. Perhaps he'd been married and divorced, or seriously hurt by a relationship.

Whatever it was, she didn't feel comfortable asking him about it.

* * *

Eugene P. Smith positioned his chair so the sun would be in Madison's and Kevin's eyes if they faced him. He tossed two more Tylenol-#4 with codeine in his mouth and washed them down with a decent Pinot Noir. His aches had nearly vanished.

Watching them through the branches of a leafy plant, Smith had just lip-read Kevin Jordan's phone conversation with a friend about the money at Tradewinds Investments. A friend they planned to dine with at Stonewalls tonight.

Maybe you'll dine ... maybe you won't.

He sipped more wine and looked out the window at a group of tourists window-shopping along the street. A skinny-legged old man with baggy Bermudas and rolled-down black socks was being dragged along by an obese woman in an orange moo-moo. A young schoolboy with a blue bookbag ran past them.

Smith's mind raced back to his blue bookbag, the one his mother bought him at Kmart. He loved the multi-pocketed bookbag, just one of many gifts his middle-class parents had given him.

He'd been fortunate that his parents were decent, loving, friendly people – but unfortunate that he didn't inherit their nice and friendly genes.

Early on, Eugene knew he was different. For one thing, he didn't like kids. For another, he didn't like adults. What he did like was military games and weapons. By age fourteen, he'd hidden twelve guns and twenty-three knives under the oak floorboards of his bedroom closet.

In high school he got straight A's, and his tall, wiry frame helped him excel in basketball and track. But he was a loner, and shunned by the in-crowd cliques. Shunning never bothered him. It was like water off a duck's back.

But in college he began to realize that projecting a friendlier image would help him. He decided to learn how to *act* more sociable and outgoing. He enrolled in some drama classes and quickly realized that acting sociable worked for him. He learned how to be easygoing and friendly with people, even with people he didn't like.

After graduating with honors, he joined the CIA, the perfect venue for expressing his pent-up militaristic, aggressive tendencies. The CIA training was intense and he soon became skilled in using all kinds of weapons, and in hand-to-hand combat. After excelling in the courses at the Agency's Farm near Williamsburg, Virginia, he was stationed at the U.S. embassy in London.

There he established valuable contacts at many foreign embassies in London's posh Belgravia section. For the next seven years, Smith functioned as a CIA covert operative in Europe. He handled sanctioned and non-sanctioned assassinations against terrorists. He worked his contacts, paid them well and usually got good, valuable information in return.

But sometimes he got lies. Like from Hans Bauer, one of his contacts in Vienna. Smith had paid Bauer fifty thousand Euros for some information that turned out to be a lie. The lie led to the death of an American and a valuable Austrian contact.

Smith wanted vengeance.

One night, after gambling away some of the money Smith had given him, Herr Bauer strolled through Vienna's Volksgarten Park. Smith stepped from behind a hedge and slammed a crowbar down on the bastard's shoulder blade, dropping him like a slab of granite. Smith could still feel the sweet crunch of bone and the pleasure of cramming the silenced barrel of a .45 Magnum into Bauer's mouth.

"Remember the Ten Commandments, Hans?"

He nodded, grimacing in pain.

"Remember number eight?"

"No...."

"Thou shalt not steal. Remember now?"

"Uh-huh."

"But thou stole fifty thousand Euros from me, right?"

"Uh-huh."

"Because thou lied, right?"

"Uh-huh."

Bauer gagged on the barrel.

"Do you want forgiveness?"

"Yes, please...." Tears streamed down his radish-red face.

Bauer started to mumble something and Smith pulled the gun barrel part way out of his mouth to hear better.

"What'd you say?"

"I needed the money. I have a gambling addiction."

"Not anymore!"

Smith squeezed the trigger.

Herr Bauer's brains splattered onto the walkway like a Jackson Pollack painting. A Kodak moment so to speak.

Smith wrapped Bauer's fingers around the Magnum and fired again into the night sky, making sure there was sufficient gunpowder residue on his hand. He stuffed a computer-generated suicide note into Bauer's coat pocket, then drove back to his room at the Grand Hotel.

Four years later, Smith was offered a promotion back at Langley. He accepted, mainly because he'd become a marked man: several terrorist groups had placed a hefty bounty on his head.

But in Washington, he soon became bored with headquarters politics, and tired of listening to his co-workers babble on.... And he didn't like sitting behind a desk. He'd become addicted to action.

Six months later, he retired from the CIA and set himself up as a freelance operative. The word got around. His CIA bosses gave him several black-ops contracts which he performed flawlessly. Over the years, he evolved into one of the world's more effective and feared assassins. His hefty fees, plus some wise investments in the stock markets of Europe and Asia, had made him wealthy.

That allowed him to select only those assignments that were personally as well as financially rewarding.

Like Madison McKean.

Thirty Six

The Executive VP smoothed out her purple Hermes scarf as Harry Burkett, looking more skittish than usual, hurried into her office and sat down opposite her desk. His lips and fingers were red from stuffing pistachios into his mouth. And his squinty ferret eyes shifted from the door to the window and back rapidly, suggesting he'd rather be anywhere else.

She'd rather he was anywhere else, too. But life's vicissitudes sometimes required strange bedfellows. And Harry was the poster child for *Strange.* She pushed a button on her desk. Instantly, the office door clicked shut and her white-noise machine hissed on, preventing others from overhearing them.

Burkett whispered, "Madison knows her father did not open the Caribe National Bank account."

"The banker talked?"

"Bastard sang like a bird."

Even so, she thought, *the trail can't lead to me.*

Burkett leaned forward. "Eugene's gonna handle the banker before the son-of-a-bitch tells her the e-mail address for the account."

She nodded approval. "What about Madison and Kevin?"

"Eugene's handlin' them, too."

Kevin Jordan, she thought. Most unfortunate that he's in the wrong place at the wrong time. And while she respected him as a highly-gifted creative director, Kevin had flaws. He was a team player in a business that rewarded the ego-driven. He practiced Stephan Covey's goody-goody *Seven Habits to Success* even though any fool knew they didn't work when you swim with corporate sharks. Kevin even wasted time in soup kitchens helping drunks.

Helping Madison would, sadly, cost him his life.

"It has to look like an accident," she said.

"This accident happens all the time down there."

"And people die from it?"

"Uh-huh."

"What about Linda Langstrom at National Media?" she asked.

"What about her?"

"Did she give Madison any more information on the MensaPlan fee she uncovered?"

Burkett appeared to search his memory. "Uh ... Eugene didn't say nothin' more about that."

"Tell our friend at National Media to find out what Langstrom knows. Fast."

"Right."

She picked up her newspaper to let Burkett know he was dismissed. He bolted from the room.

Watching him walk away, she couldn't help but think: *dead man walking.* Harry Burkett was a risk. Too nervous, too weak, and too likely to cave in to save himself under police questioning. And when the police discovered Burkett regularly engaged in criminal sexual conduct with underage girls, they'd come down very hard on him. *Hard enough for him to give me up in a plea bargain. Won't happen, Harry.*

Turning back to her desk, she noticed a pink message slip from another nervous man: Peter Gunther. She thought back to when Gunther, ComGlobe's Director of Mergers and Acquisitions, phoned her a few weeks ago in a panic. Gunther, whose career hinged on consummating the ComGlobe-Turner merger, had learned to his horror that Mark McKean planned to vote against the merger and thereby defeat it.

"You have to change McKean's mind!" Gunther had said.

"We tried."

"And...?"

"He refuses to change it."

"Why?"

"He won't resign our long-standing clients who have product conflicts with ComGlobe clients."

"Even though he'd make forty-five million dollars or more?"

"Even though, Gunther."

"He's nuts! Nothing can stop the consolidation of the ad industry. And ComGlobe will increase Turner's business ... and media buying clout ... and international resources! For chrissakes, the money will roll in!"

"It's not about money for him."

"It's *always* about money!"

She decided to let Peter Gunther rant a bit.

"What would change his vote?" Gunther sounded like what he was – a man clinging to his job by his fingernails.

"I'd have to think about it." Actually, she had thought about it, and knew exactly what would nullify McKean's vote. But she wasn't about to tell a loose-lipped bozo like Peter Gunther.

"You know," Gunther whispered, "we'll make it *very* much worth your while if you persuade McKean to vote for the merger."

Finally, he coughs up the bribe, she realized. "How much worth my while, Peter?"

Long pause. "How does six million in a numbered Swiss bank account sound?"

"About four million short."

Gunther sputtered and cleared his throat. "Jesus Christ! Ten million is absolutely impossible! Maybe ... seven!"

"Gunther?"

"Yeah?"

"Ten, or the price goes to twelve million next week."

She heard him harrumph, and rattle his papers like Rush Limbaugh.

"All right, goddammit, ten! But you better deliver!"

"Like the U.S. Mail."

"*How* will you change his vote?"

"It's better if you don't know."

He paused. "What are you plan – "

"Good bye, Gunther," she said, hanging up.

And now, almost a month later, as she looked out at the sunny Manhattan skyline, she realized her ten million dollar merger bonus was just days away.

And she'd earned it, after all she'd put up with in life. She glanced at the photo of her parents, and remembered the day they died in a fatal car accident. She was six. She remembered the two abusive foster families, the rape by Merle Lee, her rejection by T. Remus Burdine and other harsh events that had molded her, perhaps damaged her in ways. But these events, she knew, also had made her stronger.

Today, she could handle adversity and stress that would crush most people. She also could focus her determination like a laser to get what she wanted.

Life's brutal lessons had been her ladder to success.

A ladder Madison McKean, Daddy's Little Pampered Princess, never had to climb. What had Madison done to deserve her silver-spoon life? Her CEO title? Nothing.

The EVP thought back to when Mark McKean told her he would vote against the merger. She knew his mind was made up. Which meant there was really only one solution: force him to resign. So she sent Harry Burkett, posing as Mark McKean, to deposit her 8.7 million dollars in the Caribe National Bank. Then she drafted the anonymous e-mail memo accusing McKean of misappropriating the money from Turner Advertising and demanding his resignation.

But McKean had refused to resign.

And now he's dead.

And even though Madison succeeded him as CEO, she's being dethroned far away on the island of St. Kitts.

Thirty Seven

Bradford Tipleton eased his chunky Lincoln Navigator out of the Caribe National Bank parking lot and appeared to head home for the evening.

Eugene P. Smith followed in his rented Mazda, a scuzzy, unnoticeable klinker with red vinyl seats and a Daffy Duck air freshener. Three minutes later, Smith couldn't help but smile when Tipleton parked, squeezed out of the seat and trundled into a bakery called *La Dolce Doughnut.*

Smith watched Tipleton nod to a skinny woman behind the counter. The woman immediately placed eight large chocolate eclairs oozing white cream into a pastry box.

Clutching the box, Tipleton walked outside and drove off. Within seconds, the banker had stuffed an eclair into his mouth. At the next stop sign he crammed down another, puffing his cheeks out like a blowfish.

Amazed, Smith shook his head, then followed Tipleton past the Horatio Nelson Museum. Soon traffic slowed beside an ancient one-story building. A plaque said it was the first synagogue in the Ca-ribbean, built in 1688 by Sephardic Jews from Brazil. Smith remem-bered reading that Alexander Hamilton was born in Nevis and that his mother was most likely Jewish.

Minutes later, Smith followed the banker to a gray, three-story stone house overlooking the sea. Tipleton parked and walked inside with his pastry box.

Through his binoculars, Smith watched him plop down on a sofa, turn on the television and begin sucking the sugar cream from yet an-other eclair. Watching the banker gorge himself reminded Smith that *he'd* soon be having dinner with his two new best friends, Madison and Kevin, back in St. Kitts.

Smith grabbed his briefcase, walked up and tapped Tipleton's dol-lar sign door knocker.

Tipleton opened the door with an expression that suggested he rarely had visitors. "Yes...?"

"Mr. Tipleton, My name is Eugene P. Smith. My friend at Jarvis & Chamberlain Investments in Manhattan recommended you. He said my money would be very well protected with you and your bank."

Tipleton looked at him, then down at his briefcase. "That's true, but perhaps tomorrow during banking hours -"

"Unfortunately, I must leave Nevis tonight. And I'd prefer no one saw me deposit this money at your bank, if you catch my drift."

Tipleton appeared to catch his drift.

"Might I inquire as to how much we might be talking about?"

"A modest deposit to start with."

"How modest?"

"Only six million U.S."

Tipleton snorted like an eclair had backed up into his throat.

"But next Thursday I'll deposit eleven million Euros."

"Please come in, Mr. Smith."

Grinning like the Cheshire cat, Tipleton led Smith inside to a large living room with a beige sofa and matching chairs arranged around a five-foot by three-foot monster television tuned to Chef Emeril preparing stuffed pork chops.

"Would you care for something to drink or eat, Mr. Smith?"

"Sounds great."

* * *

Fifteen minutes later, Smith watched Bradford Tipleton's enormous body slump to the floor and flail about, his eyes bulging big and white, as life drained from them.

Amazing, Smith thought, *how the graceful sea wasp and its delightful chironex fleckeri toxin create such a violent reaction in man. Even a man as obese as Tipleton....*

Thirty Eight

M adison and Kevin hurried past Caines' Rent A Car on Princes Street in Basseterre. They were running late for their seven o'clock dinner with Kevin's banker friend, Craig Borden. She hoped Borden could shed more light on the mysterious 8.7 million dollars transferred to Tradewinds Investments.

She looked down at her town map. "Stonewalls is only a block ahead."

"Impossible!"

She looked up and saw Kevin leaning against Stonewalls' entrance. "Gee, they moved it," she said, smiling.

They stepped inside the Caribbean restaurant. They found themselves surrounded by tourists, locals and a skiddle-drum band bonging out Bob Marley's "One Love." Businessmen were hunched over their drinks at a large wooden bar that reminded her of the monkeypod wooden bar in Pub 222, a terrific bar in St. Charles, Illinois. Madison had spent a couple of Thanksgiving breaks with Linda Langstrom's family in the charming town near Chicago.

"May I help you?" asked a stunning young woman with skin like polished ebony and a silk blouse as red as her lipstick.

"Reservation for McKean. Sorry we're a little late."

"Not to worry."

She led them through the crowded restaurant to a breezy outdoor garden with banana trees, bamboo and purple-flowered bougainvillea. As they sat down, a waitress in a short mini skirt that showcased her long, shapely legs sashayed up to the table. "Fancy a drink to start?"

Madison pointed to a wall poster. "What's in that Stone drink?"

"Dark cavalier rum, Amaretto, coconut rum, triple sec, pineapple, orange juice, grenadine and a dead iguana...." She winked.

"Sounds nutritious. I'll have one."

"I'll have two," Kevin said.

The waitress arched her eyebrows at Kevin.

"One's for my pal who's arriving any minute."

The waitress nodded, then weaved her way through a group of men who parted for her like the Red Sea opened for Charlton Heston.

"Where did you meet Craig?"

"High school football. In college we were roommates. Now, we're guardians of each other's spiritual growth."

"Poor Craig...."

Kevin laughed.

She liked how he laughed, and how his relaxed banter always seemed to calm her. When she was with Kevin, she worried less about corporate machinations, secretive banks and the tall psychopath trying to kill her. Which reminded her. She looked around to scan the restaurant, but saw no one who even remotely resembled her attacker.

The waitress placed three Stone drinks on the table.

"Here's to loose-lipped bankers!" Kevin said, grabbing his Stone.

They clinked glasses and sipped some.

The potent rums hit her stomach like a line drive. Chills actually fingered down her back.

Kevin blinked and coughed. "This drink has a different name in Manhattan."

"What?"

"Drano."

Suddenly, Kevin jumped up and hugged a tall, handsome man in a gray Italian-cut suit. Craig Borden had the powerful shoulders of an athlete: six-four, dark brown hair, blue eyes, and teeth worthy of a Crest commercial. He looked like he could charm or muscle his way through just about any situation.

"Meet Craig Borden, banker *extraodinaire*."

"Hi, Craig." She shook his hand.

"Nice to meet you, Madison."

"That's your libation," Kevin said, pointing to Craig's drink.

"Ah, yes ... the Stone. I had one last month. Fortunately, I'm next on the transplant list."

They laughed, clinked their glasses and sipped their drinks. Moments later, the waitress came by and took their dinner orders.

"So, Madison, tell me about this incredible bank account."

Madison explained everything and Craig listened, jotting down the account number and other specifics.

When she finished, he said, "I checked around and learned that our affiliate bank in the Caymans sometimes works with Tradewinds Investments. Tomorrow I'll have our manager see if he can learn anything about this account."

"Think he can?" Madison asked.

Craig shrugged and raked his fingers through his hair. "It could prove very difficult. These offshore banks are cloaked in secrecy. The more secret the better. But they're also susceptible to pressure from their governments and from their Caribbean banking regulators, and to some extent from our Senate Banking Committee."

Borden sipped his drink, then continued. "And you have some pressure. Your account involves the police, a possible homicide, plus two attempts to murder you, Madison. All that should help loosen their tongues."

"But if it doesn't?"

"Then it'll take more time to get information. Either way, I'll call you tomorrow with an update."

The waitress placed their meals on the table. Madison breathed in the savory aromas of her garlicky chicken kabob and Kevin's blackened grouper and Craig's sauce-slathered pork ribs. One bite told her the food was as delicious as it looked.

After dinner, Madison headed toward the ladies room, and on the way paid the bill. In the restroom, she reapplied her lipstick, smiling wide to make sure her teeth weren't smudged with red. Earlier today, Kevin told her she had a terrific smile. The compliment had made her heart pump faster. Even now, it did.

Slow down, girl....

She checked the tiny scab by her ear. It was healing, but it reminded her that the Tall Man was out there looking for her. This afternoon, Kevin bought two large fishing knives at a sporting goods store. He'd given her one and shown her how to use it. And she *would* use it, if necessary.

She returned to the table and announced they were free to leave. Both men thanked her for dinner, pushed their chairs back, and made their way past a sunburned family of four, an elderly priest wearing a beret, and a rugged-looking man in wraparound sunglasses who looked like a forty-year-old Clint Eastwood.

Outside, the ocean breeze carried the sweet scent of lavender. She breathed it in and realized that she hadn't felt this relaxed in two weeks – thanks to good friends, good food, and the brain-numbing Stone drink.

A perfect night, she thought, as they walked down the street.

Craig thanked her again, flagged down a taxi and headed back to his hotel.

Madison and Kevin strolled on down the street. She looked out at the Caribbean, shimmering like black satin under a fat white moon.

* * *

_____

Eugene P. Smith, loosened his priest's collar and adjusted his Jesus beard. Madison, Kevin and the tall banker had just walked past his table and headed outside. He'd easily lip-read their conversation while pretending to read *Spirituality* magazine.

Smith crossed himself, placed money on his check and walked outside.

He watched the banker leave in a taxi, then followed McKean and Jordan. As he passed a television shop, he noticed a face on all TV screens. A *familiar* pudgy face.

Smith paused to read the announcer's lips ... "a Nevis banker, Mr. Bradford Tipleton, was found dead in his home tonight after a pizza delivery man observed his body through a window. Mr. Tipleton appears to have died from a heart attack."

And stay tuned folks, Smith thought, *that's not all!*

Thirty Nine

H arken to yon tinkle!" Madison said, cupping her hand to her ear as she and Kevin walked through the reception area of Ottley's Inn.

"Tis the tinkle of nightcap glasses, methinks," he said.

"Tis! Tis!"

Although she didn't need any more alcohol after drinking the Stone, she wanted to ask Kevin again how certain agency people got along with her father. "I thought we might go back over things. See if we missed anything."

"Makes sense."

They strolled toward the outdoor patio and sat at a table facing the long, narrow swimming pool. The water lapped against the sides and shimmered like ribbons of silver under the white moon. Tall palm trees stretched toward the stars. Seconds later, an elderly waiter shuffled up to their table and smiled.

"Compari and soda, please," Madison said.

"And you, sir?"

"Grand Marnier."

The waiter nodded and headed toward the bar.

Madison looked up at the imposing shadow of the volcano, Mount Liamuiga. She'd read it was created one million years ago from magma roaring up from miles beneath the sea. The island's first humans, the Arawak Indians, appeased the angry volcano by tossing living human beings into its abyss. Yesterday the Tall Man had tried to add her to the tossees.

The waiter placed their drinks on the table. They sipped some, sat back and sort of melted into the warm tropical night.

Kevin gestured toward the palm trees and stars. "I feel like a kid at camp."

And you look like one, she thought, noticing how the breeze had tousled his hair. The moonlight glinted off his eyes, and the pool reflections rippled across his high cheekbones. Kevin was not *GQ* pretty, but handsome in a hunky *Outdoor Life,* Pendleton shirt way.

"I keep asking myself," she said, "who at the agency is capable of doing this to my father?"

"Me too, but I still have no clue."

"Is there *anyone* my father was really angry at?"

He paused. "Not that I know of."

"Anyone *really* angry at him?"

Kevin shook his head. "As you know, he got along well with most people."

"Except recently with all the directors who favor the ComGlobe merger."

"Yeah, except them." He sipped his Grand Marnier.

"Anyone else been acting suspicious recently?"

He closed his eyes. "My sense is that Leland Merryweather is up to something."

"Really?"

"Yeah. The other day I was in his office when he got a call from London. He got excited and asked if I would mind stepping out. I did, but paused a moment and heard him whispering 'the money is coming.' And two days ago, when I walked into his office, he and Finley Weaver and Dana Williams stopped whispering."

"Trading recipes?" she said, smiling.

"For poisons maybe. But Karla Rasmussen also might be up to something. She and Dana were working in her office with the door shut for five hours last Sunday, and the Sunday before that."

"Interesting. How did Karla ever reach such a top executive position, besides schmoozing people with her obvious warmth and charm?"

Kevin smiled. "Her brains, for the most part."

"There's another part?"

Kevin's face reddened and she wondered why.

"Well, there's a rumor that years ago when she was much younger and shall we say more curvaceous, she might have used her other body parts."

"Yikes!" Picturing cold-hearted Karla in the throes of lovemaking was like imagining Reverend Jerry Falwell leading a gay rights parade.

"Yeah, but on a less catty note, clients do respect Karla's marketing and advertising savvy. And she's tenacious as hell in pursuing and grabbing off good accounts."

"Is she married?"

"Once upon a time."

"What happened?"

"Lasted about a year. Word is, the good man simply up and disappeared one night."

Madison couldn't stop herself from envisioning Karla pushing the poor man's corpse into a backyard grave. "Was her sainted husband in advertising?"

"No."

All of a sudden, Kevin put down his Grand Marnier and stared at her, his large blue eyes wide.

"What?"

"Her husband...."

"What about him?"

"He was an international banker."

Madison sat forward. "As in offshore banking?"

"As in an offshore bank in the Cayman Islands."

She blinked. "Where Tradewinds Investments just happens to be located!"

"Yeah. I'll ask Craig to see if her husband still works in the Caymans." He flipped open his phone, called Craig and left a message.

She realized that coincidences were stacking up fast against Karla Rasmussen. "What's Karla's background?"

Kevin looked down at the shimmering water. "Poor family. Parents died early. Then some foster homes. Won a college scholarship. *Summa cum laude.* Got her Master's from a prestigious East Coast school. Today, she's quite wealthy, thanks to some very smart investments in Manhattan real estate and the stock market in the seventies. In fact, she's had more than enough money to retire very comfortably for many years."

"So why hasn't she?"

"Money! She can't seem to get enough. Probably driven by her dirt-poor childhood. Also, she craves power. But bottom line, money drives Karla."

"Like the money she'd get from the ComGlobe merger."

"Like that."

A tiny hummingbird fluttered across the pool toward her, then swooped over to Kevin and paused as though reminding her that he was a cool guy ... like she needed a reminder.

"Thank you, Kevin."

"For what?"

"For being here, helping me, and, well ... everything."

He shrugged.

"And for believing in my Dad's innocence."

"That's easy."

"It means a lot to me, really." She placed her hand on his.

He looked at her. "Actually, Madison, I feel like I've known you for years. Your Dad often bragged like you were the Second Coming."

"Please tell me he *didn't* show you my baby pictures?"

"Cute butt...."

She laughed so sharply the waiter spun around in Heimlich-maneuver mode. She waved him off.

For the next few minutes, they went back over all the Turner executives, even ComGlobe executives and clients, trying to eliminate suspects, but were unable to. She found herself more and more frustrated by the lack of hard, incriminating evidence against any one individual. She also found herself hypnotized by the moonlight glimmering on the water. Moments later, she stifled a big yawn.

"Sleep beckons, boss."

"Yep."

They stood and strolled back toward her room, greeting the muscle-bound security guard, Benny, seated at the end of the hall. At her door, she turned and faced Kevin, hoping her feelings for him were not flashing like neon lights.

"Breakfast at eight?" she asked.

"Sounds good."

"What time's our flight back?"

"Six p.m."

"That gives us a whole day here," she said.

"Yeah. Maybe Craig will find out about Karla's husband, and the account at Tradewinds."

She nodded. "And maybe the Royal St. Kitts police will find the Tall Man."

"Don't worry about him, Madison. Benny is right here. And I'm only four doors away."

"That's very comforting."

He smiled as they looked into each others eyes a few moments. Then, very slowly, he leaned toward her. Her heart raced as she realized he was going to kiss her. She closed her eyes, waited....

"It's healing nicely." he said, looking at the small scab on her cheek.

"Oh, yeah ... it is." She breathed in his cologne.

"I'd kiss your boo-boo to make it better, Ms. McKean, but kissing the boo-boo of one's CEO seems like gross sucking up. Sort of conduct unbecoming an underling."

She thought, *This CEO would welcome a little conduct unbecoming from THIS underling....*

As though reading her thoughts, he leaned forward, kissed her cheek and said, "Until breakfast."

"OK."

"If you arrive first," he said, "could you please do me a huge favor."

"Sure."

"Order me a bowl of Count Chocula."

"Deal." Smiling, she entered her room, closed the door, leaned against it, and realized she really liked a man who really liked Count Chocula.

What the hell was happening to her?

If she'd learned anything over the last few years, she'd learned to not let her heart control her life. Yet, here she was, following her heart and drawing closer to Kevin each day.

Somehow, she had to slow down and stop herself. Now. She didn't have the emotional strength to sustain a relationship with him. She could barely summon the strength to handle her new responsibilities.

She had to back away from Kevin.

Hard as that would be.

Forty

"Damn...."

Madison looked up from her breakfast and saw Kevin pouting.

"No Count Chocula?"

"Nope," she said, smiling. "Just these soft banana pancakes slathered with gobs of cholesterol."

"They look yummy."

You too, she thought, noticing that the only thing bluer than his Izod shirt were his eyes. His wet hair was combed back as though he'd just stepped from the shower.

Kevin sat down beside her.

"Coffee, sir?" asked the young waitress.

"Yes, please, and some of those delicious looking pancakes."

The waitress nodded and placed a newspaper on their table. "Here's *The Democrat,* our local paper."

Madison thanked her, then scanned the front page until her eyes locked on a story in the lower corner.

"My God! 'Local Banker, Bradford Tipleton, Dead at 36. The medical examiner says the cause of death appears to have been a heart attack!" She closed her eyes, felt nauseated, pushed her food away. "Heart attack? I don't buy it."

"Me either."

"First, my Dad is accused of depositing funds into Tipleton's bank and that night my father dies. The next day, I learn of the bank account and that night a man tries to kill me. Later he tries to push me into a ravine. Then, Tipleton gives us information about the account and that night Tipleton dies."

"Too many coincidences."

She nodded.

"On the other hand," Kevin said, "Tipleton was quite obese."

"But only thirty-six."

"Heart attacks can happen at any age."

She nodded. "Especially when lethal poisons or drugs are injected into the blood stream."

"By someone like your attacker."

"Yes, but how would he even know Tipleton talked to us? We didn't tell anyone except Craig Borden, and we didn't tell Craig until *after* Tipleton's body was found at 7:16 last night."

"Tipleton must have told the wrong person."

She nodded. "I should tell the local detective about this." She took out Detective Johnstone's card and dialed the number. He picked up after three rings.

"Detective, this is Madison McKean."

"Ah, Ms. McKean. Are you feelin' better today?"

"Much better, thank you."

"Good. Unfortunately, we've still had no luck finding your assailant. And finding him, I should think, will soon prove more difficult."

"Why?"

"Two cruise ships are docking here in a few hours. Thousands of folks comin' ashore. Many of them tall, thin Caucasian men."

"I see. But I'm calling you about the young Nevis banker who died last night."

"Oh, yes, I saw that on the telly. Bradley -"

"Bradford Tipleton. Yesterday, he gave me some privileged information about a suspicious account at his bank. And now he's dead. Only thirty-six."

"A heart attack, the TV newscaster said."

"I'm not so sure."

Pause. "Really?"

"Yes. Will there be an autopsy?"

"At his age, I should think so. But would you be suggestin', ma'am, that Mr. Tipleton did not die of natural causes, that his death was related to the information he gave you?"

She paused. "Well, yes, I think so."

"But there was no evidence of foul play."

"True, but as you know, two days ago, after I talked to Mr. Tipleton, a man tried to kill me. Then yesterday, Mr. Tipleton gave me some highly confidential information, and a few hours later he's dead."

Detective Johnstone remained silent for several moments.

"Interesting connection, Ms. McKean. I'll check his autopsy findings. When are you flying home?"

"Six tonight."

"I'll ring you back when I know more."

"Thank you, Detective."

She hung up and filled in Kevin.

The waitress set down Kevin's banana pancakes. He pushed the plate aside, his appetite obviously gone.

"So what's next?" he asked, sipping his coffee.

"I have to make some phone calls."

"Me, too."

"Wait!" she said, looking out at the royal blue Atlantic sparkling in the sun. "We have our phones, right?"

"We do."

"We have sunny beaches?"

"We do."

"We have swim suits available in the gift shop."

"We do," he said, "But we also have something else."

"What?"

"The Tall Man...."

Her body tensed up as she pictured the crazed attacker. "Maybe he's left St. Kitts, or is still recovering from his fall."

"Or maybe he's fully recovered and still here."

"But we have our hunting knives. And I could wear my blonde wig and funky disguise again."

"That didn't exactly fool him in New York."

"True...." she agreed.

"You *really* want to go to the beach?"

She nodded.

"Suggestion."

"What?"

"Benny, your security guard. He's armed. Maybe we can hire him to take us?"

Fifteen minutes later, Benny was driving them past magnificent vistas of the Atlantic shoreline, heading toward a secluded beach called Sand Bank Bay. She felt safe when she saw Benny's bulging muscles and even safer when she saw his bulging handgun beneath his shirt.

Minutes later, Benny parked near a sun-bleached wood sign that read *Sand Bank Bay.*

"The beach is just over that bluff," Benny said as they got out. "I'll be up here watchin' over you."

"Thanks, Benny," she said.

She and Kevin walked up to the bluff's summit and stared down at the most breathtaking, pristine beach she'd ever seen. There wasn't another person on it.

"It's like a giant postcard!" she said.

"Yeah, let's put our stamp on it!"

"Ugh!"

They strolled down from the steep bluff, their feet sinking in the warm sand, to a nice spot near the south end of the bay. They spread out their beach towels, plopped down, and gazed out at the blue-green water rolling onto the white sand beach.

"First the phone calls, then the water?" Kevin said.

"Sounds like a plan." She dialed her Boston flat and then her father's apartment and picked up a some "sorry to hear about your father" messages. Next, she checked her office calls. None were urgent. And no more clients had fired the agency!

"Really?" Kevin said on his phone. "When?" He listened for a few more moments and hung up.

"That was Craig Borden. He just talked to his banking buddy in the Caymans. The money was wire-transferred out of Tradewinds Investments two hours ago."

"Transferred *again?*"

"Yeah. To a bank in Curacao."

She shook her head in frustration. "They keep moving the money."

"So it's harder to trace."

Madison wondered if she'd ever learn who was behind the money.

"Did Craig find out anything about Karla Rasmussen's husband?"

"Fred Rasmussen was never seen or heard from after he disappeared that night in Manhattan eighteen years ago."

Another dead end, she thought. Maybe, another dead man.

"Did you tell Craig about Bradford Tipleton's death?"

"Yes, and Craig promises he'll be extra careful."

She nodded, but still worried about Craig, and Dean Dryden on his yacht, and her best friend Linda Langstrom at National Media. What if her assassin knew they were helping her? What if he'd already sent hitmen after them?

"Don't worry," Kevin said. "Craig played tight end in college. The guy's made of steel!"

So are bullets, she thought.

* * *

Eugene P. Smith crouched behind the thick bushes on the bluff above Sand Bank Bay, focusing his powerful TC military binoculars on Madison and Kevin, the only two people on the mile-long beach.

Smith reached over and patted the unconscious head of young Benny, the bound and gagged security guard. Poor Benny never saw the heavy blackjack that dropped him like a sack of cement.

Smith worked his powerful binoculars up Madison McKean's long shapely legs, then slowly up to her breasts which, he noted, filled her bikini top quite nicely. The woman oozed sexuality.

And here, he could enjoy her oozing sexuality, since any DNA evidence would be destroyed in saline ocean water, where her body would be found. Once again, things had worked out to his advantage.

Smith turned and looked at Nigel, the local thug he'd hired this morning. Nigel was six-six and weighed over three-hundred pounds, most of it in his chest and shoulders. His mud-hued face was dominated by an enormous, bulging brow that suggested excessive steroid use. Nigel's Anglo, African and Caribbean-Indian genes had swirled together to create a towering, powerful, but decidedly dim-witted Neanderthal. He squinted at Madison through slity dark eyes that looked like hyphens.

Smith watched her rub sunscreen lotion on her face, legs and shoulders.

"Everything ready, Nigel?"

Nigel looked down at the large black bag in his hands. "Uh-huh."

"She's a pillar of pulchritude, *n'est ce pas?*"

"Huh...?"

"She's beautiful, right?"

"Uh-huh."

"Does she turn you on, Nigel?"

Nigel grinned.

"Like a closer look?"

"Uh-huh."

Forty One

Harry Burkett felt good as he strolled along East Ninety-Third Street in his new Z-Coil tennis shoes. He liked how they made him three inches taller and how they gripped in the rain puddles. He also liked how the rain cleaned all the scum off the sidewalks. Too bad it didn't clean off the *human* scum too, he thought, as he passed a teenager with zits, purple hair and several chrome rings drooping from her eyebrows and lips. She was moaning about someone stealing her coke, and she wasn't talking cola.

Burkett felt like dropping a few bunker-busters, big 4,600 pounders, up the street in Spanish Harlem, vaporizing all the putrid human waste - all the slimy junkies, pimps, hookers, dealers and payoff-grabbing cops. Vaporize the bastards!

Now *that's* ethnic cleansing, he thought.

Four blocks later, he reached into his gray jogging suit and checked his .45 caliber SIG-Sauer. The gun felt as soothing as it did the day he yanked it from the severed hand of a Iraqi soldier whose torso lay twenty feet away. Just touching the gun brought back pleasant memories of the Gulf War.

And soon, the gun would give him another pleasant memory, he thought, looking up at Linda Langstrom's apartment building. He turned up the volume on his headphones linked to the hardline phone in her apartment. Last night, behind her building, he cut through the cheap fence, popped open the building's old phone control box and tapped into her line.

Seconds ago, Langstrom had answered the phone and her words were coming through like she was walking beside him.

"I discovered where the consulting fee has been deposited all these years?" Langstrom said.

"Where?" A young woman asked.

"Offshore bank on the island of Macau. A numbered account with no name."

"How'd you find that out?"

"A friend at CitiBank. She also discovered that two months ago the money was withdrawn from Macau and deposited in another offshore bank in the Caribbean."

"Which bank?"

"Hang on ... here it is ... it's down in Nevis ... the Caribe National Bank."

Burkett swallowed hard. Langstrom had just linked the consulting fee to the account at Caribe National!

"That's the bank where my father's account was!"

She's talking to Madison!

"The account was in my father's name, but he did not deposit the money."

"Incredible."

"Yeah. Somehow we've got to find the name of the original depositor sixteen years ago."

"I'll ask my friend at CitiBank to try and dig it out."

Very bad idea, Burkett thought.

He began to walk faster, but then their voices grew faint. He remembered he had to stay within two hundred feet of the apartment.

Turning quickly, he stumbled into a sidewalk hole and had to steady himself for a moment.

Suddenly, his feet felt cold. He looked down and saw he was standing in icy, ankle-deep rainwater.

"*SHIT!*" he yelled, stomping water from his brand new Z-Coils. Enraged, he walked back toward her apartment, squishing with each step.

"There's something else you should know, Linda."

"What?"

"The Caribe National banker I talked to yesterday is *dead!*" Harry Burkett smiled. Eugene P. Smith strikes again!

"Jesus, what happened?"

"They suspect heart attack. But I think murder."

Langstrom breathed out. "Be careful down there!"

"I will. You too, Linda."

When Langstrom hung up, Harry Burkett yanked out his cell phone and speed-dialed the Executive VP.

"*Now* what?" she said, bitchy as usual.

"Linda Langstrom over at National Media has linked the consulting fee to the account at Caribe National Bank, and she told Madison."

A long pause. "What else do they know?"

"That's all," Burkett said. "But Langstrom plans to ask a friend at Citibank to try to uncover the name of the original depositor."

"A waste of time," she said. "But Langstrom and Madison are asking too many questions about the account. I don't want banking authorities placing a Suspicious Activity Report on it, or investigating it."

Me either, Burkett thought, *since I'm the guy who posed as Mark McKean and deposited the money into the Caribe National.*

The EVP was silent for several moments. "Langstrom's a problem. You know what to do."

"Yeah."

"Destroy her hard drive, e-mail records, disks."

"Right."

"Take her jewelry and valuables."

"I'll make it look like a robbery...."

"... that went *very* bad," she said.

"Yeah, yeah."

"And wear gloves."

He hated when she told him how to do his work. "Yeah, OK."

"And what about Madison and Kevin?"

"Eugene's planning a beach party for them. Nice, huh?"

Burkett heard a click. No goodbye. No "nice job Harry." Just a click. What a bitch!

On the other hand, she always gave clear orders. Not the ambiguous, chickenshit, cover-your-ass orders he got from his Army commanders: "Respond with appropriate and commensurate force." For Burkett, there was only one appropriate response: blow 'em away.

Harry Burkett phoned his contact at National Media and explained what he wanted the man to do.

Then Burkett walked into a nearby alley and checked his SIG-Sauer.

* * *

After hanging up from Burkett, the EVP watched the heavyset mailroom employee deliver her mail, then limp away. She thought back to the short-leg limp of Merle Lee Jarvis, her second foster father, the most cruel and abusive man she'd ever known. Even now, her skin crawled at the memory of fat, sweaty Merle Lee pinning her to the cold, wet garage floor and raping her on her twelfth birthday.

"*I'm* your birthday present!" he laughed. The pain had been excruciating and she knew she had to do something, or he would rape her every day. Then, like a miracle, she saw something beneath his workbench, a bright yellow box ... a box that might save her life.

Three nights later, when Merle Lee shouted for her to make his nightly Jim Beam, she went to the kitchen, took the yellow box and prepared a very special Jim Beam. She handed him the drink and watched him raise the tall, iced tea glass to his mouth. He gulped down several greedy swallows and smacked his lips.

As she turned to walk away, he grabbed her breast. "This feels good."

She pulled away from him. "Not as good as I'll feel!"

He stared back, obviously wondering what she meant. One second later, he knew. The potassium cyanide in the rat poison hit him like a line drive. His eyes shot open and he started breathing rapidly and gasping. He stared at her, his lips mouthing, "Help me...."

She watched him slump to the floor and begin to convulse. She watched foamy saliva bubble from his lips. She watched his eyes jerk about. She watched Merle Lee Jarvis pass out and choke on his own vomit.

She'd intended to teach Merle Lee a lesson, make him deathly sick so he'd never touch her again. But when his eyes went all glassy and rolled up, she realized she'd poured in too much rat poison.

Too bad, she'd thought.

On the other hand, rats deserved to die.

Forty Two

Madison filled her lungs with the fresh, tangy salt air sweeping off the bay, then breathed out slowly. She scooped up sand and let it trickle through her fingers.

Everything seemed perfect. The sun was warm, the sky blue, and the breezes nice and cool, like the guy next to her. She looked over at Kevin all sprawled out and concluded he sprawled out about as well as a man could. His well-defined muscles glowed like buffed marble in the sun.

She had to force herself to turn away.

"Hey, Kevin...?"

"Yep?" His eyes remained closed.

"Should we open up a new branch office down here?"

"Nope!"

"Why?"

"We should move the whole damn agency down here."

She smiled. "Why?"

"I don't know a client, or prospective client, who wouldn't love to boondoggle down here for a weekend conference or meeting!"

"Me either."

Some clients, she knew, chose their ad agency based on how close it was to good restaurants rather than how good the agency's advertising was ... sort of like choosing your brain surgeon because his office is near The Four Seasons.

Madison's phone rang. Caller ID read *Turner Advertising*.

She picked up. "Hello?"

"Hi, Madison, it's Alison Whitaker."

"Oh, Alison. Actually, I was about to call you."

"Why?"

"I wondered if you learned anything more about who might have accused my father?"

"No ... unfortunately nothing yet. But I did learn one thing."

"What's that?"

"That asking questions about your father can be hazardous."

Madison gripped her cell phone tighter. "What happened?"

"Some thug attacked me last night."

"My God, Alison, are you all right?"

"I'm fine. But as I was walking back from Lou's Deli near my apartment, a large SUV – a Lincoln, I think – pulled up beside me. A big man in a dark raincoat jumped out and pushed me into an alley. He slapped me around a bit, then threw me against a fire escape where I picked up a one-inch gash behind my ear."

Madison felt like steel bands were tightening around her chest.

"He grabbed me and said, 'Stop asking questions about Mark McKean or you'll wind up just like him.' Then he got back in the SUV and drove off. That was it."

Madison swallowed a dry throat. "Alison, I'm so sorry. You should be home."

"I'm fine, really."

"Are you sure?"

"Yes. But I phoned to warn you. They may come after you when you get back to Manhattan."

They're after me here, Madison thought, but decided not to alarm Alison further. "Thanks for the heads-up."

"Are you back in the office tomorrow?"

"Yes, bright and early."

"Be careful," Alison warned.

"You, too."

Madison hung up, placed her cell phone under the thick beach towel, then filled Kevin in.

He shook his head in disbelief. "Whoever the hell is behind this has their hired thugs everywhere."

"Except on this secluded beach, thank God." She noticed they were still the only people in sight and was relieved that Benny and his handgun were watching over them from up on the bluff.

Madison took another breath, laid back down and tried to calm herself. She closed her eyes and listened to the breezes hissing through the sea grass and the seagulls twittering overhead. She smelled the sweet fragrance of nearby flowers. And soon, she felt a cloud cast a shadow over her face ... but oddly, only her face.

Opening her eyes, she saw the silhouette of a bearded man wearing a wide-brimmed hat and sunglasses standing directly over her. Beside him, stood a giant of a man, carrying a black bag.

"Ultraviolet rays are harmful to your skin," said the man with the hat.

Madison's heart stopped. *The Tall Man.*

"So are bullets," he added.

Kevin started to sit up, but the giant's shoe slammed him back down on the towel.

She squinted at two gleaming handguns aimed at them.

"Abandoning me in that ravine was rather rude," the Tall Man said.

"I sent an ambulance."

"And the cops."

Where are our knives? Madison wondered, then remembered they were in her beach bag six feet away. She looked up at the bluff, but didn't see Benny. Turning back, her fingers nudged her cell phone beneath the folded beach towel. She felt the phone's corners, located the 9 and 1 buttons and punched 9 1 1.

"What do you want?" Kevin asked.

"Blind obedience. Right, Nigel?"

"Uh-huh."

She thought she heard the 911 operator's muffled voice through the towel as a large wave crashed ashore. Madison lifted the towel a bit and decided it was time to get loud.

"Please don't shoot us!" she shouted. "*Please!* I'm begging you – don't shoot us!"

Tall Man turned toward her. "Shoot you? You're going to have an accident. And don't bother shouting. Benny won't hear you. He's rather ... indisposed."

She prayed Benny was only indisposed.

"How can we have an accident sunbathing on a quiet beach?"

"Water sports accidents. They happen all the time, right Nigel?"

"Uh-huh."

"At *Sand Bank Bay?*" she said. A massive wave crashed ashore and she realized the operator couldn't have heard "Sand Bank Bay."

"There are no water sports here at – " Another wave smothered her words "Sand Bank Bay."

"Oh ... but there are about to be. Like snorkeling. A fun sport. Right, Nigel?"

"Uh-huh."

"That's why we bought you new snorkels. One hundred percent dry. Not a drop of water gets in." He motioned with his gun for them to stand.

Holding her towel in front of her, Madison slid the slim cell phone into her bikini brief. Fortunately, the brief had a short ruffled skirt that covered the phone's slight bulge. She stood up.

"I need my beach bag," she said.

"You need to *WALK!*" Tall Man said, pushing her forward.

The two men nudged them down to the south end of the beach.

There, the giant pulled two blue snorkels from his satchel.

"Top of the line snorkels," Tall Man said. "Look how easily the mouthpieces swivel."

Nigel took out two diving masks and began to adjust the straps.

Tall Man unscrewed the top of an eyedropper-like bottle, then carefully deposited drops of a pale yellow liquid into the mouthpiece tube of each snorkel.

"Epoxy," Tall Man said. "Seals all that nasty seawater out."

"You mean it seals our death in," Madison said.

Tall Man's lips bent in a smile.

Perspiration blanketed Madison's skin as she realized she was within seconds of dying on this beach. She had to keep the Tall Man talking. Maybe someone would walk onto the beach. Maybe the 911 operator had heard her.

"What about Bradford Tipleton?"

"What about him?"

"Did he feel pain?"

"Poor Porky Pig. The man had an unfortunate mouth disease. He talked too much. Led to a fatal heart attack, I'm told."

"You *murdered* him."

"I put him on a diet."

This caused Nigel to laugh so hard that mucus shot from his nostrils.

Madison checked the beach again, then the bluff and the hills beyond. Still no one. She looked at Kevin, who slowly turned his back to her, revealing the handle of a knife sticking from his trunks. He was obviously waiting for the right moment to attack ... which would get him shot, maybe killed.

Because of *her!* She'd pushed Kevin to go to the beach. If he died here, she'd be responsible.

Tall Man dripped more liquid into each snorkel tube and mask.

She heard the distant cry of a seagull. Looking around, she didn't see the bird. Again she heard the shrill sound, but now it sounded a bit different.

Could that be a siren?

"Let's go snorkeling!" Tall Man said, handing Madison and Kevin each a snorkel and mask.

Nigel forced them out into the water up to mid-thigh. The water was cold and she began to shake.

"Snorkels and masks on now!"

She and Kevin stalled, pretending to adjust the straps on their masks.

"If you're thinking of swimming away, think again...." He pointed over their shoulders.

She turned and saw large black fins slicing through the water only one hundred yards away. She couldn't tell if they were sharks or dolphins.

"Reef sharks," Tall Man said. "Vicious bastards. If I shoot you, your blood will draw them fast. So, you decide: snorkels or sharks? Either accident works for me."

Shivering, Madison looked at Kevin who nodded toward the snorkels.

Slowly, she raised her snorkel toward her face. As she did, she heard the high-pitched cry again.

Not a gull – a siren!

But ... heading AWAY...

Kevin blinked that he'd also heard it.

Suddenly, a commercial jet roared overhead, drowning out all sound.

"Masks on *now!*" Tall Man shouted, angry, raising his gun.

They stalled a moment, then inched the masks up toward their faces. Madison pretended to stumble when a wave hit her.

Nigel moved through the water toward her.

Kevin's hand inched behind his back toward his knife.

The roar of the jet faded. Then the cry – a *siren* – was back, loud and unmistakable and closer!

Tall Man and Nigel spun toward the siren.

Madison looked and couldn't believe her eyes. Two police cars, lights flashing, sirens blaring, a mile down the beach, raced toward them.

Tall Man glared at her, clearly enraged that she'd somehow contacted the police.

"You will pay for this," he said, as he and Nigel sprinted away.

Kevin ran from the water and threw his knife at them. The handle bounced off Nigel's thigh. The two men disappeared behind a nearby hill. Seconds later, she heard a car start and speed away.

Madison and Kevin ran toward the approaching police cars. One car veered toward the two escaping men. The other stopped near Kevin and her.

Two officers jumped out. A short man with sunglasses hurried over to them. "You folks okay?"

"Yes. But how'd you know -?"

"Our new 911 system automatically triangulates all call locations. We knew exactly where you were."

Madison explained that Benny was injured up on the bluff and pointed where he was. A policeman ran up over the bluff, and seconds later appeared with Benny standing, rubbing his head.

Madison and Kevin gave the policemen a detailed description of the Tall Man and Nigel. He immediately phoned in the descriptions.

"We'll drive you back," the officer said.

"Thanks," Madison said.

Kevin looked at her. "How does the airport sound to you?"

"Like a day at the beach?"

Forty Three

What the hell is MensaPlan? Linda Langstrom kept asking herself as she sat in her apartment, trying to make sense of the puzzling consultant's fee on her laptop screen.

All she knew was that her company, National Media, had paid the fee for many years to a consulting company named MensaPlan. She'd never heard of MensaPlan, and when she researched it on line in the *RedBook,* in *Bacon's* and other media manuals, she found no evidence the company had ever existed.

Even more suspicious was how the MensaPlan annual fee, which appeared to be a tiny fraction of one percent of Turner Advertising's total network media expenditures, was hidden within the Turner Advertising's *Incidental Network Expenses.* Over the last decade of financial records she'd been able to access, the fee appeared to have added up to several million dollars.

The money was going into someone's pocket. Consultants were common in advertising. They made agencies smart on subjects fast. If an agency needed to understand the airline business, the auto market, health care, or the baba ganoush eating habits of pregnant Shiite Muslims, they hired a consultant.

Clearly, the hidden nature of the MensaPlan fee, plus the total lack of information about the company, raised the ugly specter of concealment or fraud. Someone at National Media was skimming money for personal gain, or kicking money back to an individual at Turner Advertising – perhaps in return for Turner Advertising buying large chunks of media time from National Media.

Either way, it broke the law. She feared she'd uncovered the tip of a financial scandal, one that might implicate some of her company's top executives. And if they were implicated, they could be terminated – but probably not before they terminated her. She remembered what happened to whistleblowers at Enron and Worldcom: fired, demoted, or banished to a corner in the smelly basement.

So now what? She had to inform her boss, Darryl Stenson. Darryl had been at National Media over twenty-three years. He might have heard of MensaPlan. But if he hadn't, he would know how best to proceed. She dialed his number.

"Hello...."

"Hi, Darryl, it's Linda."

"That's odd...."

"What is?"

"I tried to phone you earlier, but my cell phone kept crashing."

"What'd you phone about?" she asked.

"The new ESPN rates for *Monday Night Football*. Considine-Schiff Advertising wants to buy fifteen spots."

"Great! For which client?"

"LubTech's new motor oil called ZOOOOM."

"Makes sense."

"Yeah, but you called me, Linda. What's up?"

"Something that disturbs me."

"Global warming? Hanging chads?"

"Funny you should mention 'hanging.'"

"Why?"

"Because someone at our company might get hanged soon."

Darryl paused. "You have my attention."

"Log onto our company's Intranet and I'll show you what I've found."

"My laptop's at the office."

She paused and looked around her living room. "Well, if you don't mind a messy apartment, I could show you here."

"What's this all about?"

"A consulting company fee that National Media has paid out for sixteen years."

"Who's the consulting company?"

"MensaPlan."

Darryl paused. "Don't recall it."

"Nor do I. In fact, I don't think it exists. And the fee's kind of hidden in Turner Advertising's Incidental Network Expenses. It only shows up when you click on the *Ancillary Media Services*. This consulting fee makes no sense at all."

"Frankly, a lot of *consultants* don't make sense. Bunch of flimflam artists. They take our thoughts, repackage them as theirs, hand them back in a fancy binder, then roll their big fat fee out in wheelbarrows."

"But some are legit."

"Yeah, I guess so. You still on West Ninety-Third?"

"Yes."

"See you in ten minutes."

She hung up, glanced around her flat and realized that she'd become a housekeeping slut thanks to focusing on the mysterious fee and her normal workload. Her clothes and stuff were lying everywhere. Now, Darryl was coming over. And later, so was her sister, Pam, who could spot dust from the Space Shuttle.

Linda rushed through the apartment picking up and vacuuming for the next few minutes.

What if Darryl's hungry? she wondered. She opened the refrigerator and saw an old slab of lasagna that had mutated into something like lung disease. Two shelves down, she saw a fresh wedge of Stilton cheese. She could serve it with some Carr's Crackers.

She changed into her new pink velour sweatsuit, brushed her teeth, and started to fix her hair when the doorbell rang.

She hurried over to the door and peered through the peephole. Darryl's smiling face stared back at her. She opened the door and he handed her a bunch of white daisies.

"Who's a nice boss?"

He smiled.

"They're lovely. Thanks, Darryl."

She led him into the kitchen, arranged the daisies in a vase, then placed them on the coffee table in the living room.

"So, what's with this strange fee?"

"Over here." She led him to her laptop where he pulled a chair up beside her.

She logged into National Media's Intranet. Within seconds she entered the company's financial records and moved the cursor down to the MensaPlan consulting fee.

"Look," she said. "Annually, a fraction of one percent of the total Turner network media buys has been trickling into MensaPlan."

Darryl's eyes grew serious. "But you found no info on this Mensa-Plan?

"No."

His brow furrowed. "How'd you discover the fee?"

"By accident. My friend at Turner Advertising asked me to check out some media rates. The rates were OK, but when I dug a little deeper, I noticed this fee buried in Turner's records."

Linda felt a sudden breeze and wondered if she'd left a window open. "I think someone here is skimming money, or passing it along to someone at Turner Advertising."

"Makes sense," he whispered, dabbing sweat from his face. "Who else knows about this?" Darryl looked very concerned.

"Just my friend, you and me."

"And *ME!*" said a man behind her, as his shadow crept onto her screen.

She spun around and stared into the eyes of a muscular man standing a few feet away, pointing a gun at Darryl and her. The hair on the back of her neck stood up.

"Hands over your head!" the man said.

Her heart pounding, Linda put her hands up.

But Darryl refused to.

Then, to her amazement, Darryl stood up and walked toward the door without looking back at her or the man.

My God ... Darryl's in on this, she realized. *He left my door unlocked for this man....*

At the door, Darryl paused, but still didn't look back at her. "I'm so sorry, Linda. I begged her to offer you two hundred thousand dollars to forget the MensaPlan fee. But she didn't trust you. I tried, really...."

Darryl walked out and shut the door.

A sickening feeling welled up in her stomach and she thought she would be ill.

The intruder, whose gun had a silencer, took out a CD, loaded it into her computer, then tapped in a series of commands. Her computer began to click and make weird whirring sounds.

"Whoops, I hit the wrong key. All your files and your hard drive are being fried – as in permanently destroyed!"

He grabbed all the CDs on her desk and stuffed them into a bag.

"You should leave now," she said.

"Why?"

"There's a tiny spy cam outside my door. It videotaped you entering my apartment."

"Yeah, right...." Big grin. "I checked and didn't see any cameras."

"It's only one inch wide. The police installed it after a burglary a month ago. It's live, 24/7 to the precinct. Police interns watch it non-stop. The police have you on video entering my apartment."

He blinked as though trying to remember her hall.

All she needed was a few seconds. She'd run to her bedroom, deadbolt the door and race down the fire escape.

Keeping his gun on her, he slowly backed over to the apartment door and pushed it open. Then he leaned into the hall and glanced above the door.

She ran....

One second later, she heard a muffled thump, like a gunshot.

Something hit her in the back.

She froze. The room started to spin.

She felt herself falling, felt her head hit the corner of the coffee table, felt warm blood spill onto her face and mouth, saw the white daisies scatter across her arm.

Then the daisies faded to black.

Forty Four

A t 35,000 feet Madison looked out her window as the Air France Airbus 300 began its descent into the New York area. Her *life* was also descending, into a deadly world from which she couldn't seem to escape. Her father's frantic phone call, his death, the attempts on her life and Kevin's, the death of Bradford Tipleton, the mugging of Alison Whitaker in an alley ... when would it all end?

Not in Manhattan, she knew.

She looked over at Kevin dozing peacefully beside her.

Ironic, she thought, that losing her father, a man she loved deeply, had somehow brought her to Kevin, a man she might grow to love ... if she could find the courage to love again.

From the seat pocket, she pulled out a *Time* magazine and thumbed through it. She paused at an ad for MedPharms, whose rates she'd discussed yesterday with Linda Langstrom. That reminded her to try phoning Linda again. Calls to her from the St. Kitts airport had gone unanswered.

Fortunately, the Airbus was equipped with a new on-board cellular phone system that permitted passengers to use cell phones above 10,000 feet. She dialed Linda. After four rings, she prepared to leave another voice message when she heard....

"Langstrom residence." A man's voice. Deep. Serious.

"Is Linda there?"

The man paused. "Are you related to Ms. Langstrom?"

His voice sounded icy, official. Something had happened. Something bad. "Yes, I'm her half-sister, Madison," she lied. "May I please speak to Linda?"

He paused a moment, then breathed out slowly. "Ma'am, I'm Detective Rashid with the NYPD. I'm sorry to inform you, but Ms. Lindstrom appears to have been the victim of a breaking and entering this afternoon."

Madison winced at "victim."

"She's in the ER at St. Anthony's."

"Is she –?"

"It's bad, ma'am. But her sister, a Pam McCarthy, found her shortly after the incident."

Madison felt like she'd been punched in the stomach.

Her mind spinning, Madison managed to mumble goodbye and hung up. Her eyes filled as she turned toward Kevin and told him what the detective said.

Kevin placed his hand on hers.

"They got her," she said. "She's in the hospital because of *me!*"

"No...."

"Yes, I involved her in this consulting fee."

"No, Linda discovered the fee, remember? Not you."

"Yeah, but I agreed that she should check into it further."

He shook his head. "Linda wanted to check into it further for her company's sake. Don't blame yourself."

Kevin made sense, she knew. But there was only one thing that would ease her growing sense of guilt: Linda's full and complete recovery. And based on what the detective said, she may not recover at all. Madison closed her eyes and prayed for her best friend.

Thirty minutes later, the Airbus touched down at JFK and taxied to a gate. As Madison and Kevin started to exit the plane, a young blonde female flight attendant stopped Madison. "Are you Madison McKean?"

"Yes."

"A passenger said this fell from your purse. He asked me to give it to you." She handed Madison a postcard.

Madison glanced at the card with a picture of Sand Bank Bay. Walking ahead, she flipped the card over and felt blood drain from her face.

"What's wrong?" Kevin asked.

She read the card aloud.

> *"Madison, Kevin,*
> *My esteemed colleague, Nigel, and I apologize for leaving you two so abruptly on the beach this morning while we were all having so much fun. Please keep this card as a friendly reminder.*
> *See you ... real soon.*
> *Your tall, handsome admirer"*

Quickly, she scanned the passengers swarming around her in the terminal. There were several tall men, but none resembled her attacker.

But she knew he was there.

Watching her....

Forty Five

After clearing customs, Madison and Kevin took a taxi for her apartment. En route, she called St. Anthony's Hospital and again claimed to be Linda Langstrom's half-sister. She was told that Linda had slipped into a coma. No visitors allowed. As Madison hung up, her eyes again filled with tears.

Minutes later, their cab driver, a blue-turbaned Sikh, stopped in front of her apartment. Looking up at her windows, she felt the cold, silent darkness behind them. Kevin asked the driver to wait, took her suitcase and escorted her toward the entrance. Then he stopped cold.

What's wrong?" she asked.

"This."

He held up the postcard.

Chills shot down her spine.

"He might have followed us from JFK," Kevin said.

She nodded and checked the night shadows and nearby cars for any sign of her tall attacker. She didn't see him, but knew he could be watching her even now.

"Two days ago, they changed my apartment locks and upgraded building security. I'll be fine, Kevin."

"If the security system couldn't stop him a few nights ago, the new system probably can't stop him tonight."

Deep down, she feared the same thing.

"I have a suggestion," he said.

"What?"

"Chez Jordan."

"Running water?"

"Indoor toilets even."

"Wow! Offer accepted, but I need some clothes upstairs."

Kevin put her suitcase back in the taxi and asked the driver to wait a few minutes. The driver nodded and went back to humming a Ravi Shankar melody on his CD player.

One minute later, she unlocked her father's apartment door and froze. Furniture tipped over. Drawers yanked open, files scattered, cushions tossed, a blue Chinese vase shattered on the hardwood floor beneath the bay window.

Suddenly, a loud snap somewhere down the hall.

The intruder's still here! she realized.

Before she could stop Kevin, he'd grabbed a poker from the fire-place and moved silently down the carpeted hall.

Her tension mounted as she heard him opening doors and rattling windows. One long, suspenseful minute later, he came back.

"No one here!"

"But the noise?"

"Window blinds."

She looked down at her father's scattered papers. "They're searching for some clue they think Dad left me. But I've looked twice and found nothing!"

He nodded.

They walked to her bedroom. Dresses, blouses and underwear were thrown everywhere. Her mattress was flipped over, even her pillow-cases had been yanked off. Feeling violated, she closed her eyes and forced herself to take another deep breath.

She walked into her closet, lifted a dress from the floor and noticed her hand was shaking.

Kevin placed his hand on hers. "It's OK, Madison, you're safe now."

She nodded, but didn't feel safe. She felt afraid and overwhelmed by everything. Someone had killed her father, nearly killed her and Kevin, probably killed Bradford Tipleton, shot Linda Langstrom, mugged Alison Whitaker and ransacked her father's apartment. Her life was spinning out of control ... and suddenly, so was her bedroom. She felt dizzy and leaned against the wall.

Gently, Kevin turned her around, eased her into his arms and held her. Her sobs began slowly, then came so fast she had trouble catching her breath. She remained in his arms, feeling safe and comforted.

Moments later, she managed to whisper, "I'm OK now."

"You sure?"

"Yes." But she was still trembling.

"Detective Loomis should check the apartment for prints," he said.

She nodded and eased away from his arms. She grabbed a blue suit and a white linen blouse for tomorrow, then they hurried down to the lobby. They told the security guard about the break-in, then got back in the taxi and headed toward Kevin's apartment.

On the way, she briefed Detective Loomis by phone.

Minutes later, the taxi stopped on a narrow street of older row houses and they got out.

Kevin gestured toward a charming old four-story building. "Home Sweet Brownstone."

"It is sweet." She liked the English-style blue door and brass knock-er, and the tiny side garden with red flowers, birdbath and a park bench. The windows were tinted light lavender, like windows she remembered seeing near the Anne Frank house in Amsterdam.

Kevin unlocked the front door and they stepped into an elegant turn-of-the-century foyer. She was surrounded by warm, reddish-brown woods, paneled walls and a polished mahogany staircase. The wood smelled wonderful.

"It's stunning, Kevin."

"So's the view from my loft," he said ushering her into a tiny elevator.

Four floors later, they got off and he unlocked his apartment door. They stepped into a small living room dominated by a floor-to-ceiling window that ran the length of the room and gave her a breathtaking view of the city.

"You're looking at the Triborough Bridge, Riker's Island, the Bronx and the LaGuardia runway."

"Wow!"

"Wait until you see dawn."

"Your girlfriend lives here?"

He laughed. "No girlfriends these days."

Hmmmm!

He led her over to some glass shelves that displayed a collection of New York Yankees baseball memorabilia – a Mickey Mantle bat, a Yogi Berra glove, and sports figurines. One wall held a colorful, signed Leroy Neiman art print of former New York Mets star Dave Kingman.

"You forgot to tell me something," she said.

"What?"

"You be rich."

"No, I be damn lucky. My college buddy inherited this building. He lets me stay here for peanuts in return for managing the three other tenants. Easy work, since one tenant is in London for two years and the other two live in Florida seven months a year."

He led her over to the bookshelves filled with volumes on advertising and marketing. She noticed one entire shelf was crammed with books on Poland.

"What's with all the Polish books?"

He seemed to hesitate.

"I like European history."

"Polish history especially?"

Another pause, then a nod. "My parents came from a small village in Poland."

"Jordan doesn't sound too Polish."

"How about Jowarski? Dad anglicized it to Jordan so he'd get hired."

"You mentioned your dad died. Where is your mom?"

"Last year, I finally persuaded her to move from their small house in Camden to Manhattan so we'd be closer."

"I'd love to meet her."

"How's your Polish?"

"*Dają mnie piwo,*" she said.

He laughed. "Give me a beer...."

"An essential phrase in south Boston."

"True. But my Mom, the English, so good, she don't speak."

"I'd still love to meet her."

He seemed a little reluctant, perhaps embarrassed by his mother's English. "OK...."

"Get nailed with a few Polish jokes growing up, Kevin?"

"Oh, yeah."

She nodded. "In England, I got nailed with Irish jokes."

"Really?"

"Yeah. You know, like an Irishman calls up British Air reservations and asks. 'Could you be tellin' me how long it takes to fly from London to Boston, ma'am?'

'Just a moment, sir.'

'Thank you very much,' says the Irishman, hanging up.

Kevin laughed.

"My great-great-grandparents only spoke Gaelic when they immigrated here from County Cork. They'd been potato farmers."

"Funny you should mention potatoes."

"Why?"

"We Polish do neat things with them."

"Like what?"

"Vodka."

"I'll drink to that!"

Smiling, he led her over toward the tiny wet bar and took a bottle of Wyborowa Vodka from the mini fridge. He poured two glasses over ice and handed her one.

They strolled over to his drive-in-theater-size window, sipped their drinks and looked out at the city lights.

"Best seats in the house," he said, gesturing toward the three-section beige leather sofa.

She sat down and was pleased when he sat near her.

"Watching the headlights crawl across the bridge is therapy," he said. "Doze-off therapy."

"I'm too uptight to doze off."

He looked at her. "Linda Langstrom...?"

She nodded.

He placed a comforting hand on hers. She felt heat rush through her. Then he clicked a remote control device and a familiar guitar rhythm filled her ears.

She smiled and said, "*I Walk the Line.*"

He nodded. "Wow! An urbane sophisticate like you knows the songs of a country boy like Johnny Cash?"

"I love Johnny's songs. Dad did, too."

They sipped their vodkas, listening to the familiar, boom-chick-a-boom-chick-a-boom of the rhythm guitar, watching the car lights wink through the girders of the Triborough Bridge. Kevin was right. The lights were therapeutic. She nestled down in the supple leather and moments later was delighted when he placed his arm behind her.

She was completely attracted to the man beside her and completely terrified because she was. What was she getting into?

Johnny Cash sang, "I walk the line...."

I am too, Johnny....

"If you get sleepy, just drift away," Kevin said.

How about I drift closer?

She sensed he wanted to drift closer, too, but held back, probably because he felt conflicted about a relationship with his boss – like she felt conflicted about a relationship with her employee.

She thought about the conflicts for a few moments. Then she de-

233

cided, *Screw 'em!*

"Kevin...."

"Yes?"

"Thank you again, for everything. For tonight." She looked into his eyes, praying he saw the depth of her feelings for him. He blinked as though he did, started to speak, then paused.

"Madison ... I...."

"What is it?"

He paused again, then slowly leaned forward and gently pressed his lips to hers.

Yes! she thought, as she pulled him into her arms. She felt the phenomenal heat of his body, felt her heart racing. His, too.

Within seconds, they drifted toward his bedroom.

Forty Six

The following morning, Madison sat at her desk thinking of Kevin, remembering the warmth of his lips, the softness of his touch, the moment their souls merged and changed her life....

Yet, some part of her still feared the change, the closeness, the risk of commitment....

"The BioFirme meeting has started."

Madison looked up and saw Christine at the door.

"Oh, thanks, Christine."

Madison was attending meetings to learn more about her clients – and who might have accused her father.

BioFirme was an amazing new skin-firming treatment formulated specifically to tighten the skin of women over the age of fifty.

She walked down the hall and stepped into the meeting room. Karla Rasmussen, Alison Whitaker, Dana Williams, Leland Merryweather and others were engaged in a heated discussion about the Bio-Firme media plan, the agency's recommendation of magazines, television and other media geared to reach BioFirme's target audience.

Madison was amazed to hear them debating whether to run a Bio-Firme commercial on the Super Bowl, at a cost of two-and-a- half million dollars for 30 seconds. Football didn't seem like the best venue to talk to saggy-skin females over fifty.

"Look, it's simple," Karla Rasmussen said, straightening her Hermes scarf. "The client wants his commercial on the Super Bowl. It's the largest television audience of the year. Over 130 million Americans watch it! And statistics prove women watch it."

"*Younger* women," Alison Whitaker countered. "Not women fifty and older."

Madison agreed with Whitaker.

"Women that age do watch it," Rasmussen shot back. "In fact, *forty million women* watched the Super Bowl last year! That's ten million more women than watched the Academy Awards!"

That fact surprised Madison, but she saw something in the media plan that concerned her. "There's a risk here, Karla."

"What risk?" Rasmussen challenged.

"*When* this commercial will run. Late in the third quarter."

"So?"

"So by then, if one team is way ahead, many viewers will have already switched to another channel, wasting most of our client's money."

Rasmussen simply shrugged and folded her arms.

Madison leaned forward. "Karla, you said our client requested this Super Bowl commercial?"

"Yes. He and his CEO, Martin Wellbourne," Rasmussen said.

Alison Whitaker asked, "Did they say why they want their commercial on the Super Bowl?"

Rasmussen looked like she'd rather not say why. "Yes. They want their pals at the Harvard Club to see the commercial."

"Brilliant marketing!" Whitaker said, sarcasm dripping from each word.

Time to referee, Madison thought. "Well, the client can spend their money any way they want. But from my perspective, spending $2.5

million for thirty seconds on the Super Bowl to reach saggy-skin wom-
en over fifty is like spending $2.5 million on *The Julia Child Show*
to recruit Navy SEALs. You may reach some, but not many. I would
suggest we recommend an alternative: a smarter, $2.5 million dollar
plan, a mix of TV, newspapers, magazines and other media specifically
designed to reach the over-fifty female market."

Heads nodded. Rasmussen seemed unconvinced.

Madison excused herself from the meeting and headed back to her
office to review a presentation. As she settled in at her desk, she saw
Kevin had phoned. She dialed his extension and he picked up.

"Hi there...." she said. Her body grew warm at the sound of his
voice. "I'm the girl that you bewitched, bothered and bewildered last
night until I finally granted you my considerable favors."

"Roxanne?"

"You're fired, Jordan," she said, laughing. "By the way, did you hear
from Craig about the money in Tradewinds?"

"He just left me a voice message suggesting we have lunch around
one."

"Works for me."

"I'll swing by your office about 12:30."

"See you then."

For the next thirty minutes, she worked on the presentation. As
she moved a file aside, she noticed a memo from Alison Whitaker and
realized she'd forgotten to ask how her injuries were healing from the
mugging the other night.

Madison hurried down to Whitaker's office. Alison was on the
phone and waved her to a beige leather chair beside her desk.

Madison sat down, and looked around. The decor was as elegant
and refined as Alison. Her teak desk was spotless and held a thin laptop, a BlackBerry, a chrome in-and-out tray, and a crystal paperweight.
Fresh daisies graced a nearby cherry credenza. Above the credenza
hung autographed pictures of Alison with Rudy Giuliani, George W.
Bush, and Barack Obama.

Whitaker hung up and smiled at Madison. "What's up?"

"I just came by to see how you're recovering."

"I'm healed! Look!" She leaned forward to show a small bandage behind her ear. Then she pushed up the sleeve of her blouse. "And these bruises will fade soon."

"You were lucky, Alison."

"Very. But not when it came to finding anything about your father's accuser. I asked our computer guy, Harley, or Harry what's-his-name, if he could locate the e-mail or the backup. He couldn't. And yesterday, I flat-out asked Karla what she knew."

"And...?"

"She denied knowing anything about anything."

What a surprise, Madison thought. "What's your take on Karla?"

Whitaker took a deep breath and paused a moment. "Well, as you know, she's very opinionated. She's also very smart and tough. Even ruthless at times. And, of course, she's filthy rich."

"Really? Where's her money come from?"

"No one knows for sure. But she has a huge apartment near the Dakota overlooking Central Park and a condo in Aspen. She also has a villa in the Caribbean, on one of those little islands, maybe St. Barts."

"St. Kitts?" Madison's heart pumped faster.

Alison nodded. "Maybe."

"One more question...."

"Sure."

"Do you think Karla sent the e-mail accusing my father of misappropriating funds and demanding he retire?"

"You mean, so he couldn't stop the ComGlobe merger?"

Madison nodded.

Whitaker fingered her crystal paperweight for several moments. "I don't know, Madison. I *do* know that she's hell-bent for that merger. And, she's a very determined woman. If we put the two together ... well, I suppose it's possible she sent the e-mail."

"What if my father discovered she was behind the e-mail and threatened to tell the police? What if she had him killed and made it look like a suicide?"

Whitaker blinked, looked out the window, then turned back. "Well, murder is a long way from an accusation. I just don't know. But...."

"But what?"

"Well, I guess when it comes to money, nothing Karla did would surprise me. The woman's obsessed by it."

"She'd get millions from the merger."

Whitaker nodded. "Many millions."

Madison stood up. "Thanks, Alison, for speaking frankly. And I'm relieved that you're healing so quickly."

She smiled and touched the Band-Aid behind her ear.

Back in her office, Madison called St. Anthony's Hospital again to check on Linda Langstrom. The nurse said she was still in a coma, but that Linda had responded to a command to squeeze the doctor's hand, and had even mumbled her own name. Very encouraging signs. Madison's eyes watered up with the news. She hung up and continued working on the presentation.

Moments later, she looked up and saw Kevin chatting with Christine in her outer office. He looked terrific wearing a blue button-down shirt, dark blazer and tan slacks. Last night he'd looked more terrific wearing nothing.

"Ready for lunch with Craig?" he asked her from the outer office.

"Starving," she said.

As they walked outside, she couldn't help but worry about Craig Borden.

Bad things were happening to people who helped her.

Forty Seven

M adison and Kevin walked into Granny Colasanti's popular new Italian restaurant off Canal Street in Manhattan's financial district. The cheerful young raven-haired greeter led them through the spicy scent of oregano, garlic and Italian sausage, then past red tablecloths with Chianti bottles and hunched-over bankers whispering about convertible debentures. "O Sole Mio" wafted from the red speakers on the walls.

She saw Craig Borden in a corner booth, talking on his cell phone and waving them over.

As they sat down, an elderly waiter with eyebrows thick as hedges hurried over and handed them menus.

Craig snapped his cell phone shut. "Their linguini is incredible, especially with garlic and clam sauce. That's what I'm having."

The waiter nodded his approval.

"And those cannolis," Craig said, pointing at the desert trolley, "are to die for."

Or from, Madison thought, as she stared at the six-inch cannolis oozing thick cream.

Live dangerously, she told herself. "I'll have linguini and a cannoli."

"Works for me," Kevin said.

The waiter smiled and walked off.

Craig pointed at his cell phone. "That was my associate in the Caymans. He learned the $8.7 million was just transferred three hours ago to a Curacao bank, Millennia Trust, N.V."

Madison leaned forward. "Did he by any chance learn the name of the person behind the account?"

"No. And learning it will be tough. Curacao is part of the Dutch Antilles, and Dutch bankers' lips are sealed tight."

"Any way to pry them open?"

"Crowbar! Curacao's got very strict laws that prohibit bankers from revealing account information to anyone without the express *written* consent of the account holder. And this account holder, the man who claimed to be your father, expressly wrote that no one, not even immediate family members, be given any information."

"What if a banker does give out information?" Kevin said.

"Possibly jail time, plus serious fines."

Madison's hopes took a nosedive. "So, now what?"

Borden checked his watch. "So, in a few hours I'm flying to Barbados for a meeting tomorrow morning. Millennia Trust has a branch office there and my pal, Philip, works in it. I helped him out with a similar situation a year ago. So maybe he'll reciprocate."

"What if he refuses?" Madison asked.

"Then I'll remind him how Millennia Bank's image could be hurt, maybe devastated, by having its name associated with murder investigations, and U.S. Congressional banking committee inquiries."

"And what if he *still* refuses?"

Craig smiled. "Then, Phil and I will play our game."

"What game?"

"'I gotta pee.'"

"Now...?"

"No, the game's called 'I gotta pee'. See, Phil and I chat in his office for a while. Then he says, 'Excuse me, I gotta pee' and leaves his office. I look over at his desk and damned if I don't see the papers with the exact information I came to get. So I memorize the info or photograph it. Phil comes back, we chat and I leave. Bottom line, Phil's told me nothing, given me nothing. I took it. He can't be responsible for a visitor snooping at stuff on his desk, right?"

Madison simply shook her head and smiled.

The waiter set their meals in front of them. Madison took a bite of the lemony-garlic linguini and it was delicious.

All of a sudden, something occurred to her. "What about the bank statements for the account?"

"What about them?" Kevin asked.

"The bank must have mailed them to an address."

Borden nodded. "They did. But only to an e-mail address. In fact, all account transactions have been by e-mail. The account holder logs on with a password, does his business, then logs off. All electronic. No paper trail."

"And the e-mail address is also protected?" Madison asked.

"Absolutely."

"Maybe Dean Dryden can help," Kevin said.

"Who's Dryden?"

"A very savvy computer hacker pal of mine. Maybe he can discover the e-mail address."

"Ask him to try. Give him the account number and the names of the banks. I'll also try to get the e-mail address and the dates the money was wire transferred. The wire transfers should have been confirmed by e-mails."

Madison's hopes rose, but still she was worried about the safety of Craig Borden and Dean Dryden. Even though they insisted on helping her, she feared that the Tall Man would find out. Once he did, he or his henchmen would try to stop them.

Like they stopped Linda Langstrom.

* * *

Eugene P. Smith watched Madison McKean, Kevin Jordan and the banker stand up from their table and leave Granny Colasanti's. Smith had lip-read their conversation through the tinted mirror behind the restaurant's crowded bar.

"They've left," he said into his cell phone.

"Where are they going?" Harry Burkett asked.

"McKean and Jordan are heading back to the agency. Borden's going to Barbados."

"Why Barbados?"

"To squeeze his pal at Millennia Trust for the name of the original account holder."

Burkett coughed. "Jesus....! You've *got* to handle Borden and his banker pal!"

"I will, soon as you deposit another fifty grand in my Brussels account."

Burkett sputtered and cleared his throat.

"Make up your mind, Harry. If I don't catch the flight, and Borden talks to the banker ... and the banker traces the account back ... well, you know how bad things could get for you and our friend, the EVP."

Long pause. "You'll get your goddammed money!"

Smith smiled as he hung up and sipped the rest of his Glenfiddich. Then he phoned American Airlines and booked a first-class seat on Borden's flight to Barbados.

Barbados ... a banker's paradise ...

Except for nosy bankers.

Forty Eight

M adison sat at her desk, flipping through a thick stack of phone messages. She paused on one from Dana Williams and thought back to their recent conversation.

Why had Dana been so nervous when she mentioned the argument with my father? Were they arguing, as she claimed, over an advertising campaign? Or the ComGlobe merger?

Or had her father discovered, like Madison had, that Dana was involved romantically with Lamar Brownlee, the CEO of Griffen Girard? Was Dana simply sleeping with the enemy? Or planning to bring him some highly profitable Turner clients?

"Madison...?"

She turned and saw Christine, her secretary, walking toward her.

"Here's your travel packet. Everything you need's inside." Christine handed her a brown zipper folder.

"Thanks, Christine. I can hardly believe it."

"Believe what?"

"That I'm actually going to the Cannes Advertising Festival in

France!"

Christine smiled. "Promise me you'll have some fun."

"Just going is fun." Madison had dreamed often of attending the prestigious Cannes Advertising Festival, the ad industry's version of the Academy Awards. And now she was attending, thanks to the festival *Président* who'd asked her to deliver the presentation her father had been scheduled to give. Even though she was no expert on the subject – namely, the advantages of smaller affiliated agencies versus the giant global systems – her father was an expert, and had written a terrific first draft of his speech last month.

And even more terrific, Kevin was going. Two of his truck television commercials were in the running for the festival's highly coveted *Lion D'or.*

"You have a moment, Christine?"

"Sure." Christine sat in the chair beside the desk.

Madison wondered how best to raise the subject, then simply said, "My father and Dana Williams...."

The muscles in Christine's face tightened.

"They worked well together for a long time, right?"

Christine nodded.

"But I heard Dana became quite angry with him a few days before his death."

"Well, yes."

"Any idea why?"

Christine took a deep breath, paused, then looked at Madison. "I suppose you have a right to know...."

Know what?

Christine checked the door as though making sure no one could overhear, then turned back. "Dana had a ... strong romantic interest in your father."

Madison's jaw dropped open. Her father was at least twenty-five years older than Dana.

"She first pursued him one year after your mother's death, but he was still in mourning. Dana tried again the next year. He *still* mourned your mother."

"He mourned her every day."

"Yes, but at our last Christmas party, after everyone got a little tipsy, Dana really latched onto him. They danced some, and went on to the afterglow party with a bunch of us. Dana stayed glued to him, then dragged him off to some other parties, maybe even spent the night with him. She was very serious, your father was not! He tried to break it off politely, but Dana persisted. She can be quite, ah ... possessive."

Christine paused, took a deep breath. "Then about two weeks ago, I heard Dana in here with him. She was quite angry. It sounded personal. When she came out, she had fire in her eyes."

Hell hath no fury like a woman scorned, Madison thought.

Christine started to say something else, then stopped.

"Whatever you say will remain between us," Madison said.

Christine nodded, checked the door again, then whispered, "Five years ago, Dana had a very nasty divorce. She fought against it tooth and nail. After the divorce, she actually stalked her ex-husband, demanding they get back together. He refused. But she kept stalking him."

"Then one day, she showed up uninvited at his family reunion where he'd brought his new girlfriend. Dana became enraged and threatened him. They had to escort her from the party. The next morning, her ex-husband was found dead in his home. Thirty-four years old. Cause of death was inconclusive. The police suspected poisoning, but the toxicologist found no trace of poison. They interviewed Dana three times, but never charged her. She refused to take a lie detector test."

Madison was stunned by what she'd just heard. *Dana's husband divorces her and then dies under mysterious circumstances. My father refuses her advances and then dies under mysterious circumstances. And while she's being turned down by my father, she's involved with the CEO of a competitive agency.*

"You and Kevin should leave for the airport now," Christine said, standing up.

Madison nodded, still shocked by what she'd learned about Dana

Williams.

"Have a safe trip, Madison."

"We will."

She and Kevin would wear disguises and leave from the building garage in a windowless plumber's van, driven by Neal Nelson, her guard. Nelson would make certain no one followed them to JFK Airport.

Kevin and she would be in France having fun.

The Tall Man would be in Manhattan having a fit trying to find them.

* * *

Craig Borden looked out the window of his non-stop American Airlines flight at the lights of Barbados blinking up at him from the dark Caribbean. He liked Barbados, especially jogging on the white sand of Crane's Beach and conducting business over shrimp focaccia and Cuban cigars at the Lone Star restaurant.

But what he loved most about Barbados was Miss Sarah Featherstone, the brilliant, funny, drop-dead-beautiful young bank officer with large brown eyes and a smile as enchanting as a Caribbean sunset. On his last visit, they'd gone out for dinner for the second time and he'd laughed harder than he had in years. He would phone her after meeting his banker pal, Philip Carter.

The 737's tires slammed down hard at Grantley Adams Airport near Bridgetown. Craig breezed through customs, then flipped open his cell phone and called Carter, who picked up on the first ring.

"So Philip Carter is working late again! I'm impressed."

"You'll be more impressed with what I found."

"Which is?"

"I'll tell you in thirty minutes at Nelson's Arms."

"OK. Dinner's on me."

"Just a drink, Craig. My girlfriend's promised me spiritual comfort tonight."

"You dating a nun?"

"Ha ha ha," Carter said, hanging up.

Borden stepped outside, breathed in warm humid air that smelled of flowers and diesel fuel, then settled into a blue Mercedes taxi.

"Nelson's Arms, please."

* * *

Eugene P. Smith had lip-read Borden's conversation. Four years ago, Smith had been to Nelson's Arms. He remembered that Lord Nelson's statue was just down the street.

He signaled the next taxi, got in, pulled out three crisp one-hundred-dollar bills and leaned over the front seat.

"These are yours if you beat that taxi ahead of me to Lord Nelson's statue by ten minutes."

The fat driver scrutinized the money, then floored the accelerator.

Smith took out his BlackBerry, logged on to the Internet and brought up the Millennia Trust Website. He clicked on *Management,* then on *Philip Carter,* the name Craig Borden had spoken into his cell phone.

Philip Carter's pink, cherubic face and bald head popped onto the screen.

Nineteen minutes later, the taxi driver skidded to a stop in front of Lord Nelson's statue, grinning like he'd won the Daytona 500. "The other taxi is at least ten minutes back."

Smith handed him the three hundred dollars, got out and watched the taxi drive off. Smith never had a driver leave him at the scene of an imminent hit. He walked quickly down the street and stepped inside Nelson's Arms. The restaurant-bar was crowded. He smelled grilled steak and heard soft jazz coming from a trio near the bar. He looked around and saw Philip Carter's bald head glowing like a polished egg in the shadowy corner. Carter was sipping beer and writing in a folder.

Smith walked toward Carter's corner. "Excuse me folks, but there's a fella named Craig over in the bar area looking for a Philip Carter. Is there a Mr. Car – ?"

"That's me," Carter said, getting up and walking into the bar area.

While he was gone, Smith leaned over and pretended to read Carter's newspaper. Then, holding the paper up so no one could see him, he squirted a clear liquid into Carter's beer. He noticed Carter's open folder. On the top page, were two words: 'Craig.' And a long, strange word starting with "B." The word probably was related to the money at Millennia. He pulled the page off and slid it into his coat. Then, calmly, he put the newspaper back down and walked toward the door. He saw Carter near the pool table area still searching for Borden.

Back outside, Smith looked through the window and saw Carter looking very puzzled as he returned to his seat.

Then the banker took a nice long sip of beer.

* * *

Craig Borden saw red ambulance lights streaking across the faces of customers leaving Nelson's Arms. *Another café coronary,* he assumed.

He walked inside and saw paramedics jackknifed over a man on the floor in the far corner.

"300!" a young paramedic shouted. "Clear!"

The crowd backed up.

"Hit it!"

He heard a loud *THUMP!* – and saw a man's arm rise and drop.

Craig moved through the crowd and checked the heart monitor line. Flat.

"Hit it!"

THUMP!

Craig inched closer and froze. He was looking at *Philip Carter.* Craig's eyes went out of focus. He felt like he'd been kicked in the chest and had to steady himself against the bar.

He watched the paramedics try several more times to revive him, unsuccessfully. Then, slowly, they put away their defibrillator paddles, lifted Philip's body onto a gurney and rolled him outside.

Craig's mind was numb. He tried to make sense of what he'd just witnessed. He walked over where Philip had been sitting and noticed an open Millennia Trust folder. The top page had been ripped off, but he saw the indentations of two words on the second page. He could only make out an "r" and a "g." He took out his pencil and began rubbing the lead over the indentations. Slowly, C R A I G emerged, and then below it, a strange, long word.

Blanchectar

Blanchectar? A name? A place?

Whatever it was, Phil had wanted him to see it.

The ambulance doors slammed shut. Craig turned and watched the long red vehicle drive away with the body of his friend. *How the hell could a healthy, thirty-three-year-old man who breathed effortlessly when we jogged four miles in 87-degree heat last month suddenly drop dead?*

It made no sense ... unless he was murdered ... because he was examining the mysterious bank account. But how would anyone even know he was examining it? *I told no one his name.* Did he mention it to the wrong person at his bank?

Suddenly, Craig felt like the pub's walls were closing in on him. He took a deep breath and hurried outside, devastated by the painful realization that his good friend was dead, perhaps because of him.

Dazed, Craig wandered down Broad Street.

Forty Nine

CANNES, FRANCE

Madison and Kevin gazed up at the Carlton Hotel as the afternoon sun glanced off the glass casing on the clock above the entrance. She'd seen the magnificent old hotel in movies, but none had captured the stately charm of its façade, still fresh and white despite a century of wet Mediterranean winters.

To her left, the yacht-studded harbor of Cannes sprawled out toward the *Palais des Festivals,* the massive convention center where the Cannes Advertising Festival was now taking place. Weeks earlier, the same center had held the famous Cannes Film Festival, drawing swarms of movie stars, studio moguls, paparazzi and bug-eyed fans here for a glitzy week of high hopes and low cleavage.

Madison was amazed at how the Advertising Festival had grown from a few hundred professionals in the early sixties to over nine thousand attendees this year – four thousand more than the Film Festival. Understandable, since the ad industry was a $600 billion dollar business and the film industry $100 billion.

For one week, ad people sat in auditoriums watching a few thousand television commercials. Everything from beers that promised to keep you skinny, to cars that promised you fifty miles per gallon ... from deodorants that promised to keep you dry to hemorrhoid creams that promised to end your "infernal rectal itch."

Most commercials were funny, some provocative, some flat-out dumb, and a few, brilliant.

Madison and Kevin strolled into the Carlton's distinguished lobby and looked around at the glittering crystal chandeliers, gleaming marble floor, intricate gold leaf trim and stately white columns.

"There's a name for all this," she said.

"Motel 6?"

Laughing, she elbowed him.

Two famous New York advertising gurus walked past her. She recognized the successful professionals who clearly earned the right to be here. *What did I do to get here? Have a successful father?* Suddenly, she felt like the little donkey surrounded by the big Clydesdales in a Budweiser commercial.

Minutes later, she entered her suite and found herself looking at the kind of understated luxury that European hotels do so naturally. A massive bed, royal-blue drapes, tasteful chairs and sofa, fresh flowers and a breathtaking view of the sun-drenched Mediterranean.

She hurried next door to Kevin's suite and saw it was identical to hers.

Kevin gestured around his room. "In French class we said, *'Le luxe n'est pas un péché,'*"

"Huh...?"

"Luxury is not a sin."

She checked her watch. "But being extremely late to a big event is."

"What event?"

"The VIP, ComGlobe-sponsored cocktail party downstairs. It started forty minutes ago. I'm committed to go. You wanna come?"

* * *

Fifteen minutes later, Madison, wearing her low-cut strapless black dress with its long, slutty slit up the side, handed her VIP invitation to a young woman who escorted her and Kevin in his classic tux into a palatial banquet room. She saw sixty or so heavy-breathers mulling about. Most were nursing drinks, schmoozing and undoubtedly gossiping about which juicy ad accounts were vulnerable, which CEOs were in trouble, which agencies were looking to buy agencies, and which agencies were looking to be bought.

They took glasses of champagne from a white-coated waiter.

"Obviously," she said, "the Cannes festival is about watching commercials, *and* wheeling and dealing."

"*And* stealing creative directors," he added with a grin.

"What! Someone *already* approached you here?"

"*Three* someones."

"You're joking!"

"Nope. They left kissy-kissy, come-work-with-us messages on my room phone."

She was shocked. "You told them you were happy?"

"Yeah ... I lied."

"These headhunters have no shame!"

"But they have *money!*" he said, grinning.

And Cannes, she knew, was *the* place to flaunt it, the perfect venue to steal hot creative directors and executives with fistfuls of bonus money and fat salaries. The last thing she needed was Kevin working for a competitive agency.

"Ah, you've arrived, Ms. McKean," said a soft male voice.

She turned around and saw a short, pudgy man in his mid-fifties wearing an expensive black suit. His silver hair was combed straight back from a high forehead and pink, jowly face. His red-rimmed eyes and stained tie suggested the empty champagne flute in his hand wasn't his first of the night.

"Peter Gunther of ComGlobe," he said, extending his hand. "Welcome to our little soiree. It's a delight to finally meet you, Ms. McKean."

She shook his hand. "Nice to meet you, Mr. Gunther," She remembered his name from her father's ComGlobe file.

Kevin introduced himself.

Gunther turned to her. "Please accept my heartfelt condolences for your father's passing."

"Thank you." She knew his condolences probably weren't *that* heartfelt, since her father wanted to block Gunther's merger.

"And congratulations for being named as the new chair of Turner Advertising."

"Thank you again."

"As you know, your father and ComGlobe were having excellent discussions on the mutually beneficial Turner-ComGlobe merger."

She nodded.

"We believe that the merger would greatly enrich the depth and diversity of the services you could offer your fine clients."

"Except the four fine clients we'd be forced to resign."

"Well...." Gunther shrugged, then snatched another champagne flute from a passing waiter and gulped down half.

Madison wanted to level with him. "Mr. Gunther, we're flattered by ComGlobe's interest in Turner. But to be fair, I should tell you I plan to vote against the merger just like my father would have. Our company is doing well, and our clients prefer our agency's independence."

"Yes, but with ComGlobe you would remain perfectly independent. Nothing would change."

She marveled at how easily Gunther had just lied. "But ComGlobe's history suggests things do change. When ComGlobe took over Ferguson-Felix-Folster Advertising, three-hundred twenty people wound up on the street."

Gunther's jowls turned bright red. "Just a staffing realignment."

He made it sound like they rearranged some paper clips.

Kevin's cell phone went off. He pulled it out, listened a moment, then gestured for Madison to follow.

"Excuse me, Mr. Gunther," she said, "but business beckons."

Gunther started to speak, but she was already walking away.

She followed Kevin to a quiet corner where he answered the call and mouthed to her that it was his secretary, Barb. His eyes grew serious. A minute later, he hung up and faced her.

"What's wrong?" she said.

"Barb played me a voice message from Craig Borden in Barbados. Craig's banker friend, Philip Carter, dropped dead in a bar five minutes before Craig was to meet with him."

Her mind spinning, Madison sat in a nearby chair, praying his death wasn't connected to the bank account, but knowing it somehow was.

"They think it was stroke or heart attack."

"How old was he?"

"Thirty-three."

"Jesus!" She looked at Kevin and whispered, "The Tall Man!"

"Either he followed Craig to Barbados or had someone there do his dirty work."

She said nothing.

"But Craig found a word that Philip wrote down."

She looked up. "What?"

Kevin grabbed a paper napkin and wrote:

Blanchectar

They stared at the single word, wondering what it meant.

"A name? A place?" she asked.

"Maybe. But Craig couldn't find *Blanchectar* in the phonebook or on the Internet. He tried to send an e-mail to it, but it came back 'delivery failed.'"

"Still, it could be the account name we've been looking for."

"Or simply a friend of Philip Carter's."

"Or ... the Tall Man."

Fifty

Peter Gunther wasn't worried. The EVP had promised him she'd deliver the Turner-ComGlobe Advertising merger, and for ten million dollars she damn well better deliver it. Gunther's only fear was that one of his competitors might sneak in and offer Madison McKean a better deal – before Turner's directors voted on the ComGlobe merger in a few days.

After all, WPP, Havas, and IPG, at one time or another, had each tried to persuade Mark McKean to merge Turner Advertising with them, but he'd politely said no to each. Still, they might approach Madison, sweet-talk her, promise her the moon, and because she was young, and because IPG and WPP had fewer client conflicts than ComGlobe, there was a chance they might persuade her.

Which meant it was time for Gunther to launch his torpedo of disinformation into the Cannes festival.

He strolled into the Carlton's famed *Bar des Célébrités*, a lavishly decorated bar with mauve Baker chairs tucked in small hushed alcoves, soft yellow lighting and even softer jazz filtering over from the piano player.

Gunther saw who he was looking for immediately. *The boys.* His competitors from IPG, Havas, WPP and the other advertising conglomerates. Like him, they'd spent the night schmoozing their major clients and sniffing around parties for disgruntled clients with fat ad budgets.

Gunther picked up a Bowmore scotch from the bartender, then walked over and joined the boys.

"So, Gunther, hear any juicy gossip tonight?" asked Yves Tournier, the tall, handsome director of acquisitions for Publi-Service, a Paris-based global advertising conglomerate.

Gunther tossed down half his single malt and felt the wonderful heat.

"Yeah, *very* juicy."

"Let me guess," Tournier said, grinning, "ComGlobe is buying Exxon Mobil!"

The boys laughed and clicked their glasses like athletes giving each other high-fives.

You bastards won't laugh when I pull off the Turner merger! Gunther thought. He turned to make sure no one else was listening, then leaned forward and whispered, "Turner Advertising has *big* trouble."

Their smiles vanished and they leaned forward.

"What trouble?" Tournier asked, all business now.

"They're about to lose three major clients."

The boys froze.

"Who told you this?" Tournier whispered.

"A very reliable source."

"Who?"

"I can't reveal his name."

"OK, OK, which clients?"

Gunther leaned close to them. "One is World Motors. Another, MedPharms. I don't know the third."

They reacted as he knew they would, like sharks smelling blood. He could almost hear their greedy little minds devising schemes to scoop up the two big profitable accounts for their own agency system.

"But that's crazy! *C'est fou!*" Tournier said, "Turner Advertising is an excellent agency. They have two World Motors commercials up for a *Lion D'or.* And Turner's MedPharms ads won several Effie Awards last month. Why would these clients leave an award-winning agency?"

Gunther shrugged. "Who understands what clients do?"

"How much money are we talking?"

"If all three clients leave, Turner's will lose $397 million in annual billings." He loved stuffing big numbers into their gullible minds.

The men shook their heads in amazement. Two of them drained their drinks and signaled the waiter for another round.

"This is a fucking *hémorragie!* Tournier said. "A blood bath, no!"

Gunther nodded.

"Why are these clients leaving?" Tournier asked.

Gunther checked over his shoulder and whispered, "They're nervous because Mark McKean's daughter took over as CEO."

"Why nervous?"

"She's too young. No experience. Doesn't have Mark's savvy. The Nat-Care client has already left. I also hear Mason Funds Ltd. is talking to another agency. And, she's a loose cannon."

"How so?"

"She resigned their FACE UP client, a nice guy named Maurice Dwarck, just because the guy wanted to change his ad a bit."

The boys looked shocked.

Gunther nodded. "At any rate, we at ComGlobe have lost all interest in Turner Advertising."

"Publi-Service just did, too," Tournier said.

Gunther silently congratulated himself.

He was enjoying this. He could see them crossing off Turner Advertising as a merger candidate, and spreading the rumor as soon as they left the bar. Within minutes, everyone who mattered in the business would know big clients were bailing out of Turner Advertising. Even though it was just gossip, and even though the clients would deny it, everyone knew clients always denied rumors. The damage would be done. The big conglomerates would back away from Turner Advertising like it had leprosy, leaving ComGlobe as Turner's only suitor.

Mission accomplished, Gunther thought, signaling the waitress for another scotch.

Fifty One

Madison sat with Kevin in one of the five lecture auditoriums of the *Palais des Festivals,* preparing to give her presentation. She was also recovering from this morning's vicious rumor that three of her major clients were about to yank their business out of Turner Advertising.

She feared the rumor might be true. After all, she'd lost the Nat-Care business her first day, and a good agency was trying to steal her Mason Funds account.

She immediately phoned her World Motors and MedPharms clients in a panic. They assured her the rumor was absolutely false and that they had no intentions of leaving Turner Advertising. They also promised to kill the rumor with the media and at any festival parties they attended. Meanwhile, Kevin had phoned their other clients and learned all was well with them.

But was it really? she wondered.

Today, a client might tell you "We're delighted with your agency," and next week tell you, "We're moving our ad account to Frick &

Frack." When you ask why, they'll say, 'Oh ... our chairman's girlfriend started working there.'

Madison looked around the nearly-filled auditorium and felt herself growing more anxious. In minutes, she would make a presentation to hundreds of people who probably knew more than she did about her topic, namely the advantages of smaller independent agencies versus the giant conglomerates. Fortunately, her father, an expert on the subject, had written a superb rough draft of the speech that she and Kevin had polished.

After her speech, they would attend the big awards show to see if either of Kevin's television commercials was lucky enough to win a coveted *Lion D'or*.

"Nervous?" Kevin asked her.

"Oh, yeah."

"Why?"

"I'll probably make some horrible *faux pas*."

"Like what?"

"Like passing out or frothing at the mouth."

He smiled. "Far worse *faux pas* have been made here."

"Really?"

"Did you ever see the shocking commercial for a Norwegian newspaper that they showed here?

"No."

"A guy in the men's nude sauna peeks through a hole in the wall into the women's nude sauna, and wouldn't you know it, he becomes sexually ah...."

"Aroused?"

"Yeah, that's the word. Then one of the women confronts him and he hides his arou ... you know, by drooping the Norwegian newspaper over it ...."

"Over his arousal?"

"Yeah. Like he was hanging clothes on a line."

Madison laughed.

Behind her she heard a young woman say, "Mademoiselle

McKean?"

"Yes?"

"Ees time for to check your microphone."

"OK," Madison said, feeling less anxious thanks to Kevin's story. They stood and strolled toward the podium at the front of the auditorium.

* * *

At his desk, Detective Pete Loomis bit off a big chunk of his juicy New York Stage Deli corned beef sandwich and watched a huge glop of Russian dressing splatter down onto his case file. He wiped the glob off, leaving a pink skid mark. His desk phone rang and he answered it.

"Loomis..."

"Detective, my name is Alistair Johnstone. I'm a detective with the Royal Police Force down in...."

Static crackled in Loomis's ear. "Sorry, where?"

"St. Kitts ... in the Caribbean. Madison McKean gave me your name."

"Oh yes, she gave me yours as well."

"We've just identified the man who attacked Ms. McKean down here."

"That's terrific!" Loomis said, grabbing a pencil.

"The name on his passport is Arnold P. Nichols."

Loomis wrote down the name.

"But that's only one of his seven aliases according to Interpol. I'll e-mail you their entire file on him. His birth name is Eugene P. Smith."

Loomis jotted down that name too.

"Mr. Smith is a very nasty chap indeed. Ex-CIA. Been a paid, freelance hitman for years. Multiple felony indictments pending against him in seven countries. All professional assassinations."

"Any recent photos?"

"No. Just an old one from his CIA days years ago. It's been computer-updated, but that won't help."

"Why not?"

"Mr. Smith is a master of disguise. Probably why we couldn't find him down here. All we know is, he's forty-one, six-feet-two, thin, and commands huge fees as an assassin. He can be very charming if need be, but it's a facade. In Qatar, he blew up a home he thought was a terrorist's, but it was a small orphanage. Seven children died."

Loomis pushed his half-eaten sandwich away. "We'll put out a state-wide APB for him now."

"Good idea, but you may not find him."

"Why's that?"

"Barbados customs officials just told me that a man using one of his aliases, Antoine Cravatte, flew out of there yesterday morning."

Loomis felt his gut churn. "Flew *where?*"

"Paris. Then down to Cannes."

"*Shit!*"

"What's wrong?"

"McKean's in Cannes."

"Good Lord!"

"I'll alert her immediately!" Loomis said.

They hung up and Loomis called Madison's cell phone. He heard a clicking sound and realized her phone was switching him to voice mail. He left her a voice message warning her about Smith. Then he called Kevin's number, got voicemail again and left him a similar message.

Loomis reached into his coat pocket for the paper with the name of their hotel.

The paper was not there.

Fifty Two

Eugene P. Smith finished his Glenfiddich as he sat in the elegant *L'Amiral* bar of the famous Martinez Hotel in Cannes. A few feet away, a pianist, who looked like Sam in *Casablanca,* sang "Ramblin' Rose," in a voice as buttery as Nat King Cole's.

The bartender pointed at Smith's empty glass. Smith nodded and moments later the barman placed a fresh scotch in front of him. Smith sipped some, then scanned the well-dressed customers surrounding him. He recognized a couple of French movie stars at a corner table.

Smith checked his watch. A little later, he'd go handle Madison.

He liked Cannes, the glamor and glitz, the unapologetic wealth that personified the town. But sometimes it went too far. Like the penthouse suite seven floors above him. It was one of the world's most expensive hotel accommodations. The per-night rate was $37,200 dollars. Obscene!

But not as obscene as the pudgy Saudi prince he'd watched in the Cannes casino a few hours ago. The prince, about twenty-five, was playing roulette, betting thirty thousand dollars with each spin of the wheel, barely noticing if he won or lost, barely noticing the busty blonde carefully placing chocolate-covered strawberries in his mouth. A cute waitress told Smith that the prince had lost seven million dollars over the last three weeks, but never once tipped her for all the champagne she'd brought him.

Cheap bastard! Smith thought. Probably supplied money to terrorist groups. *Maybe I'll eliminate him for free.*

Sipping more scotch, he noticed three nice-looking women walk in and sit down at a nearby table. His eyes zeroed in on the tall brunette. He blinked to be certain. It *was* Nina. Incredible. After all these years she still looked terrific.

He thought back to when Nina Brower and he had trained together at the CIA Farm in Williamsburg. She was smart, attractive, and tough enough to outperform a few male colleagues in some physical endurance tests. He remembered when she won the midnight navigation test by crawling though the snake and tick-infested forest and reaching the test's pre-set coordinates before the boys.

After graduating, Nina and he were stationed in London where they teamed up to assassinate an Al Qaeda operative who'd murdered an American judge vacationing there. They also teamed up in bed.

But a few months later, when Smith was posted to Cairo and Nina was sent to Buenos Aires, the distance seemed to pull them apart.

Now, years after they'd both left the CIA, Smith realized Nina still looked great. He told the barman to send a round of drinks over to her table. The waiter delivered the drinks and Smith watched her ask him who'd sent them. The waiter nodded toward Smith. Her eyes lit up as she recognized him. She excused herself from her friends and strolled over toward him, bringing her drink.

"Eugene P. Smith lives!" she said, kissing his cheek.

"He does. What brings you to Cannes?"

"Corporate Security," she said. "I work for a company that does sophisticated security systems for multinational companies."

"Fun?"

She shrugged. "Not as exciting as the old days."

"*Our* days?"

She smiled. "Yeah, our days. And what brings Eugene P. Smith to Cannes?"

"Like you, corporate security."

"What kind."

"The kind where one executive feels more secure if he eliminates the competition."

"So to speak."

Smith smiled and held up his scotch.

She clicked her glass to his and they sipped some.

"Maybe it's time we revisit old memories," she said.

"How about upstairs in Room 507?"

"Give me fifteen minutes."

Smith heard a knock on his door. He opened it and Nina strolled in, looking drop-dead gorgeous in a slinky black dress that looked like it had been sprayed on. She was also wearing a new fragrance imbued with human sex pheromones. Whatever the fragrance, it worked. Within minutes they were making love like they had in London.

Later, lying spent in each other's arms, she turned and whispered in his ear, "You serious about retiring?"

"This is my last assignment."

"Really?"

"Yeah."

She looked pleased that he'd said that.

"What about you?" he said.

"I'm quitting in three months. I just inherited my parents' farm outside Tampa. A condo developer offered me eight million for the land."

Smith smiled. "Sell. Retire. Enjoy."

"That's my plan."

Eugene P. Smith glanced out the window at the long row of multi-million-dollar yachts lining the Bay of Cannes. Maybe he should buy a yacht, cruise away from those who wanted his head on a platter, and settle down.

With a little plastic surgery and new ID, he could sail to some exotic island in the Caribbean. Hell, he could buy the island. Disappear with Nina. They could live like a king and a queen. The more he thought of it, the more he liked the idea.

But first he had an old debt to settle.

And it was time to settle it.

Fifty Three

Madison looked out at the more than four hundred festival attendees staring at her as she gave her presentation. So far, heads had nodded agreement, mouths had laughed at the jokes, and no one had thrown tomatoes. All positive signs.

She began to relax a bit, thinking she might actually make it through the speech.

One second later, she did not.

She saw him.

The Tall Man. Thirty rows up, standing next to the Exit. Tall, thin, familiar shape. Narrow face hidden in shadows. Dark eyes locked on hers. His hand held something shiny and black.

Her pulse started pounding so loud she feared the audience could hear it through her lapel microphone. She sipped water and continued speaking, but with an audible tremor.

In the first row, Kevin seemed to realize something had upset her. He looked around the auditorium, then back at her. She directed him with her eyes to where she'd seen the Tall Man, but the man was gone now.

Don't panic, she told herself. *Calm down, finish the speech. One page to go. He won't shoot you here. Not in front of all these eyewitnesses!*

Or will he?

Her hands trembling and palms sweating, she continued reading, and managed to finish her presentation to enthusiastic applause. As she stepped quickly off the podium, delegates swarmed around her, offering congratulations.

She thanked them, but Kevin hurried her away from the crowd. "Did you see him?" he asked.

"Yes."

"Where?"

"Up there."

The overhead lights suddenly came on, flooding the room.

She scanned the departing attendees and saw no one even remotely similar to the Tall Man. As she looked back up to where she'd seen him, a tall thin man walked through the Exit and stood in the same spot. A teenage usher. He held a black two-way radio.

"Whoops!" she said, pointing to the usher. "I overreacted."

He smiled. "*Under*reacting is not an option."

"Nor is missing the main event!" she said, pointing to the Exit.

Seconds later, they merged with the noisy crowd hurrying into the magnificent, tiered Grand Auditorium de Louis Lumiere for the festival's final awards ceremony. She looked around at the twenty-three hundred other attendees, each hoping and praying for a highly coveted *Lion D'or.* Laser beams danced across the stage curtain and along the massive, low-hanging balcony hovering over the main floor. Suspense hung in the air like static electricity. Music, soft and atmospheric, filled the darkened room.

As they walked down to their row, Madison heard at least six different languages being spoken. They settled into their plush red seats. Kevin began drumming his fingers on his knees.

"*Now* who's nervous?" she said.

"That would be me."

"Why?"

"Bloc-voting."

"You mean when European judges and others combine to vote lower scores on North American commercials?"

"Yeah, but also North American judges bloc-voting lower on commercials from other countries. It happens when you've got 127 judges from 31 countries. Remember 1991?"

"Vaguely."

"The bloc-voting was so bad the festival president threatened to humiliate certain judges by having them publicly justify their very high marks for their own country's very ordinary commercials."

"But didn't the new computerized voting system fix the problem?"

"Not completely."

Suddenly, a blast of trumpets filled the room. The festival president strolled out and for the next twenty minutes everyone watched some brilliant, creative, provocative and hilarious *Lion*-winning commercials. Then the festival president announced, *"Madams et monsieurs, la catégorie d'auto.* The automobile category."

Madison watched Kevin lean forward and grip his armrests.

The president continued, "And one *Lion D'or* has been awarded to ... Campbell-Ewald Advertising for their 60-second Corvette commercial." The commercial flickered onto the big screen, spellbinding Madison for the full minute. The audience exploded in applause as the winning copywriter jogged to the stage and accepted her award.

"And another *Lion D'or* is awarded to ... Turner Advertising for their World Motors Scamper II SUV commercial."

"YES!" Madison shouted, causing the people near her to smile.

Kevin shot his arm in the air and grinned like a kid. The projectionist ran the commercial and the audience roared their approval.

Kevin bounded up onto the stage and thanked the jury in perfect English and halting French. Then he smiled directly at Madison and she felt like she would burst with pride for him. Minutes later, they were even more shocked when Kevin won a silver *Lion* for his pickup truck commercial. Winning two *Lions* was very rare. Other agencies would offer to double or triple Kevin's salary. She'd have to match the offers to keep him.

After the awards ceremony, and still floating on air, they left the *Palais des Festivals* with the crowds strolling back toward the hotel parties along the *Croisette,* the romantic palm-treed boulevard that hugged the Bay of Cannes. Darkness had fallen. The hotel lights glittered around the bay like diamonds on black velvet. A soft, warm breeze rolled in from the sea.

Could this night be any more perfect? she wondered. Her speech had gone well. Kevin had won two prestigious awards, and she was walking arm in arm with a man she cared deeply for, thousands of miles away from a man who wanted to kill her.

* * *

In *Le Petit Bar* of the Carlton Hotel, Eugene P. Smith sat on the corner bar stool, sipping his second cup of strong coffee, and still savoring his amorous rendezvous with Nina Brower. The more he thought about her, the more he liked the idea of disappearing with Nina to some faraway island. Retiring. Forever.

But first, his final job. Now that the Awards Show was over, he watched the door more closely. Minutes later, he was rewarded with the sight of Madison McKean and Kevin Jordan strolling past and heading toward the elevators.

He waited a few minutes, drank the rest of his coffee, then walked out to the lobby and settled into a big leather chair. He pretended to read the *International Herald Tribune,* but in fact he watched for a man he'd seen earlier. Thirteen minutes later, the man strolled by. Smith put the *Trib* down and followed him onto an elevator.

"*Etage, monsieur?* Floor, sir?" asked the man, a tall elderly room-service waiter.

"Four, *monsieur, merci,*" Smith said, smiling.

The old man punched Four, smiled back, then faced the door.

Smith stared at the base of the old man's neck. Lots of thick, bushy, gray hair, a veritable forest. Perfect for hiding a microscopic puncture from the syringe cupped in Smith's left hand.

Smith grabbed the old man and injected him an inch above the hair line. He flailed a second, stiffened, then slumped. The elevator door opened, and Smith carried him out into the hall, then into a nearby housekeeping room. There, he removed the man's white coat and tie and put them on. A perfect fit. He hid the waiter behind a tall shelf stacked with bath towels. The 2.5 grams of chloral hydrate, the equivalent of a very strong Mickey Finn, would keep the old guy asleep for about five hours.

Smith adjusted his reddish-brown goatee and mustache, a disguise McKean had not seen. Nor had she seen his cheeks puffed out by collagen injections, or the foam hump behind his left shoulder. Now, he was an unfortunate hunchback, a feeble old room service waiter she'd most certainly take pity on.

From the corner of the room, he took a small room service cart with a silver serving dish. He rolled it into the hall, then turned the corner and headed toward McKean's room. He stopped at her door, leaned close and listened. He heard her laugh.

He knocked on the door.

"*Service de chambre* ... room service," Smith said as he flicked his Glock's safety off.

"Just a moment," she said.

Seconds later, the door opened and a fifty-year-old woman smiled out at him.

Who the hell is she?

"Sorry, but we didn't order room service."

Smith *knew* this was McKean's room. He'd checked twice.

"Is Ms. McKean here?"

"No. We just checked in. Ms. McKean must be the woman who checked out of this room minutes ago. The desk manager said we were darn lucky to get it." The woman grinned like she'd just won the lottery.

Smith felt like shooting her between the eyes.

Fifty Four

Madison breathed out slowly as she and Kevin settled into the plush leather seats of the gleaming white Learjet.

The lap of luxury, she realized, looking around the cabin. They each had their own entertainment center, video monitor, personal computer, and stereo headphones. The galley had sterling silver cutlery and monogrammed Royal Doulton china.

"Feeling pampered?" Kevin said, rubbing the supple leather armrest.

"Feeling *safe.*"

He nodded.

Detective Loomis had phoned and told her that her attacker was in Cannes. Two minutes later, she and Kevin checked out of the Carlton, hurried out the back door and into a waiting taxi. Loomis advised them to immediately leave Cannes by non-commercial airline, if possible.

It was possible, thanks to nearby *l'Aeroport Cannes Mandelieu,* a small, modern airport, where the hotel concierge had arranged for them to charter a Learjet from a fleet that whisked VIPs in and out of Cannes daily. She'd almost choked on the thirty-nine-thousand-dollar cost, but Evan Carswell insisted she leave Cannes. The cost would be absorbed in the corporate travel budget.

Now, as the jet taxied onto the tarmac, she looked out the window and saw a halo of haze hovering over Cannes. Once again, she'd evaded the Tall Man, a man Detective Loomis said was named Eugene P. Smith, a man she believed would stop at nothing until he killed her ... or was stopped by the police.

Moments later, Madison felt herself thrust back into her cushy seat as the twin Learjet engines propelled the aircraft down the runway and up into the inky sky. She looked down at the dark Mediterranean, furrowing like black silk up to the shore. Along the docks, rows of white yachts were lit up with the bright lights of festival parties.

My party's over, she thought. Back home, she'd have to focus on the upcoming ComGlobe merger vote. Feeling exhausted, she sipped more champagne, and seconds later, yawned.

She placed her hand on Kevin's hand.

"Bon nuit, mademoiselle."

She rested her head on his shoulder, and somewhere over the Atlantic, they drifted off to sleep.

* * *

Eleven hours later, Madison and Kevin sat in Café Cubana on Lexington Avenue, drinking their second cup of strong, Cuban coffee. The high-caffeine, sugary brew, plus the Salsa music blasting from a boombox behind the grill, had jump-started her jet-lagged brain. After sleeping through most of the flight and the refueling in the Azores, they landed at JFK around five in the morning. They taxied to Kevin's apartment, showered and dressed for work.

Kevin put his coffee mug down and handed her a tiny earplug connected to his cell phone.

"Listen in."

She held it to her ear and heard a phone ringing.

"Dryden...."

"Hey, Dean, it's Kevin and Madison."

"Hey, guys. So how was Cannes?"

"Breathless!" Kevin said.

"Cannes ... St. Kitts ... Manhattan. Wow, you ad biggies sure get around."

"So does the $8.7 million."

"Really?"

"Yeah, we tracked it to a bank in the Caymans and then to a bank in Curacao."

"Good work."

"But dangerous. A guy's trying to kill us."

Dean Dryden was silent. "Are you OK?"

"We're fine, Dean, but two bankers who were helping us are dead, probably murdered by the same man. Also, a woman helping us at National Media was shot. She's in intensive care."

"Jesus...."

Madison signaled Kevin that she'd like to say something. He handed her the phone.

"Dean, it's Madison. I'm concerned."

"About what?"

"You. The person behind this always seems to know who's helping us. And like Kevin said, those helping us are dying or getting seriously injured. So, if you want to back off from this, I'll certainly understand. In fact, I'd feel better if you did."

Dean Dryden was silent for several moments. "I appreciate your concern, Madison. But our boat basin here has security like Fort Knox. Just two days ago, the guard stopped some computer salesman trying to fake his way onto our dock to visit me. And there's no way they can learn I'm helping you. My computer network has a very sophisticated series of firewalls, hieroglyphical encryptions and hacker alerts. Even top cyber-sleuths can't find out where I operate from."

"You're certain?"

"Ninety-nine-point-nine percent certain. But if, by some incredible stroke of luck, they discovered my computer's location, my computer would instantly beep out a *Hostile Incursion* alert. If that happens, I'll pull up anchor and cruise to my hideaway on the Maryland coast. Also, Madison, these are bad people. They need to be stopped! So, I'm gonna ride this horse all the way to the barn, God willing."

Madison prayed God was willing. "Thank you, Dean."

Kevin leaned close to the phone. "By the way, my banker pal, Craig Borden, just discovered the e-mail address to which Caribe National Bank sent all account correspondence on the $8.7 million."

"That's great! What is it?"

Kevin gave him the address and the dates of recent e-mails. "Can you track these e-mails to the recipient?"

"To the computer the recipient used."

"How?"

"Every computer on the Internet has an Internet Protocol address, the IP. It's in the e-mail's header."

"Is the header that stuff at the top of the e-mail?"

"Yeah. It can tell me the exact route taken by the e-mail, all the way from the sender's IP number to the recipient's."

"So we'll see who the recipient is?"

"We'll see the computer the recipient used. Let's just hope the recipient picked up the e-mails on the same computer."

Madison began to feel hopeful that they might get some answers.

"Hey guys, the guard just signaled that I have a visitor. Talk to you later."

They hung up.

"If anyone can locate the computer, Dean can," Kevin said.

Not if they locate Dean first, she thought.

* * *

Leland Merryweather, Turner's EVP of International Operations, hung up from talking with Jarvis Smythe in London. Smythe had threatened him again, saying that if Merryweather didn't come up with money from the ComGlobe merger to buy into Smythe O'Rourke, Smythe was going to accept the offer of a British partner.

Merryweather had assured Smythe again that the ComGlobe money was coming!

The office door opened and Finley Weaver walked in and sat down. Merryweather pushed a desk button and his office door swung shut.

"Well...?" Merryweather said, adjusting his velvet eyepatch.

"He's ready."

"He has the IBM service uniform?"

Weaver nodded.

"And a Turner work order?"

"Yeah."

"What about the McDonald's Happy Meal?"

Weaver grinned. "He's got that, too."

"Excellent."

"And once he's here, he'll steal some stuff, including my laptop and Madison's."

Merryweather nodded his approval.

"Then, in Madison's office, he'll place the contents of the Happy Meal box in her credenza."

"You'll report the stolen laptops to the cops?"

"Yeah. They'll come, check my office and Madison's. They'll look in her credenza and be shocked at what they find there."

"Shocked enough to remove her as CEO of Turner Advertising."

Fifty Five

M adison watched Kevin present a television commercial concept to their agency executives. The commercial was for DietRxx, MedPharms' new weight loss product. According to research, DietRxx's target audience was the average American woman.

There's no such woman, Madison knew. Today, the average American woman is a stay-at-home mom, a businesswoman, brain surgeon, fork-lift operator, poet, tank commander....

"The good news," Alison Whitaker said, "is that DietRxx gives dieters ephedrine-like weight loss without ephedrine's potentially deadly side effects."

"Says who?" Karla Rasmussen challenged.

"Says MedPharms' research."

"That's totally biased research," Rasmussen said. "What does the FDA say?"

"The FDA says DietRxx is so safe they won't even require a medical review."

Rasmussen seemed surprised by the news. "Well, DietRxx must

have *some* negative complications!"

Whitaker nodded. "Less than one percent of users experience diarrhea."

"More weight loss," Kevin said.

The group laughed.

Rasmussen did not. "You won't be laughing when angry DietRxx customers sue us for false or misleading advertising. And what will ComGlobe think? Don't forget, our merger vote is in three days."

How could I forget? Madison thought.

She'd been increasingly worried that the Turner-ComGlobe merger would pass, especially since Alison Whitaker found an anonymous note saying someone presently against the merger was now planning to vote *for* it. Yesterday, Madison had again polled each director individually, and based on that poll, the merger would not pass, but only by a margin of one vote.

But what if a director had lied to her about their voting intentions? Or what if Rasmussen had blackmailed a director to lie? Or what if someone at ComGlobe bribed a director to switch their vote? Madison would never know who voted how, since the votes would be unsigned.

Minutes later, the meeting broke up. As Madison and Kevin stepped into the hall, Kevin's cell phone buzzed. He answered, listened, then led her away from the group.

"Dean Dryden is zeroing in on the location of the computer that received the Caribe National Bank's e-mail statements. He might know where the computer's located by the time we get there."

* * *

Madison watched Officer Emmett Vincent speed her and Kevin toward the Seventy-Ninth Street Boat Basin. Detective Loomis had assigned Vincent to guard her after finally persuading his captain that three attempts on her life warranted protection.

Minutes later, Vincent, a tall, muscular, red-haired man, parked beside the pier.

"You two go on in," he said, "I'll watch the dock area."

Madison and Kevin got out and hurried toward the pier. Despite Officer Vincent's presence, she moved away from a tall thin man on the dock. Even now, she imagined Eugene P. Smith hunched over Dean's body in the yacht.

"Hey, Dean," Kevin shouted as they neared the boat.

She relaxed when Dean stepped onto his deck and waved them aboard. Inside, he led them over to a large-screen computer, flanked by an empty Domino's Pizza box and a bottle of Jack Daniel's.

"So," Kevin said, "any idea yet where the receiving computer is located?"

"Not yet, but we'll know soon," Dean said, tapping away on the keyboard.

"How do you locate the address?"

"With new FBI software."

"How'd you get their software?" Madison asked.

"I designed it."

Dean typed at warp speed, filling the screen with words and symbols that only he seemed to grasp. Then he typed in another command and the screen filled with a map.

"Gotcha!" Dean said, putting his finger on the screen.

"Where?" Kevin asked.

"Fifth Avenue and Forty Second."

"That's near the Mid Manhattan Library," Kevin said.

"It's *in* the library," Dean said. "Probably someone's using a public-access computer to pick up the bank's e-mails."

Madison slumped down in a chair. "Which narrows our search down to only eight million people...."

Everyone stared at the screen.

Another dead end, she realized. Frustrated, she looked out at the Hudson River where a barge stacked with garbage slid by. Seagulls circled above the garbage. One large bird flew over to a pole on the dock. Halfway down the pole, Madison noticed a tiny camera aimed at the yachts.

"Security cameras!" she said, standing up.

Kevin nodded. "The library's gotta have them. Keep people from stealing keyboards and mouses."

* * *

Minutes later, Officer Vincent parked his blue and white NYPD sedan in the "No Parking" space near the Fifth Avenue entrance of the Mid-Manhattan Library. As Madison and Kevin started to get out, Vincent's car phone rang. He grabbed it and signaled for them to wait.

Madison watched Vincent's eyes grow serious. Something was wrong.

"Yeah, OK, I'm on it!" Vincent said. He hung up and looked at them. "We've got some nut case walking around with a suitcase full of explosives over near Seventy-First and Amsterdam. Sergeant Webber wants me over there now. I'll be back as soon as possible. Please stay inside the library until then."

Madison nodded, suddenly more worried about an explosion on a crowded Manhattan street than being left unguarded.

* * *

Nine blocks away, behind a large dumpster in an alley, Harry Burkett took the police phone that Sergeant Webber had used to call Officer Vincent.

"Well done, Sergeant Webber," Harry said, keeping his Glock 9mm on the back of Webber's head. "Just enough quiver in your voice to be authentic. You could be on *Law & Order*."

Webber said nothing.

Burkett swung a large blackjack down hard against the base of Webber's neck. The policeman froze, wobbled a bit, then slumped to the ground. Burkett tied the unconscious man's hands and legs and taped his mouth.

"Pleasant dreams," Burkett whispered, removing his beard and sunglasses as he walked from behind the dumpster.

* * *

Madison and Kevin hurried through the revolving door of the Mid-Manhattan Library, then zig-zagged through a class of school kids, past the catalogs counter to the information desk in the middle of the room. A thirtyish librarian with large brown eyes framed by straight, brown, shoulder-length hair looked up from her computer and smiled.

"May I help you?" she asked. Her nameplate read "Emily Sea-borne."

"Do you have public-use computers?" Madison asked.

"Yes. On the fourth floor. For library card holders."

"Actually, we're wondering if you have video surveillance of the computers?"

Emily Seaborne stared back.

Madison explained. "One of your library computers has been used to access e-mails connected to some assaults and possible murders. The NYPD is investigating."

Emily Seaborne's eyes widened. "Yes, we do have video surveillance, but any request to view the tapes must come from the police."

"I'll phone Detective Loomis now."

"Well, normally, the Detective should be here asking, but just have him fax or e-mail me the request on official NYPD letterhead." Emily Seaborne gave her the fax and e-mail information, then handed her a desk phone to use.

Madison dialed Detective Loomis's direct line at the precinct. The phone rang three times and she feared she'd be bounced into his voice-mail, when suddenly someone picked up.

"Homicide," a woman said.

"Is Detective Loomis there?"

Long pause. "No."

"I need to reach him fast."

Another long pause. "Detective Loomis was just involved in a car accident."

Madison felt her blood go cold as she slumped against the information desk. *No ... not another person....*

"How is he?"

"The initial report doesn't sound good."

Fifty Six

W hat about Detective Loomis's partner?" Kevin said, "He can fax the request here. What's his name, Donley, Devlin?"

"*Doolin!*" Madison said. "Archie Doolin!"

The librarian, Emily, gestured for Madison to use her desk phone again. Madison dialed Loomis's number, heard four rings, feared voice-mail, then....

"Homicide...."

"Is Detective Doolin there?"

"Hang on."

Moments later, she heard...

"Doolin speakin'."

"Detective, it's Madison McKean. I just heard about Detective Loomis...."

Archie Doolin wheezed long and hard.

"How's he doing?"

"No word yet, ma'am."

"Detective, I'm at the Mid-Manhattan Library trying to view some surveillance videos that might show us who's behind the $8.7 million account. But the librarian needs NYPD authorization before she can let us see the videos."

"Lemme speak to her."

Madison handed the phone to the librarian.

Emily talked with Doolin a few moments, then said, "Fine, Detective. I'll wait for your fax." She hung up and nodded at Madison.

Kevin suddenly reached into his coat pocket. He pulled out his cell phone. Madison saw it vibrating in his palm.

"May I answer this?"

The librarian smiled and nodded.

"Thanks."

He took the call and Madison watched his eyes grow serious fast. He slumped against the information desk for a moment, then began pacing back and forth in front of it, his eyes wide with concern.

What now? Madison wondered.

"OK," he whispered, hanging up.

"What is it?"

"My mother."

"What hap -?"

"The doctor suspects a stroke."

"Oh, Kevin...." She placed her hand on his.

"The left side of her face was numb and she had difficulty speaking. They're rushing her to Mount Sinai."

"I'll come with you."

"No, Madison, please stay and view the videos. The sooner we know who's behind this, the safer you'll be. I'll call you as soon as I know anything more." He hurried toward the exit.

As she watched him go, she remembered how alone she felt when Detective Loomis told her that her father had drowned. If Kevin phoned and said his mother's condition was worsening or critical, Madison would hurry to the hospital. The videos could damn well wait.

Behind her, the fax machine sputtered out a sheet. The librarian read it and signaled for Madison to follow her.

They walked down a hall to a narrow stairwell that descended to a labyrinthian basement with hallways leading in many directions. They passed a book cart filled with large, dusty medical textbooks. One book, entitled *Tropical Eye Diseases,* was opened to a photo of a man whose eyeballs had been eaten by tapeworm larvae. Madison shuddered and hurried ahead.

The librarian led her into a small room.

"Over here," Emily pointed to a wall of videotapes and DVDs stacked in floor-to-ceiling shelves beside a desk with two VCR and DVD players.

Emily took out two DVDs.

"These are the two most recent dates you requested."

"Thank you."

"The Panasonic works better," Emily said, pushing a DVD in the slot and turning it on.

Madison hit PLAY and the screen turned snowy, then flickered into a good view of the computers upstairs. In the lower right-hand corner of the screen Madison saw the date and the time, 9:01:08 AM, one minute after the library opened. A ponytailed teenage girl in a green plaid school uniform hurried over to a computer and began tapping away on the keyboard. The camera showed a side view of the computers, not what was on the screen.

"If you need me," Emily said, "I'll be at my desk."

"Thanks, Emily."

"Happy to help."

As Emily headed upstairs, Madison watched a heavyset man with suspenders and a polka dot bowtie waddle into view. He plopped down at a computer and began typing something. She didn't recognize him, nor the next seven people who sat at the computers.

She knew she might not recognize anyone.

Whoever was behind this might have sent someone else to pick up the e-mail. Someone she had never seen.

* * *

Eugene P. Smith peered over a leather-bound St. James Bible, watching the cute young librarian emerge from the hall where she'd led Madison minutes ago.

Earlier, he'd lip-read the librarian tell McKean that police authorization by fax was all that was required to view the videos. No police needed to be present. A lucky break for Smith.

After all, he wanted Madison alone.

Like she was now....

He adjusted his gray beard and hairpiece. Then he put on rose-tinted glasses and flicked a piece of lint from his charcoal gray suit. Carefully, he adjusted the heavily starched white minister's collar around his neck. The collar was tight, and he stretched it until it felt better. Then he took out a shiny gold crucifix on a gold necklace and put it on.

He checked his reflection in a glass-enclosed bookcase and flashed his best smile. Damned if he didn't feel born-again, downright evangelical....

"The Reverend Eugene P. Smith at your service," he whispered aloud.

Fifty Seven

Central Park was a green blur as Kevin's taxi raced up Park Avenue toward Mount Sinai Hospital. He prayed that his mother was receiving treatment within the golden hour when the chance to limit her stroke damage was so much better.

But her stroke made no sense. Just last month, she passed her annual physical with flying colors. She'd never smoked, always stayed thin, walked a lot, and drank a half-glass of Polish vodka every night. Her doctor said she had the blood pressure of a woman fifteen years younger.

On the other hand, her father had dropped dead of a stroke at seventy on a Warsaw trolley.

Kevin realized he should have persuaded her to get a second physical examination just to make sure nothing was missed. And now that he thought about it, he should have done a lot of other things. Like spend more time with her, and phone her more often.

And, he should have introduced her to Madison.

Madison had *asked* to meet her, even though he'd explained about her broken English and weird old world babushkas and cabbage rolls that sometimes smelled like burnt Firestones. Still, he sensed they would have liked each other.

Now, they might never even meet.

The driver swerved around a parked ambulance and skidded to a stop at Mount Sinai's emergency entrance.

Inside the ER, Kevin walked past a construction worker holding his hand in a blood-soaked towel and a teenage girl with pinpoint pupils staring at the ceiling and a nurse pushing a gurney with an elderly man spitting up blood. Down the hall, a woman screamed.

Kevin approached a round-faced receptionist whose hair was swirled up in some sort of orange beehive.

She looked up at Kevin. "May I help you, sir?"

"Yes. My mother, Anna Jordan, was rushed here a short time ago. The doctor said she was suffering a stroke."

"Let me check." Louise turned back to the screen and tapped on her keyboard. "Is that J-O-R-D-A-N?"

"Yes."

More tapping, waiting, then more tapping. Then she switched to another computer and typed in something. Moments later, she turned and looked up at him.

"Sorry, but I don't find her name here or in our main hospital admissions. Also, ER has received no call that she's being brought in."

Kevin was stunned by the news.

"Who told you she was being brought in?"

"Dr. Arthur Telvin."

She frowned at him. "I spoke with Dr. Telvin an hour ago. He's in his London hotel room."

Kevin slumped against the counter. His mind was spinning as he walked over and sat down in a chair. What the hell was going on? Did he get the doctor's name wrong? Was EMS performing a procedure at her home?

Quickly, he dialed his mother's apartment.

She answered on the first ring and the air drained from his lungs.

"Mom, you OK?"

"Sure, OK. With Ester I play canasta. Why you ask?"

"Oh, just wondered, Mom. Listen, I'll explain later, OK? I've gotta run. Bye."

As he hung up, reality hit him like a rock. Eugene P. Smith had suckered him away from the library.

Madison was in danger.

Kevin dialed Madison's cell phone. It rang twice, then bounced into voicemail. He left a message for her to get out of the library fast.

But he sensed it might already be too late.

Fifty Eight

Madison fast-forwarded the video to a man with gray hair and a gleaming aluminum briefcase sitting down at a computer. She'd never seen him before, nor the last seventeen people who'd used the library computers over the last twenty minutes.

She forwarded to a young female ... then to identical male twins in red NYU jogging suits ... to a hefty woman with a short, skinny bald man ... a Hasidic boy with heavy school books ... a blue-collar worker with a bad limp... an old man with shaky hands.

She knew she might be wasting her time. The person behind everything might have worn a disguise.

As she fast-forwarded to two Asian boys, she heard a *thump* in the hall behind her. It sounded like a book had fallen. She tightened her grip on a nearby cassette.

Another thump. *A footstep....*

Madison spun around and looked at the door.

Nothing. Silence.

Then ... footsteps ... louder.

Her stomach balled up tight.

"Any luck?" Emily asked as she walked in and plopped a thick dictionary down on a nearby shelf.

"Oh, not yet."

"Well, you're welcome to stay after we close in a few minutes."

"Thanks. That's very kind of you."

"When you're ready to leave, just dial 23 and Marvin, our security guard, will come and escort you out."

"Thanks again, Emily."

"You're welcome." The librarian smiled, picked up a thick green tome entitled *Black's Law Dictionary* and left.

Madison was relieved that she wouldn't have to rush through the videos, and even more relieved that a security guard knew she was down here.

For the next ten minutes, she watched an ongoing parade of business professionals, students and seniors tapping away at the keyboards. None looked the slightest bit familiar.

Suddenly, the lights went out.

She was in total darkness.

She began to panic ... then realized it was closing time. The basement lights were probably on a timer.

She flicked on the desk lamp, which gave her just enough light, then turned back to the VCR screen. She fast-forwarded to two middle-schoolers in blue uniforms, two nuns in black habits, a thick-hipped woman in red Spandex.

Something creaked out in the hall. A floorboard? A wooden bookshelf? A ventilation duct, maybe? She listened. Silence.

Relax, she told herself.

* * *

Eugene P. Smith loosened his minister's collar as he stared through the tiny crack in the door at Madison McKean. *So similar,* he thought. Same color hair, same tall curvaceous figure, same long neck and high cheekbones.

So similar to Lori....

Lori Laurent. Smith met her in his university drama class. She'd been drawn to acting for the same reason he had: to learn how to fit in better with others. In *A Room With A View*, their on-stage romance continued off-stage and soon Lori moved into his apartment.

After graduation, they planned to go to Washington while he began training at CIA Headquarters. But her mother's sudden, terminal cancer forced Lori to remain in New York. To help pay her medical expenses, Lori got a job as a secretary at Turner Advertising. One evening, as Mark McKean was rushing off to catch a flight, he asked her to hand deliver an important new business proposal to a Manhattan address by the 10 p.m. deadline. She took a taxi, delivered the proposal to an address in north Harlem fifteen minutes early, then came right back outside.

But her taxi had fled the high crime area.

As she waited for another taxi, two men dragged her into an alley, then raped and brutalized her.

Seven hours later, Lori Laurent died in Downtown Hospital.

Her death devastated Smith and filled him with rage.

A month later, he tracked down the two gangbangers who'd raped her. He dumped the two corpses, minus their genitals, in the same alley where they'd left Lori.

But Smith's rage was not quenched. He transferred it to Mark McKean. After all, McKean should have asked for an extension to deliver the package the following day. Or had a man deliver it. And because he didn't, Lori was dead.

But his daughter, a few feet away, was very much alive.

Smith removed the syringe from his pocket and looked at its eerily translucent liquid. So lethal ... so painful ... and so appropriate for the woman who'd proven more elusive than any of his other victims.

Smith squirted droplets of the toxin into the air. The flow was perfect. Within three minutes the toxin would stop her sweet little heart. The medical examiner would wonder why her heart failed, but he'd never test for sea wasp venom since she died in a library. He would, however, test for opiates and be shocked to find a lethal amount of heroin in her blood.

Smith would inject the heroin into her arm where the medical examiner couldn't miss the puncture, and the venom under her toenail, where he'd be least likely to check.

Smith watched her rake her fingers through her thick brown hair. He grew excited as he imagined her life force slowly draining away ... like it once drained away from Lori Laurent.

And even though the Executive VP had just phoned him and told him *not* to kill Madison, because the EVP had the votes she needed to pass the ComGlobe merger, Smith would kill Madison anyway. It was get even time.

Madison McKean for Lori Laurent.

Fifty Nine

Why isn't Madison answering? Kevin wondered as his taxi raced back toward the Mid-Manhattan Library. She would have left her cell phone on to hear the update on his mother's condition. But maybe her battery died again. Or maybe the library had one of those cellphone-blocking systems.

No. My cell phone worked in the library.

Why isn't she answering?

Deep down, he knew why.

Eugene P. Smith.

Kevin tried dialing her number again, but misdialed as the taxi swerved around a cement mixer and threw him against the side of the cab. At a red light, he dialed again and listened.

Nothing.

He slammed his phone shut.

He'd let Eugene P. Smith sucker him up to Mount Sinai. Smith must have been in the library all the time, probably watching them, somehow overhearing their plans. Then, he called pretending to be Dr.

Telvin. Amazingly, Smith had used the specific medical terminology of a cardiologist and a voice tonality completely different from the one he'd used on Sand Bank Bay. The man was a linguistic chameleon as well as a master of disguise. Had Smith also diverted Officer Vincent to a bogus terrorist situation?

Meanwhile, Madison was alone, unprotected, and by now injured or....

Sick with worry, he dialed Detective Loomis's number to ask Detective Doolin to speed police over to the library. After several rings, the phone was picked up.

"Loomis."

Kevin wasn't sure he'd heard correctly. "*Detective* Loomis?"

"Yeah. Who's this?"

"Kevin Jordan. You sound fine."

"I am fine."

"But your car accident?"

"Big-ass lie. We're trying to find the bastard who started it!"

"Probably the same man who just lied to me about my mother's stroke."

"Who?"

"Eugene P. Smith."

Loomis cursed under his breath.

"Smith lured me away from Madison at the Mid-Manhattan Library. She's there alone."

"But Officer Vincent's guard –"

"No. Vincent was pulled over to that terrorist situation, some guy with a suitcase bomb."

"What terrorist situation? Jesus H. Christ! Hang on."

Loomis shouted to someone and seconds later came back on the line. "There's no active terrorist incident going on in Manhattan right now! How could Smith send Vincent –"

"I don't know, but right now Smith has Madison all to himself in the library. And she's not answering her phone."

"I'll meet you there in about ten minutes."

By then she could be dead, Kevin feared.

They hung up. Kevin felt like steel pincers were tightening around his head. He phoned the main library number, hoping a security guard might pick up, but got a recording.

Then he realized something. Smith had called him. Kevin hit the *Last Call Received* button. Caller ID displayed *Unknown Number.* Kevin hit the re-dial button, praying that the ringing would distract Smith, or at least alert Madison. He waited for the ring. Nothing. He tried again. Nothing. Smith had turned off his phone.

Frustrated, Kevin snapped his phone shut, then leaned toward the taxi driver. "Please hurry!"

"Can't."

"Why not?"

The man pointed ahead.

Kevin looked and saw traffic frozen solid in all directions.

Sixty

Madison freeze-framed on a tall woman who seemed to intention-ally turn away from the camera as she walked toward the com-puters. Her bulky rain coat concealed the shape of her body while her high collar, sunglasses and scarf hid most of her face. Yet, something about her seemed familiar. What was it?

Then she knew.

The scarf! That purple pattern scarf!

Madison thought back over the last few days. *Karla had worn a scarf that color in the board meeting. And she walks sort of stiff like that.*

And Dana Williams wore a similar colored scarf a few times.

The woman on the screen sat down at a computer and appeared to log onto the Internet. Madison pushed the PAUSE button to study her profile, but the picture began to jiggle. She pushed PLAY again, hoping the woman would face the camera. She didn't.

She has to show her face when she leaves.

Behind her, Madison again heard a strange sound in the hallway. A soft, scuffing sound.

Was Emily back? No. She would have left when the library closed twenty-five minutes ago. Madison snapped to full alert. Her heart was pounding. Ten seconds, twenty. No more scuffing. No sounds. Perhaps she'd been mistaken.

Then, behind her, the door creaked open and her neck muscles tightened. A shadow moved across the video screen. *A large shadow.*

Please be the security guard.

She turned slowly and looked into the dark, empty eyes of Eugene P. Smith. He was dressed as a minister. Her breath caught in her throat.

"Praise the Lord!" he said, grinning. "I've found my prodigal daughter."

In his hand, he carried a syringe filled with a clear liquid, its needle gleaming in the dark room. Her mind racing, she inched toward a side door that led to another hallway.

"Sorry I missed you in Cannes," he whispered.

"We left after the Awards Show."

"Without celebrating with me?" He took a step toward the side door, cutting down her angle of escape.

She had to buy time. "May I ask you something?"

"You may."

"Who's behind this?"

"Sorry, that's confidential."

"Why confidential, if you're going to kill me?"

"You make an excellent point. So does this syringe!" He waved the point of the needle toward her face.

She leaned back and swallowed a dry throat. "Who hired you?"

"Someone who doesn't like you very much."

"Someone I work with?"

"Reasonable assumption."

"Karla Rasmussen?"

"Persistent, aren't you?" A smile revealed his small, white teeth.

"It's *her*, isn't it?"

Another thin smile.

"Be a good soul and hand Reverend Smith that naughty video you were watching."

"I didn't recognize anyone on it."

"That's because someone on it wore a disguise. My disguises work. Remember the old man with a cane on your flight from St. Kitts?"

"You were the old man? You left the Sand Bank Bay postcard?" She pretended surprise, even though she and Kevin had figured it out.

He took a slight theatrical nod.

"Where'd you learn disguises so well?"

He smiled knowingly. "You'd like to hear my nice long bio, so the righteous Officer Vincent will get back to save you, like a sweet Hollywood ending, dissolve to black. Sorry, but the only thing dissolving to black around here is you. So just hand me the video."

Now or never, she knew. Somehow she had to distract him long enough to run out the side door – *without* getting injected by the needle. She reached toward the DVD player and hit EJECT. The disc popped out, and she leaned over and pulled it free.

Pretending to be defeated, she turned slowly to hand him the DVD. When he reached for it, she threw it at his face.

He jumped back as she ran for the side door.

He grabbed her sleeve, ripping it.

She threw a DVD case at him.

He ducked and raked the syringe needle across her bare forearm, bringing drops of blood to her skin.

Crazed, she threw a heavy stapler at him, hitting his hand and knocking the syringe under the desk. When he bent down to pick it up, she yanked free, ran out the side door and sprinted down the hall.

Turning the corner, she found herself running down another hall lined with doors, some open, some closed. She had no idea where she was going. Seconds later, she faced a dead end.

She heard his footsteps coming.

Trapped, she ran back up the hall, opened a door marked "Janitor," went inside and closed the door. She saw a mop and quickly wedged it under the door handle lever and against both sides of the door frame.

She prayed it would hold.

She heard him sprint past her. When he reached the dead end, he began coming back, opening doors and closing them, checking rooms, working his way back up the hall toward her room.

She was trapped.

Inching backward in the darkness, her heel touched something solid. She reached down and felt cold steel, a metal pipe two feet long. She picked it up and gripped it like a baseball bat.

Smith opened the door next to hers. Moments later, he shut it.

Through a thin crack in the door frame, she saw him step toward her door, stop and stare at it. Did he see her? Perspiration covered her skin and her arm burned where the poison syringe had drawn blood.

Smith grabbed the handle of her door, turned and pulled. The mop-brace held. He jiggled the handle harder, but it still held. He continued staring at the door. Then, slowly, he walked to the next door, opened and closed it. She listened as he opened two more doors, and then walked down the hall toward the video viewing room.

Then she heard nothing.

Maybe he's left. She waited a full minute, two....

Silence.

She unclenched her teeth, then quietly pulled the mop handle from the door handle. She grabbed the steel pipe and eased the door open an inch. He was not in the hall.

Suddenly, the door was jerked from her hand – and Smith's needle was slashing down toward her neck.

Ducking sideways, she swung the steel pipe hard, hitting him hard above the ear. Stunned, he froze, then slumped against the door and slowly dropped to one knee. She sprinted down the hall and up the stairs to the first floor.

"Help!" she screamed, running into the library, hoping the guard would hear her.

Warm blood skidded down her arm onto the floor, leaving a road-map of red drops. She pressed her sleeve against the needle cuts to stanch the flow.

Behind her, she heard Smith coming after her. Any second, he'd turn the corner and see her. She ducked between two tall bookshelves and hid herself in the shadows next to a bookcase ladder.

Through a gap in the shelves, she saw Smith tracking her blood. He stopped where the blood drops stopped. Then he lifted his head and sniffed like a jackal catching his prey's scent.

And he appeared to catch the scent of her perfume, because he walked directly toward her bookshelf. She was blocked in by the bookshelves and the wall. Her only way out was the way in. He'd see her instantly.

He began to move along the bookshelf as though he knew where she was on the other side. Then he stopped two feet away. She froze.

Smith pushed two large books through onto the floor beside her and looked through the opening. Madison ducked back just in time. He pushed several more large books onto the floor, wobbling the shelf a bit, then reached through the opening, missing her by inches.

It was only a matter of time before he saw her.

The bookshelf wobbled. Can I topple it over on him?

Soundlessly, she climbed the ladder on the bookcase behind her and sat on the top rung. Then she placed her feet on the bookshelf next to Smith.

"Love that light floral scent, Madison. Allure is one of my favorites."

The fact that he knew she wore Allure sent shivers down her spine.

"The game is over, Madison. This time I win!"

Maybe not, asshole!

With all her strength, she pushed her legs against the top of the bookshelf. It tipped, then suddenly crashed down hard onto Smith, burying him beneath hundreds of heavy volumes and the thick oak shelf. He gasped loudly, but she heard him moving about.

She jumped from the ladder and ran out into the library hall, shouting for the night guard.

No response.

Maybe Smith killed him....

Behind her, she heard Smith crawling from beneath the bookshelf. Soon, he would catch up to her.

Out of the corner of her eyes, she saw a red light on the wall. She ran over and yanked the alarm lever.

Instantly, an ear-splitting horn blasted off the library walls. Red lights flashed everywhere.

When she glanced back, she saw Smith freeze, then turn and hurry the other *way,* toward the entrance.

She stopped, leaned against a bookshelf and took several deep breaths.

Seconds later, she heard keys jingling and saw a heavyset security guard wearing iPod earphones jog into view. He raised his flashlight beam to her face.

"You pull the alarm?"

"Yes."

"You the lady what Emily said was in the basement?"

"Yes. A man attacked me."

He yanked his gun out. "Where's he at?"

"He went toward –"

Suddenly, they heard two gunshots, followed by glass crashing onto the floor. The night guard, gun in hand, hurried toward the sound, Madison close behind. They ran around the information desk, and headed toward the entrance. When they got there, she saw the shattered window through which Smith had escaped.

A minute later, a taxi screeched to a stop. Kevin jumped out and ran toward the door.

"He's with me," she said.

The guard unlocked the door. She hurried outside and ran into Kevin's arms.

"What happened?" he asked, looking down at the blood on her forearm.

"Smith may have injected me with poison."

Sixty One

Harry Burkett brushed lint from his green orderly's shirt as he pushed the supply cart down the hall in St. Anthony's Hospital. He checked his fake ID badge. It looked genuine. He'd created it on his office Mac.

He felt juiced. Just like he was back in his Special Ops unit, back in Desert Storm, whacking Iraqis. He loved clear-cut missions like the one he was on now. A mission always snapped his brain to attention, focused it like a laser, reminded him of something that he learned very early in life.

Eliminate anything that can harm you.

Like his drunken, abusive father.

And Linda Langstrom.

One very lucky broad, he thought. With all that blood pouring from the bullet wound he'd put in her back, she should have bled out and died right on her apartment floor.

But no, her busybody sister showed up and rushed her to St. Anthony's. And even worse, Langstrom was slowly coming out of her coma and expected to make a full recovery. Which meant she could finger him as her assailant.

No way he'd let that happen.

He saw her room number down at the end of the hall.

Behind him, he heard hushed female voices. Looking back, he saw a short, fiftyish nun in a white habit at the nurses' station talking to an older nun behind the counter. The short nun glanced at him. He nodded, but kept walking, just an orderly on his rounds.

A few feet further, he pushed his cart into Langstrom's room and closed the door halfway. She lay in bed, partly hidden in shadows, IV tubes feeding into her arms. He walked over and looked down at her face. It was bruised, swollen and bandaged from where she'd bashed it against her coffee table.

He took out the small glass vial that he'd bought from his buddy at the U.S. Army's chemical weapons facility at Fort Detrick. His buddy bought several vials from a laid-off worker at a Russian chemical weapons plant. They were worth every ruble.

Burkett pulled on a pair of latex gloves. He rechecked them for tiny holes, but found none.

His heart pounding, he looked back at Langstrom. He wondered where on her body he should apply the clear, slightly viscous liquid in the vial?

Then he noticed the shoulder of her hospital gown was pulled down.

* * *

"Who's our new orderly?" Sister Rose Angela, the head floor nurse, asked.

Sister Bernadine peered up from behind mountains of insurance forms. "What new orderly?"

"Muscular man. Five-seven. Tinted glasses. Weird tennis shoes with black springs in the heels. He just went into Miss Langstrom's room."

"That's odd."

"Why?"

"Dr. Lyons said everything was fine in there ten minutes ago."

Sister Rose Angela's radar went on alert. Neither she nor Sister Bernadine had been informed a new orderly was substituting for DeVon Washington tonight. Although turnover among orderlies was high, substitutes were still required to check in at the floor desk. "I'll go find out."

Sister Rose Angela headed toward Langstrom's room at the end of the hall. Halfway down, Sister Bernadine called out to her, "Sister Rose?"

"Yes?"

"Mrs. Miele just pushed her medical alarm button. Could you check her?"

"Certainly," Sister Rose Angela said, hurrying back two rooms. As she entered, she saw that ninety-four-year-old Elena Miele had somehow slid down between the guard rail and the mattress, entangling her arm and shoulder in several IV lines and monitor cables.

The two women smiled at each other.

"Where do you think you're going, young lady?

"Out for some *vino*! Wanna go?"

"Later." Chuckling, Sister Rose Angela lifted the silver-haired woman back onto the bed, untangled her lines, fluffed her pillow and promised to sneak some linguini to her tomorrow, if her doctor agreed.

Back in the hall, Sister Rose Angela hurried down to Linda Langstrom's room and entered. She was shocked to see the new orderly, his back to her, bent over Langstrom.

"Is there a problem?" she asked, growing concerned as his hand eased back from Langstrom's upper body.

The man spun around, clearly surprised.

"Oh ... the patient ... she started breathing real funny, making noises, you know? So I hurried over to check her out. I was just gonna ring for a nurse."

Sister Rose Angela stared at him, her instincts telling her the man was lying. She felt a shiver of fear run down her spine.

Was he a mercy killer? Twenty years ago, she'd unknowingly worked alongside a friendly young doctor who quietly murdered seven patients by giving them 20 percent Lidocaine injection instead of 2 percent. Since then, she rechecked every suspicious death on her floor.

Sister Rose Angela walked over and read Linda Langstrom's monitors. "Well, her vital signs look normal and she seems to be breathing fine now. I'll watch her for a while. And I'm sure you have other work before your shift ends."

He seemed frustrated that she'd interrupted him.

"You're new at St. Anthony's, aren't you?"

"Yeah, started yesterday. Still learning my way around, you know?"

"Of course. What's your name?"

He hesitated a second. "Joe ... Joe Richardson."

"Where's DeVon tonight?"

"Oh ... I heard DeVon was tied up."

"Will you be on this floor a lot, Joe?"

He paused. "Uh, yeah, they said mostly the fourth floor and maybe this one."

Again, she sensed he was lying. She'd check him out when Human Resources opened in the morning.

"Very well then, Joe. I'll monitor Ms. Langstrom now. So get along with you ... and in the future please check in with the nurses' desk first. That's hospital policy."

"OK," he said, pushing his cart from the room.

* * *

Burkett could feel the nun's eyes burning holes in the back of his head as he rolled his cart toward the elevator.

Just rubbing the VX nerve agent onto Langstrom's skin would have killed her within six minutes. But no, the nosy nun showed up before he could apply the VX.

Next time, Langstrom wouldn't be so lucky.

———

And he knew exactly when the next time would be....

Meanwhile, the night was still young.

Like Jennifer, who was meeting him at the Westwind Mall in forty minutes.

Sixty Two

"Y ou were attacked in the library?"

Madison spun around at her desk and saw Karla Rasmussen standing a few feet away. How long had the woman been standing there?

"Oh, it's just a minor scratch. Nothing serious," Madison said, again relieved that the ER doctor found no poison in her blood last night.

"That's good. By the way, did Linda Langstrom over at National Media ever get back to you on whether we're paying too much for our MedPharms TV advertising?"

"Yes," Madison said, picturing her friend lying semicomatose in a hospital bed. "She told me our MedPharms rates are two percent less than what comparable clients pay for the same TV shows."

"That's good news."

Yes, Madison thought, *but not as good as the fact that Linda should fully recover. Or is that bad news for you, Karla?*

"Well, I'm glad you're OK, Madison, but right now I'm off to a client meeting."

As Karla hurried away, Madison noticed that her straight-back stride was quite similar to the stiff gait of the woman Madison had seen in the video at the library last night. *Was that you in the video, Karla?* Sadly, they might never know, since Eugene P. Smith had taken both DVDs last night.

Madison's cell phone rang. The Caller ID window read, *Craig Borden.* Why was Kevin's banker friend calling?

"Hi, Craig."

"Hey, Madison. I tried to reach Kevin, but he's out."

"He's at a client conference and dinner until late tonight."

"I just got some new information."

"What?"

"Remember '*Blanchectar*,' the word my colleague, Philip Carter, wrote down in the Barbados bar...?"

Madison closed her eyes at the mention of the deceased man. "Yes, I remember."

"Well, Philip's secretary just told me that right before he went to the bar, he'd traced the $8.7 million bank account back sixteen years to the original depositor's name."

"Blanchectar?"

"Yes."

"That's great!"

"So is Blanchectar's address from sixteen years ago."

"You have the *address?*" Her heart was pounding.

"3907 Brunsman Street, apartment B5. Over in Newark."

Madison jotted down the address, which she knew was just across the Hudson River. "Maybe someone in the area remembers Blanchectar."

"Someone should. It's an apartment building."

She thanked him, hung up and immediately phoned Detective Loomis.

"Homicide."

"Is Detective Loomis there?"

"No. Loomis and Doolin are taking depositions up in Attica.

They're back in here late tomorrow afternoon."

"Do you have Detective Loomis's cell phone number?"

The man hesitated. "Why you gotta call Loomis?"

She explained everything. He gave her Loomis's cell number and she dialed it. After four rings, she was bounced into voicemail.

She left him a message telling him about Blanchectar's Newark address. She then buzzed her secretary. "Christine, could you please ask Officer Vincent to come in."

Christine paused. "Don't you remember?"

"Remember what?"

"He's attending his daughter's grade school graduation."

She'd totally forgotten. "Oh...."

"Want me to phone him to come back now?"

"No, no. That's an important family event."

Frustrated, Madison leaned back in her chair and considered what she should do next. Identifying Blanchectar was the key to everything: Blanchectar was behind the $8.7 million ... and maybe her father's death ... and maybe the effort to ram through the ComGlobe merger. Surely someone near the Newark address would remember what Blanchectar looked like. Madison knew she should wait for Detective Loomis and Officer Vincent and Kevin, but they were not around. And time was critical.

The ComGlobe vote was tomorrow.

Opening her purse, she looked at the Beretta .25 pocket pistol Kevin had given her after last night's attack in the library. He'd shown her how to use it – and she *would* use it, if Smith attacked her again.

But how could she visit the Newark address without Smith knowing it? The man seemed to know every move she made. And her earlier disguise had failed miserably. She stood and paced back and forth near her window. As she turned back to her desk, she noticed a copy of *Business Week*. It was opened to an ad for office copiers. She stared at the ad, then quickly grabbed the phone and called a producer in her broadcast department.

"Ginny, do you still have the stuff we used for the office copier ads yesterday?"

"Sure. It's in Wardrobe."

"I'll be right down."

Fifteen minutes later, Ginny led Madison over to a large three-way mirror. Madison smiled at the person smiling back at her. Curly black wig, black slacks, black windbreaker with red logo on the pocket – and chestnut brown skin, thanks to Ben Nye theatrical makeup. She was a Hispanic Xerox service technician. Her ID badge read Angela Martinez.

Service people came and left the building every few minutes. Smith would barely notice them. And he certainly wouldn't pay attention to a dark-complected one.

Ginny handed her a Xerox tool bag. Into it, Madison placed her purse with the Beretta.

She left the agency through the delivery entrance in the rear of the building. The security guard didn't recognize her as she walked past him. She headed down two blocks to Fifth Avenue, making sure no tall, thin men were following her. She saw none. To be certain, she entered a fashionable Manolo Blahnik shoe store and watched out the window for a few minutes. A saleswoman kept frowning at her Xerox uniform as though Madison was befouling her store's image. Madison felt like asking if she had anything under 20 bucks?

Satisfied that Smith had not followed her, Madison went outside, got into a taxi and handed the Newark address to the driver, a chubby, round-faced man with a Haitian accent.

Twenty minutes later, the taxi pulled over to the curb at 3907 Brunsman. She was in a ghetto, not what you'd expect of someone with $8.7 million in a bank.

Many stores and buildings appeared abandoned. On the corner stood the burnt-out shell of an old Baptist church. In a nearby alley, street dogs ripped open a garbage bag. Overhead, thick clouds darkened the street. She opened the black tool bag, reached into her purse, and flipped the safety off her small Beretta.

"Can you wait for me?"

"Sorry, I gotta a pickup over at Rutgers."

Madison checked the street again. "Could you please wait until I get inside?"

"Sure...."

She paid him, then made sure no cars had followed her. Seeing none, she got out and found herself alone on the shadowy street, except for a rusted-out Honda Civic up on cinder blocks.

Beyond the Honda was a skinny, hunched-over derelict sitting on the curb, sipping from a wine bottle.

She looked at 3907 Brunsman. The gray, five-story apartment building had seen better decades. Bricks had crumbled at the corners, downspouts had slipped off the gutter and some windows had been covered with black garbage bags snapping in the wind. A scrawny cat hobbled past on three legs.

She checked the derelict. Still sipping wine. She walked toward the building, took off the wig, Xerox jacket and ID badge and put them in the service tool bag. She climbed the concrete steps and pushed a button marked "Super."

Moments later she heard an elderly woman clear her throat and cough. The woman's larynx sounded damaged. "Whuuuut?"

"Can I please talk to you about a person named Blanchectar who lived in apartment B5 about sixteen years ago?"

"No."

"It'll just take a second, ma'am."

"I wuzzn't here."

"Is there anyone in the building who lived here sixteen years ago?"

The woman hacked herself into a loud coughing fit that could have registered on the Richter Scale. "Maynard...."

"Could I talk to Maynard?"

"No."

"I'll be very brief."

"Maynard don't talk to no strangers. Probably shit-faced anyways."

"Would you accept twenty dollars to let me try?"

The door buzzed open.

———

Madison waved the taxi off, stepped into a dark hallway and almost passed out from the stench of cat urine. Beside her, a door creaked open and two tan kittens shot out and disappeared down the hall. Then a liver-spotted hand with gnarled fingers opened the door a few inches and an old woman's deeply wrinkled face appeared like a death mask in the darkness. Strands of straggly white hair hung down over rheumy eyes that were locked on the twenty dollar bill like it was the Hope Diamond.

Madison's heart went out to the poor woman.

"No guarantees Maynard'll talk," she wheezed.

"I understand."

"He's in A3, second door on left."

"Is he there now?"

"Yeah. Maynard don't go nowheres 'cept to Safeways on Wednesdays."

Madison held out the twenty dollar bill and the woman's arthritic fingers swooped it up faster than a Hoover vacuum cleaner.

Madison thanked her and stepped down the dark hall, trying not to let the cat urine or the gooey stuff sticking to the soles of her shoes nauseate her. She knocked on the door marked A3. Nothing. She knocked harder. Still nothing.

"Mr. Maynard...?"

"Don't want any."

"I'm not selling anything, sir."

"Still don't want any."

"May I give you forty dollars to ask about someone who lived upstairs in B5 sixteen years ago?"

Silence.

"Please, Mr. Maynard. It will only take a minute."

She heard shoes shuffling and several door chains rattling. Slowly, the door creaked open and she saw a thin-faced man in his early fifties with red-rimmed but intelligent eyes peering at her over unframed half-glasses. He was slim and pale and stood about five-ten. His neatly trimmed red beard covered most of a nasty scar that zig-zagged up to his forehead.

"Watch your step," he said, opening the door. "It's the maid's day off."

Smiling, she walked in and was rewarded with the sweet scent of lavender incense. She was surprised by the neat shelves of history books, novels, and an equally neat shelf of empty Jim Beam bottles. Maynard plopped down in a leather executive chair behind his desk and closed a leather bound book entitled *Herodotus, The Persian Wars.* Beside it was the same book in Greek.

"Fancy a libation?" he asked, tapping a Jim Beam bottle on his desk.

"No, thanks."

As he poured himself three inches, she looked at the wall and saw a Rutgers University diploma for *Thomas J. Maynard, PhD, American History.* Beside it was an old newspaper article headlined, *Two Die in Private Airplane Crash, Pilot Survives Wife and Daughter.* In the article was the photo of a young woman, a five-year-old girl and the pilot, Tom Maynard.

My God, she realized, *he crashed the plane that killed his wife and daughter. No wonder he drinks.*

"You want to know who lived up in B5 sixteen years ago?" he asked.

"Yes."

"No one."

"What?"

"She never *lived* in B5, never domiciled there in a strictly legal sense."

"She?"

He nodded. "She came by occasionally to pick up the mail. In that one year, she stayed overnight here maybe ... three, four times. All she had up there was a hide-a-bed sofa and one of those Admiral mini-fridges."

"What'd she look like?"

He closed his eyes a moment. "Serious woman, dark hair, attractive, well-dressed. Walked kinda straight-up, stiff."

Madison wanted to bring photos of her executives, but the Human Resources department was at an offsite conference.

"Was her mail addressed to Blanchectar?"

"Yes. But I don't think that was her name," Maynard said.

"Why not?"

"One time I called out, 'Hey, Ms. Blanchectar?' She didn't respond even though she was a few feet ahead. So I called her again, but she still didn't answer. Finally, I caught up to her, tapped her shoulder and said, 'Hey I've been calling you.' She claimed she'd been concentrating on something and didn't hear me."

"So Blanchectar probably wasn't her real name?"

"I'll wager all my liquid assets it wasn't." He gestured toward his bottles of Jim Beam.

She smiled. "If I showed you a photo tomorrow, do you think you might recognize her?"

He paused. "Well, it's been sixteen years, and I only saw her a few times."

"I understand. But it would really help us." Madison wondered if Human Resources had a photo of Karla Rasmussen from sixteen years ago.

"I'll try."

"Thank you, Mr. Maynard. How's tomorrow morning?"

"Fine. Stop by any time."

She nodded, stood and placed forty dollars on his desk.

He looked at the money. "That's very kind of you, but not necessary."

"PhDs make much more per hour these days," she said, smiling.

"Gee, maybe it's time I got back into academia."

"I'm sure academia would benefit, Doctor."

He seemed to smile at her use of his title. "Actually, the University has asked me to come back. First, though, they insist on rehab." He tapped his Jim Beam glass. "But my health care provider refuses to pay for rehab. Pre-existing condition, yada, yada.... And if I paid, well, it would cut into my drinking money." He smiled.

She smiled back. "I have a thought...."

"What's that?"

"I can easily afford your rehab, Mr. Maynard. We could consider it a loan if you like, paid back at your convenience."

Tom Maynard seemed shocked by her offer, then smiled. "That's most generous of you, but..."

"Maybe just think about it?"

He looked up at his diploma for several moments, then at the *Herodotus* leather bound history and said, "OK...."

She smiled, walked toward the door. "So, tomorrow morning?"

He nodded.

She left and, holding her breath, hurried back down the sticky hall and stopped at the front door. She phoned the taxi driver she used earlier and discovered he was driving his fare to Manhattan. She called Yellow Cab. They promised her a taxi in five minutes.

After ten minutes of breathing cat urine, she began to gag. She needed air. Seeing no one out on the street, she stepped outside, but kept her hand on the door handle just in case she had to hurry back inside.

As she breathed in the delicious fresh air, a vegetable truck rattled down the street and suddenly backfired. The sound startled her and the greasy door handle slipped from her fingers. The door slammed shut behind her.

She was locked out. The street was darker because the streetlight mysteriously had gone out while she was inside.

The derelict was no longer at the curb.

She heard something to her left. She turned and saw a dog walk quickly from the alley.

Then something else came from the alley.

Footsteps....

Sixty Three

She sipped coffee laced with Glenfiddich, savoring its taste almost as much as her imminent victory in the hotly-contested ComGlobe merger. She had the votes. The merger would pass tomorrow and ComGlobe's Peter Gunther would wire ten million dollars to her offshore account in Belize. A short time later, she would sell off her Turner shares as part of the initial public offering of stock. The IPO sale, her cash cow, would net her maybe an additional eighteen million dollars that would be wired directly to her numbered Swiss account.

Life is good, she thought.

As she fingered her gold Montblanc pen, the office phone rang. She checked Caller ID and picked up.

"We gotta talk!" said Keith Davidson, the agency's director of Internet marketing communications. He sounded even more anxious than yesterday when she'd persuaded him – some would say black-mailed him – to vote for the merger.

"Don't worry about tomorrow's vote, Keith."

"I'm not."

"Good."

"*You* should worry." His voice was hard.

Surprised by his words, she leaned forward. "Why should I worry?"

"Because I've changed my mind. I'm voting *against* your god-dammed merger!"

Every muscle in her body grew taut. She didn't need this now. "If you do, Keith, you know what I'll do."

He remained silent.

"I'll reveal everything."

Still silent.

"Have you been drinking, Keith?"

"No!"

"Then think again."

"No. My mind's made up!"

"Your mind's screwed up! Think how devastated your wife, Diane, and your children will be when they learn you've been married to that topless dancer in Paramus, and have a six-year-old biracial child with her!"

Keith Davidson did not respond.

"And Diane will be even more devastated when she sees photos of you and her nineteen-year-old sister making passionate love."

Davidson cleared his throat.

"Diane will leave you, Keith. And she'll sue you for every penny you've got! Your children will never forgive you or talk to you again!"

He sighed heavily. "That's a risk I'll take. I'm going to tell Diane everything."

He was slurring his words. He had been drinking. "You'll lose something else, too, Keith."

"What?"

"Your job."

"Bullshit!"

"I'll post your very sexy photos on our company Intranet. Every director and every employee will see them. Maybe I'll put them on the Internet with headlines like, *Ad Biggie Bangs Wife's Sister!*"

She heard him cursing under his breath.

"Listen, bitch ... if you do any of this, I'll make sure you never work in this business again."

I don't plan to after tomorrow's vote, she thought to herself. "I'll deny it all, Keith, and you'll find no proof that I loaded the photos on our Intranet."

Davidson mumbled something. "There's a word for people like you."

"What's that?"

"Cunt!"

She laughed. "I like it. Nice, short, Anglo-Saxon word. And I'll expect your vote tomorrow, Keith."

Swearing, he slammed the phone down.

She stood and started pacing behind her desk. Clearly, she could not count on Keith Davidson's vote tomorrow.

That meant she needed Eugene P. Smith again. Two days ago, when she'd obtained the necessary votes to pass the merger, she told Smith to spare Madison's life. But for some reason, he'd gone ahead and tried to kill her in the library. Obviously Smith had a personal vendetta against her.

And once again, so do I.

Madison's fatal accident – and it had to look accidental – was back on for tonight. By the time the police became suspicious and started to put things together, the EVP knew she'd be in a non-extradition country – counting her non-extraditable money.

She flipped open her cell phone and called Eugene P. Smith.

* * *

In the parking lot of the Westwinds Mall, thirteen miles northwest of Newark, Harry Burkett focused his military binoculars on three young girls strolling toward the GAP store. Jennifer, on the left, was wearing a red tank top and red hat just like she said she would. She was so beautiful. And only fifteen. The perfect age! She glanced toward the parking lot, obviously looking for his van.

Burkett's mouth went dry as he watched her and her girlfriends walk into the GAP. In six minutes, Jennifer would walk back out and place her red hat on the Mr. Pony ride near the door. She would pat Mr. Pony's nose four times with the back of her left hand. *Our little signal.*

He would then blink his lights four times and she would walk out and get in his van. He could almost feel her creamy pubescent skin, her silky blonde hair....

His dream was interrupted by the hacking cough of a frail old hunchback hobbling along on a walker. The guy was lugging a heavy bag of groceries along the row of cars ahead. He coughed hard again, opened his car trunk, then leaned on his walker, wheezing like an asthmatic.

The chubby old coot looked like he might croak any second.

As he lifted the grocery bag, it tilted, dumping cans that rolled under his car. Burkett laughed out loud. The old guy bent down to retrieve them, and a milk carton fell out, splattering milk everywhere.

"Ha!" Burkett cackled, slapping his thigh. This was better than Comedy Central. Then he felt a little guilty. He'd be old one day. Maybe she should go help the geezer. Burkett got out of his van.

"Having trouble there, mister?"

"Huh?" the old man wheezed, turning around. "Oh ... yes, I dropped some stuff. Can't seem to reach those cans beneath the car. Bum back. Korea."

"I'll help ya."

"Bless you, young fella."

Burkett knelt down, grabbed a can and handed it out to the old man.

"Thank you. You're very kind. Can you reach that Starkist Tuna behind the tire? Minerva, that's my wife, woman loves her Starkist."

"No problem." Burkett reached in and rolled the can into his fingers. He handed it up to the old man.

"Thanks again, young fella."

"Sure thing."

As Burkett inched back out from under the car, he felt a sharp pain in his neck. Suddenly his head snapped back hard and he couldn't breathe.

Reaching up, he felt a thin wire around his neck. The old bastard was strangling him! Burkett managed to wedge the tip of his little finger under the wire and pulled. But the wire cut deep.

Razor wire! Jesus...!

The old man pulled harder.

Something warm trickled down Burkett's neck and he smelled the coppery scent of his own blood. His lungs screamed for air as the razor wire cut down to the bone. His head felt like it would explode.

The old man jerked the wire hard twice, and Burkett watched the tip of *his little finger* fall down into the pool of milk, turning it pink. He stared at his severed finger, knowing there was nothing he could do, knowing he was bleeding to death in Section C3 of a goddamned parking lot of a shopping mall....

"Why?" Burkett gasped at his attacker.

The old man took off his tinted glasses and smiled.

"No use crying over spilled milk, Harry!" Eugene P. Smith said, yanking tighter.

Sixty Four

Madison and Kevin sat on his small two-seat sofa watching the Yankees-Red Sox game on television. They'd been watching it since a taxi brought her back from meeting with Professor Tom Maynard in his Newark apartment. She felt hopeful that tomorrow morning Maynard would identify a photo of Karla Rasmussen as the woman he'd known as Blanchectar sixteen years ago.

Madison also felt safe, thanks to Officer Vincent on guard downstairs in the lobby.

And now that the bulldozer in the alley had stopped working, they could actually hear the baseball announcer.

Which, of course, didn't stop Kevin from lifting his Louisville Slugger up to his lips like a microphone and doing the play-by-play. "Yes sports fans, it's the bottom of the ninth at Fenway, Yankees ahead by two, Boston at bat, three men on, two outs, two strikes. The Yanks are just one strike away from chalking up another big win in Boston."

"Not so fast, mister," she said.

"It's over. Boston hasn't got a prayer."

"Oh yeah? They've got a home-run slugger at bat, thirty-seven thousand fans cheering him on, and they're playing in Fenway!"

"Won't matter."

"Why?"

"Because my bat performs *miracles!*" He made the Sign of the Cross with it over the TV.

She smiled as the Yankees pitcher fired a fastball right down the middle of the plate. The big, muscular batter uncoiled like a cobra, and when she saw the fat part of the bat whack the ball, she *knew!* Grinning and laughing out loud, she watched the ball soar up over the Green Monster.

"Argh!" Kevin groaned. "The agony of defeat!"

"What's wrong with your feet?" she asked.

He laughed. "Enough sports!" He zapped to another channel where a surgeon was prying off a chunk of human skull, then to a Weed-Whacker commercial, then to an old romantic movie that she loved staring Greer Garson and Robert Donat.

"*Goodbye Mr. Chips,*" Kevin said. "I always liked this movie."

"Wow – a manly man who likes sentimental movies?"

"Don't tell the guys."

"The guys I know would rather watch *Goodbye Godzilla.*"

"Me, too, sometimes."

They settled in with the movie and she soon found herself swept into the romantic saga of Mr. Chips at a charming English school and the tearful scene of Mrs. Chips dying in childbirth. During a commercial, she stared out at the headlights flickering between the girders of the Triborough Bridge. The flickering was hypnotic. Another sip of wine made her yawn. Soon, she found herself nodding off and snapping awake. She noticed Kevin's eyelids were also drooping. Within seconds, she dozed off again....

CLINK!

Her eyes shot open at the sound of metal. She focused on the fire escape door at the end of the room. Behind the door's window curtain, she saw a large shadow move. Was it a passing cloud? A man?

The shadow moved again ...

A man! Tall!

She nudged Kevin awake and pointed to the fire escape door. He grabbed his Louisville Slugger, slid off the sofa and crouched beside the door.

Something jiggled into the key slot.

Madison's heart pounded. As she turned to go tell Officer Vincent, the door creaked open an inch and she ducked behind the sofa.

Slowly, the door swung open, and she saw the tall dark shape of Eugene P. Smith backlit by moonlight. He held a gun with a silencer. Squinting into the dark room, he looked around.

Then he stepped inside.

Kevin swung the bat.

But Smith sensed it coming and jerked back.

The bat hit his gun, causing it to fire. The bullet ripped into the wooden floor three inches from Madison.

Before Smith could regain control of his gun, Kevin swung the bat again, knocking Smith back outside onto the fire escape.

Smith started to raise the gun.

But Kevin batted it from his hand, sending the weapon clanging down the iron stairs into the alley below.

Madison's sighed in relief – then screamed as Smith slashed open Kevin's shoulder with a long knife, sending a red streak of blood down his sleeve.

Smith swung the knife toward Kevin's chest....

But Kevin ducked to the side, then slammed into Smith's shoulder, knocking the man back against the fire escape railing.

As Smith lunged with the knife again, Kevin's bat blocked it, causing the blade to twist back toward the assassin ... but before Smith could turn it back, Kevin grabbed the handle and shoved the blade deep into Smith's eye.

Smith froze – then began shrieking and flailing his arms....

He staggered backward, the knife still lodged in his eye. His shoe caught on the metal grating and he flipped over the railing and fell into

325

the alley three stories below.

Seconds later, Madison heard a loud *THUD!*

Then, behind her, the apartment door banged open. She turned and saw Officer Vincent, his weapon drawn, running toward them. She pointed toward the alley below.

They all looked down over the railing. Madison couldn't believe what she saw: Smith had impaled himself on the teeth of the bulldozer shovel. The blood-drenched teeth protruded up through his chest, neck, and base of his skull.

Madison and Kevin followed Vincent downstairs. In the alley, they ran around the construction barriers and bulldozer to Smith's body. His eyes were locked open, unblinking, his neck twisted at an grotesque angle. Blood was pooling in the bulldozer shovel bucket.

Vincent checked for a pulse, shook his head, but phoned EMT anyway.

He reached into Smith's blood-soaked pocket and pulled out a wallet. He flipped it open and looked at a VISA card. "Meet Eugene P. Smith."

"We've met," Madison said.

Officer Vincent reached into Smith's other vest pocket, came out with a small address booklet and handed it to Kevin. "Maybe you'll recognize a name."

Kevin began flipping through the pages as Madison read over his shoulder. She didn't recall any names, but Kevin suddenly stuck his finger on one.

"Harry Burkett!"

"Who's he?" she asked.

"A computer guy at our agency. He oversees our in-house Intranet system. Computer-savvy, but weird."

"Something else is weird," Officer Vincent said.

"What?" she asked.

"A guy named Burkett got whacked tonight in Jersey. Razor wire around his neck. Bled out in the parking lot of the Westwinds Mall."

"*Harry* Burkett?" Kevin asked.

"Yeah. That's the name."

"Jesus...."

Madison pointed to a phone number tucked next to Burkett's. "Whose number is this?"

Kevin stared at the number and frowned. "It seems familiar."

"Dial it."

He took out his cell phone, punched in the numbers and waited. Seconds later, he turned toward her, his eyes wide open.

"What?"

He shook his head from side to side.

Sixty Five

The EVP straightened her Hermes scarf as she watched Madison McKean walk into the board of directors meeting called to vote on the ComGlobe merger.

Congratulations, Madison, on escaping Eugene P. Smith last night. But your luck is about to run out.

"The meeting will now come to order," Madison announced in a no-nonsense tone as she sat at the head of the long mahogany conference table. Her hair was pulled back and held tight by a silver clasp. She wore a white silk blouse, silver necklace and a serious pin-striped business suit in midnight *black.*

The perfect color, Madison, for the funeral of Turner Advertising as an independent agency.

The murmurs quieted down and Madison nodded to Evan Carswell, the vice chairman, to begin.

"Madam Chairwoman," Carswell said, "I move that we waive the minutes and all regular business and vote now on the final merger offer made to us by ComGlobe on May 21."

"Seconded," said Raymond Sanders, corporate counsel.

All heads nodded agreement.

"The merger offer is now open for discussion."

Discussion is irrelevant, the EVP thought. *In business, only one thing counts – leverage. And I've got it!*

As Evan Carswell began rambling on about why he thought the ComGlobe merger was wrong, her mind drifted to her new life, a life she'd planned meticulously over the last seventeen years in Turner Advertising.

A life that would begin in six hours when she belted herself into the plush seat of her chartered Gulfstream. The jet would fly her to the Bahamas and from there to her favorite non-extradition country, Cuba, where she'd secured a 75-year lease on her new home, *La Casa de Campo.* She pictured the 12,000-square-foot villa with its nine bedrooms, Olympic-size swimming pool, cabanas, tennis court – all nestled into a hillside overlooking the blue-green Caribbean. She visualized her Miros on the walls, her French wines in the cellar, and her personal trainer, Carlos, in her bed, exercising her in a delightfully personal way.

A loud cough jolted her back to the meeting.

"Any more discussion?" Madison asked.

No one raised their hand.

"Then let's vote," she said, "As you know, our bylaws permit us to vote anonymously. No signature required. So please take the sheet of white paper in front of you and simply write down either FOR or AGAINST. Then fold your paper and pass it up here."

Each director quickly wrote down their vote and passed it forward until all eleven ballots were stacked in front of Madison.

The EVP watched Madison unfold the top vote, read it, then frown.

"*FOR* the merger."

She opened the next ballot and her eyes dimmed further. "*FOR* the merger."

Brace yourself, Madison. This is going to feel like someone's hammering bamboo splints under your fingernails.

* * *

The vote was off to a bad start, Madison realized, as she handed yet another *FOR* the merger ballot to Sanders.

Madison looked around the table and noticed Harold Cummings and Keith Davidson. Both looked extremely uncomfortable. A few days ago, they'd assured her they would vote against the merger. But this morning, they'd been avoiding eye contact with her. Obviously, they'd voted *for* it, most probably because they were blackmailed.

And, Madison knew who the blackmailer was....

She turned and looked at the woman, the same woman she'd seen in the library video – wearing, oddly enough, the same purple scarf around her neck. Madison wanted to walk over and tighten the scarf until the *woman* turned purple. She also wanted to ask her, *How did your phone number wind up in the little black book of Eugene P. Smith, an assassin hired to kill my father, two bankers, Kevin and me?*

But Madison didn't ask her. Instead, she opened another vote and read, "*FOR* the merger."

The blackmailer's lips creased in a faint smile.

* * *

The EVP was enjoying Madison's humiliating defeat far more than she'd anticipated. She watched her unfold another ballot. "*AGAINST* the merger."

Don't raise your hopes, Madison. It's already four to one in favor of the merger.

Again, her mind drifted to this evening when she would order the Curacao banker to transfer the 8.7 million dollars to the *Nederlandse Privé Bank* in the Dutch Antilles where she had an account. That money would be added to the $10 million dollar fee from ComGlobe's Peter Gunther and her upcoming IPO stock sale money, roughly $18 million.

For a grand total of nearly $40 million. Not a bad retirement package.

"What's the count, please?" Madison asked Raymond Sanders.

Sanders looked at his tally sheet. "Five *FOR* the merger, four *AGAINST*, two votes left."

Madison opened the next ballot. "*AGAINST* the merger."

"Five-five tie. One ballot remaining," Sanders said, dabbing sweat from his brow.

All noise in the boardroom ceased. Tension crackled like static electricity. Each director stared at the final folded ballot.

Slowly, Madison picked it up.

Sorry, Madison, but that ballot is mine. See my big blue X on the corner?

Madison opened the ballot and slumped down in her chair.

"*FOR* the merger."

The room was graveyard quiet.

Raymond Sanders whispered, "Six *FOR* the merger, five *AGAINST*. The ComGlobe merger motion passes. I'll ask our attorneys to prepare the paperwork immediately."

* * *

Madison looked over at the blackmailer, the woman who was responsible for killing Madison's father and two Caribbean bankers. The woman who'd attempted to kill her and Kevin. The woman who'd blackmailed her fellow directors.

But now, the woman was about to meet someone she could not blackmail.

Right on cue, there was a knock on the boardroom door. The room fell silent.

Madison knew that Detectives Loomis and Doolin were about to walk in and arrest the woman.

Madison walked slowly over to the door.

She opened it, looked at the men on the other side – and felt her knees buckle. She grabbed the doorknob to steady herself. She was hallucinating! But why now? Behind her, the directors gasped.

Her father, Mark McKean, several pounds thinner and using a cane, limped into the room, living and breathing and smiling right at her.

"Sorry I'm late," he said.

When he pulled her into his arms and she smelled his Dunhill pipe tobacco, she realized he was *real,* and that *real* tears were spilling from her eyes, and from his.

This was not a cruel hallucination.

Her father was alive!

"I'm so sorry, Madison," he whispered, "so very sorry. And I can explain everything."

The astounded directors gathered around him, smiling, shaking his hand, patting his back.

But one director remained seated. Her eyes, like empty black pits, stared in utter disbelief at Mark McKean, resurrected from the dead.

Detectives Loomis and Doolin walked over to her and flashed their NYPD badges.

"Alison Whitaker," Loomis said, "We're placing you under arrest for conspiracy to commit murder, blackmail and other felonies to be named...."

Everyone stared at her in shock.

The same shock Madison felt this morning when she showed Professor Tom Maynard a photo of the board of directors and he identified Alison Whitaker as the woman he'd known as Blanchector.

"This is absurd!" Whitaker shouted.

"You have the right to remain silent and refuse to answer questions. Anything you say may —"

"You're making a mistake!"

"No – we're makin' an arrest!" Doolin said, starting to cuff her.

"Get your goddammed hands off me!" Whitaker said, yanking her arm away.

"Resisting arrest is another crime, ma'am," Doolin said, pulling her wrists behind her back and cuffing her.

"You'll hear from my attorneys!" Whitaker screamed, struggling to free herself. "I'll sue you bastards for every cent this city has! I know the governor!" A fat vein bulged like a trapped worm on her forehead.

Madison watched the two detectives drag the screaming executive from the room.

Carswell closed the door, but Madison could still here Whitaker shouting obscenities.

"Madam Chairwoman...," Carswell said.

"Yes," Madison said, still clutching her father's arm to keep him from vanishing again.

"As Detective Loomis just indicated, we learned this morning that Alison Whitaker blackmailed some of our directors to vote for the merger. Whoever you are, relax. The court has enjoined Whitaker from using any information she might have intended to use to blackmail you. All her files, hard copies, and online documents, both here in the office and at her Park Avenue apartment, are now being confiscated by the authority of the District Attorney who will hold them under lock and key. You may retrieve the files related to you at a later date."

Madison heard sighs of relief.

"And because your ComGlobe votes were made under duress," Carswell said, "I move that the merger vote be reconsidered, and that we take another vote on the ComGlobe offer at this time."

"Seconded," Raymond Sanders said.

"Let's keep it simple," Carswell continued. "All those in favor of accepting the ComGlobe merger offer, please raise your right hand."

Three people slowly raised their hands.

"And all those against the merger?"

Seven people shot their hands into the air.

"The motion fails. The ComGlobe merger offer is defeated seven to three."

Madison felt hot tears fill her eyes.

Sixty Six

Mark McKean limped toward the conference room table, pain shooting up his legs with each step.

"Who beat the crap out of you?" Evan Carswell said.

"Abra de San Nicolas."

"Who?"

"A *mountain!*"

The directors stared back, waiting for an explanation.

McKean shifted weight from his bad, throbbing leg to the less throbbing leg that only had a six-inch gash. After more than two weeks lying comatose in an Acapulco hospital, his sixty-five-year-old body had awakened early this morning with more aches and pains than an NFL running back on Monday morning. Now, here in the boardroom, all he felt was overwhelming joy at seeing his daughter alive.

"Where should I begin...?" he asked them.

"I like when you died and I took over," Carswell said.

More laughs.

McKean managed a smile, remembering the fun times he'd had

with these smart, talented people over the years.

"I'll begin just prior to my unfortunate demise," McKean said. He took Madison's hand in his and again felt an overwhelming sense of guilt for the pain his suicide letter and his fake "death" undoubtedly had caused her and her brother. His well intentioned, but quickly conceived plan to fix the problem had failed miserably.

Yet, here she was, his beautiful daughter, smiling at him with forgiveness in her eyes.

"It all started with an unsigned, untraceable e-mail I received," McKean said. "The one I mentioned to you, Madison. The e-mail accused me of misappropriating $8.7 million from our company and demanded that I return the money and resign immediately." His throat was raspy from not speaking for weeks. He sipped some coffee and it helped.

"I have not misappropriated one red cent from Turner Advertising. Frankly, I don't need the money. And as many of you know, I'm not sophisticated enough in high finance to misappropriate that much money without getting caught!"

"That last bit's true," Carswell mumbled.

More smiles.

"How did you answer the e-mail?" Carswell asked.

"As it demanded. By e-mail. I said I did not misappropriate any funds and I refused to resign."

He sipped more coffee.

"What happened then?"

"I got a second e-mail." McKean looked at Madison and placed his hand on her shoulder. "That e-mail gave me a choice: resign ... or attend my daughter's funeral."

Several people gasped.

"Did you know that when we talked on the phone?" Madison asked.

"No."

She nodded. "You told me you had a vague memory of seeing the $8.7 million figure somewhere in the agency."

"Yes. I thought I saw it in our financial books, but couldn't remember exactly where. Then, after I spoke to you, I remembered. It wasn't in our financial books at all."

The directors leaned forward, waiting....

"I saw the $8.7 million on a printout of a bank statement. The statement was sticking out from a file folder on the desk of Alison Whitaker. So I hurried down to her office to ask her about it."

Suddenly, pain shot up his leg and he had to sit down.

"What'd Whitaker say?" Carswell asked.

"Nothing. She was in Boston! Where *you* lived, Madison. That's when I panicked. I thought she was up there hiring someone to come after you. I phoned to warn you, but you didn't answer."

"I was probably on the way to the airport."

He nodded. "So my next step was clear. Resign. I started writing my letter of resignation. But as I wrote, I realized something: Whitaker would not kill you if she thought I was dead."

The room went silent.

"So you faked your own suicide?" Carswell said.

McKean nodded. "I wrote my suicide letter, set up the rowboat with my coat and wallet in the East River, then caught a flight to Chicago and from there to Mexico. I used fake ID so no one could trace me. In Chicago I used a pre-paid phone to call you to explain everything, Madison, but you didn't pick up. Then I phoned you again when I landed in Acapulco, but the phone company said the phone was off the hook."

"I knocked it off during the night."

Mark McKean felt more guilt.

"Dad, why didn't you just leave me a voice message that you were OK?"

"Because the detectives would have listened to it and known I was still alive. Then, *your* life would be in danger again."

She nodded, but still looked puzzled. "But it's been over two weeks. Why didn't you phone me?"

"I couldn't." He pointed to the large bandage at the side of his head. "The doctor told me there's a hole in my skull beneath this bandage. The hole relieved pressure on my brain. When I woke up this morning at 3 a.m. in the Acapulco hospital, the doctor said I've been in a coma for the last sixteen days."

Madison tightened her grip on his hand.

"I'm OK now, sorta. Anyway, the police said that when the taxi was driving me from the Acapulco airport, a drunk driver forced us off the road. We flipped and bounced about two hundred feet down the side of the Abra de San Nicolas mountains, then slammed against some boulders. I don't remember any of it. The taxi driver was killed and I was knocked unconscious, then slipped into a coma. This morning, when I came out of it, the doctor told me the date. I told him I had to get back here for today's ComGlobe vote. He refused to discharge me, so I discharged myself, chartered a jet and landed at LaGuardia about forty-five minutes ago."

The directors stared at him in amazement.

McKean looked at his daughter. "I'm so sorry, Madison. But I decided the only way to save your life was to fake my death. Once I knew you were safe, I was going to tell the police about Whitaker. Instead ... I wound up in a coma."

Madison put her arms around him and he felt waves of relief ripple through him.

"I have just one request," Mark McKean said.

"What now? Death benefits?" Carswell joked.

"Hey – I've got my death certificate!" McKean shot back, smiling. "But what I really want, and this is important, is for Madison to remain as chairwoman of Turner Advertising. As you know, I'm retiring in eleven months anyway, and I think it's better that we don't disrupt our clients with another major change in top management. Is that acceptable?"

Heads nodded.

"Not with me," Madison said.

Her response jolted him. "Why not?"

"I'll stay," she said, "but only on one condition."

"What's that?"

"That you remain as, ah ... let's say, co-vice chairman with Evan Carswell until you retire."

Mark McKean smiled at his daughter. "OK, if the board agrees."

"The board and I happily agree, for chrissakes," Carswell shouted.

"No, wait!" said Raymond Sanders. "We have to make this official!" He tapped his tattered edition of *Robert's Rules of Order.* "I move that we retain Madison McKean as our chairwoman, and second, that we retain Mark McKean as our co-vice chairman for the next eleven months."

"Seconded," several others shouted.

"Any discussion?" Carswell said.

There was none.

"All in favor?"

Unanimous "Ayes" bounced off the walls.

"This meeting is adjourned," Carswell said. "Roll in the champagne."

"We serve champagne now?" Mark McKean asked.

Madison started laughing.

"What's so funny?" McKean asked.

"ComGlobe sent it over," she said.

Mark McKean smiled. "Cocky bastards! Let's drink it anyway."

Epilogue

W hat's our speed up to?" Madison asked Kevin as she squinted through the evergreen branches at the shimmering blue lake. "About three miles an hour! Buckle your belt!"

"Can't."

"Why?"

"Jehosaphat's wearing it!"

They smiled at the belt-harness wrapped around Jehosaphat, the big, beautiful chestnut horse, pulling their carriage down Main Street on Mackinac Island, a small island nestled in Lake Huron between Michigan's lower and upper peninsulas. A gentle breeze brushed across her face.

"What's that seductive, alluring fragrance?" she asked.

"Jehosaphat."

"No, it's sweeter."

Kevin sniffed the air. "Ah ... that would be Ryba's famous peanut butter fudge. Which, by the way, you ate an entire box of yesterday."

"I was terrified it would go bad!"

"You were terrified I'd eat some."

"That, too."

She listened to the clippity-clop of Jehosaphat's hooves. It was hypnotic, a mantra luring her into the peaceful serenity of the lush green forests surrounding them.

Being on Mackinac Island was sort of like breathing Valium, or waking up in America, circa 1850. A quiet America. No cars, trucks, or other motor vehicles are allowed on the island. You walked, bicycled, horse-carriaged or galloped your way around.

The land originally was inhabited by the Ottawa and Chippewa Indians. The pious French missionaries sailed in around 1665, followed by greedy French fur traders, then the imperialist British in 1780. Finally, the uppity American colonists kicked the Brits out in 1815.

Jehosaphat shook her head, whinnied and politely farted her arrival at the magnificent Grand Hotel, built in 1887. As they stepped onto the Grand's porch, she marveled again at its length. At 700 feet it was the longest porch in the world, and lined with white rocking chairs and decorative urns sprouting over two thousand red geraniums and a small Dixieland band playing "Basin Street Blues."

Below the hotel was the large tea garden with thousands of dazzling red tulips and the large swimming pool where Esther Williams once swam in the movie *This Time for Keeps*.

They sat down at a porch table and gazed out at the magnificent view of the five-mile-long Mackinac Bridge. She was amazed to learn that Michigan had more shoreline than Florida or California.

"Would you care for somethin' to drink, ma'am?" asked a young waiter with a thick Caribbean accent that made her think of St. Kitts. She noticed Kevin smiling at the accent.

Moments later the waiter placed their drinks on the table.

Kevin clinked his Heineken against her Chardonnay. "To the two of us."

"Maybe the three of us, after last night."

"Honeymoons sure are fun!"

She smiled, remembering their passionate nights and mornings and afternoons of lovemaking. Just five days ago, to the delight of Kevin's mother and her father, they were married in St. Joseph's Polish Catholic church in Camden, N. J. in a half-Polish, half-English ceremony followed by a completely wild and crazy reception.

Her cell phone rang and she fished it from her purse.

"Hello...."

"Detective Loomis."

"Oh, hi, Detective."

"Hope I'm not interrupting anything?"

"Not at all."

"You asked me to update you on Alison Whitaker."

"Yes, please," she said, recalling that three weeks ago, a jury had found Whitaker guilty of the murders of Bradford Tipleton, Philip Carter and Harry Burkett – and the attempted murder of Linda Langstrom, Kevin and her. She also was found guilty of misappropriating $8.7 million from National Media over many years, and blackmailing three Turner Advertising directors.

"The judge just nailed her with four consecutive life sentences without the possibility of parole."

"Sounds about right!" Madison said, feeling a sense of closure wash over her.

"By the way, Karla Rasmussen was never involved with Whitaker. Not even years ago when Whitaker called herself Blanchector."

"Good for Karla." Madison felt guilty for suspecting Karla and would somehow make it up to her. "How could I have missed the name Blanchector? 'Blanche' and 'hectar' are very loose French translations of 'white' and 'acre', or 'Whitaker.' I probably saw the word fifteen times and still didn't get the connection."

"I missed it, too." Loomis said.

Moments later, they hung up and she filled Kevin in.

"Poor Alison," he said. "From a Fifth Avenue apartment to the slammer."

"Yeah, life's a bitch."

"But this bitch got life!"

Laughing, she gave him a high five.

They sipped their drinks and listened to the band belt out "Won't You Come Home, Bill Bailey."

Suddenly, her phone rang again. *What's going on? Four days with no calls and now two calls in five minutes?*

"Hello," she said.

"Madison...." It was Evan Carswell.

"Hi, Evan."

"Sorry to bother you, Madison, but I thought you'd like to know."

"Know what?"

"I just received a phone call from the CEO of our former client, FACE UP Cosmetics."

"Why?"

"He called to say that he just shitcanned his advertising director, the lecherous Maurice Dwarck, after three secretaries filed sexual harassment suits against Maurice and the company. The CEO also asked if we'd please reconsider handling his FACE UP advertising again now that Maurice is gone. I said we'd be delighted to."

"You're right. That's terrific news!"

"But Dana Williams isn't, I'm afraid."

"What happened?"

"Our Ease-Z-Sofa client just told me that Dana tried to persuade him to move his business over to Griffen-Girard. He told her no."

So, Madison realized, Dana's relationship with Griffen-Girard's Lamar Brownlee was much more than one romantic lunch at Club '21'.

"Did you confront her?"

"Yeah."

"And...?"

"She looked like she needed an adult diaper."

Madison smiled.

"With your permission, I'll fire her ass outta here right now!"

"Do it."

"OK, but I'm afraid there's more bad news: Leland Merryweather and Finley Weaver."

"What's the problem?"

"The night before the ComGlobe vote, Christine was working late and saw a computer technician in your office putting something inside your credenza. She called Security and they called the cops who came and arrested him. Yesterday, the fake technician finally confessed to stashing a pound of heroin and a couple hundred ecstacy pills in your drawer. When the cops pressured him, he admitted that Merryweather and Weaver paid him three grand to hide it in your office. The bastards were gonna frame you for possession. Get you kicked off the board so the merger would pass."

Madison was stunned. "Where are they now?"

"I was just about to go fire their asses, too."

"Don't let me hold you up."

They hung up and she told Kevin.

"I never trusted Merryweather and Weaver," he said.

They sipped their drinks and listened to the music awhile. The waiter walked up and handed her a note saying her father had called.

She dialed his number and he picked up.

"So how's Mackinac Island?" he asked.

"Everything you said it was, and more! What's up?"

She punched her phone's speaker button so Kevin could hear.

"My attorney and I just came out of the most unbelievable meeting I've ever been in."

"What meeting?"

"Between National Media and the three Caribbean banks involved with the $8.7 million. Turns out, Alison Whitaker was planning to transfer the money to the *Banco Nacional de Cuba* after the ComGlobe merger meeting. When Millennia Trust found out she'd been arrested, they froze her money."

"Good."

"But here's what's interesting; National Media claims they can only document two-hundred-ninety-three thousand missing from their books. Not $8.7 million."

"But Bradford Tipleton told me $8.7 million was deposited."

"Yes, $8.7 million was deposited, and $8.7 was misappropriated. But National Media is terrified of bad PR. If the networks and newspapers announce that National mishandled millions of their clients' money, the company fears many of their clients would bolt for the doors!"

"They probably would. What about the two-hundred-ninety-three thousand?"

"They figure they can weather any bad PR on that. That's chump change for them."

"So what happens to the $8.4 million that's left?"

Her father started laughing.

"What's so funny?"

More laughing.

"Dad?"

"The banks declared that the $8.4 million legally belongs to the name attached to the account."

"But that's your name."

"Correct."

"But Dad, *you* didn't deposit the money."

"They know. But the banks decided that because the account had my name and my social security number and my Manhattan address on it, and because no other Mark McKean has come forward to claim the money, the $8.4 million is mine!"

She started laughing. "And who are you to argue?"

"Damn right! And after I reimburse New York City $320,000 for their costs in searching for my body in the East River, I'm donating roughly half of what's left to the New York Fire Department, NYPD and research institutes for childhood diseases, like St. Jude's Hospital down in Memphis."

"That's terrific!"

"And the other half is for you and Thaddeus to split."

She tried to say something, but couldn't. Her eyes filled. "Really...?"

"Yeah, but only after I kick the bucket!"

"You already kicked the bucket," she said, smiling. "I have your death certificate."

"Don't be a smart ass!"

"Dad, thank you."

"You're welcome. Talk to you later."

She hung up,

Kevin was staring at her. "Did I hear what I think I heard?"

"You did."

"Millions?"

"Millions."

Kevin shook his head, smiled, then started laughing. "Do I know how to pick a wife or what?"

"You do."

"You know what this means?" he said.

"What?"

"All the Ryba's fudge you want."

Also by Mike Brogan

BUSINESS TO KILL FOR

Business is war. And Luke Tanner is about to be its latest casualty. He's overheard men conspiring to gain control of a $1 billion piece of business using a unique strategy – murder the two CEOs who control the business. The conspirators discover Luke has overheard them and kidnap his girlfriend. He tries to free her, but gets captured himself.

Finally, they escape, only to discover that the $1 billion business is his company ... and that it may be too late to save his mentor, the CEO. The story takes you from the backstabbing backrooms of a major advertising agency to the life-threatening jungles of Mexico's Yucatan.

Writer's Digest gave BUSINESS TO KILL FOR a major award, calling it, "the equal of any thriller read in recent years...."

Available at Amazon.com
or mikebroganbooks.com
ISBN 0-615-11570-5

Also by Mike Brogan

DEAD AIR

Dr. Hallie Mara, an attractive young MD, and her friend, Reed Kincaid, learn that someone has singled out many men, women, and children to die in ten cities across the U.S. in just a few days. But because Hallie has no hard proof, the police refuse to investigate.

When Hallie and Reed try to find proof, they unearth something far beyond their worst fears. And as they zero in on the man behind everything, the man zeros in on them. Barely escaping with their lives, they finally convince the police and the federal authorities that a horrific disaster is imminent. But by then there's a big problem: it may be too late. *Midwest Book Review* calls DEAD AIR, "a Lord of the Rings of thrillers. One can't turn the pages fast enough."

Available at www.PublishAmerica.com
mikebroganbooks.com
or Amazon.com
ISBN 1-4137-4700-0

About the Author

MIKE BROGAN is the *Writers Digest* award-winning author of BUSINESS TO KILL FOR, a suspense thriller that *WD* called, "... the equal of any thriller read in recent years..." He writes about a world he lived – the increasingly dog-eat-dog world of international business. His years working in Europe gave him a unique perspective on global corporations. He witnessed hostile takeovers, consolidations, mergers and buyouts. He saw winning companies roll out champagne ... and losing companies roll out heads. He brings that experience to his novels, like MADISON'S AVENUE. Brogan now lives in Michigan where he's completing his next novel.

To learn more, visit mikebroganbooks.com